SACRIFICE

The Legacy Series
Book Three

Jessica Ruddick

CHAPTER 1

SITTING IN MY CAR OUTSIDE Nice Beauty where I worked, I stared at the email on my phone and the pounding of my heart scared away the butterflies that had been circling my stomach for the past three hours. I was now a high school graduate.

Well, sort of. I'd earned my GED, so technically I guessed that meant I wasn't a graduate, but the important thing was I was finished with high school.

My breath whooshed out of me in a palpable sign of relief. No more sneaking around to GED study sessions, no more hiding notes and workbooks. I didn't feel guilty for taking control of my life, but I did feel bad about lying to Bill. He'd been so good to me, especially since my mom died.

As it always did when I remembered that fact, a shock zapped through my system.

My mom died.

It was closing in on three months, but sometimes when I woke up in the morning, I still expected her to be sitting at the kitchen table, cradling a mug of coffee. Sometimes, I could still hear her in the back of my mind, bugging me about college. But worst of all, sometimes I thought I could still feel her tuck me in at night, still feel her hand brush across my forehead to smooth my hair back, still feel the brush of her lips against my cheek.

It was those times that I couldn't stop the tears from falling as I screamed into my pillow.

I'd heard people say a parent never gets over the death of a child. I wouldn't know anything about that personally, but I could tell you that dealing with the death of a parent was no walk in the park either, especially when that parent was in the prime of her life.

I looked out the driver's side window, searching for a familiar figure that had become my shadow the past few months—Xena, my former handler. I was supposed to be getting a new one, but as long as Xena was present, I knew I was in the clear, at least for today. No new handler meant no new assignments—no searching for pure souls in order to sentence them to death in the hope they'd become angels.

Also, her presence meant I had another day with Cole. No one knew he was a seeker, and I intended to keep it that way, which meant as soon as my new handler showed up, I would have to drop him like a bad habit.

The thought made my heart hurt.

I squinted, still peering into the darkness. There she was—leaning against a tree on the other side of the median. She didn't always let me see her. Since she was a fallen angel, she had the ability to mask her presence from humans. When she noticed I'd seen her, she stepped back out of sight.

She knew I wasn't ready to forgive her for her deception. Not yet. I didn't know if I ever would.

But now this email would change everything. It was the last piece of my plan.

New butterflies took up residence in my belly.

There was no reason to put off leaving anymore. Yet, I found myself whispering what had become my mantra—
just give me one more day with Cole.

MY BOSS SHENICE HAD PULLED out of the parking lot a few minutes before me, and now I found myself driving toward her apartment. I'd never been to her home—she'd never invited me—but the discussion I wanted to have couldn't be done over the phone, and it couldn't wait.

If I waited too long, I might lose my nerve.

Shenice had agreed to help me find other seekers. My mom and I had never met any, and I always found that curious. There had to be more than just the two of us. I wondered if they'd kept us apart purposefully or if it was simply a practical thing—they probably didn't want seekers all crowded into the same area.

Still, it might have been helpful to have a group of us, a support network of sorts. But maybe that was part of the ploy as well. There was strength in numbers, but keep us divided and we were less likely to rebel.

Freaking angels. I'd only ever met one—well, one that was a true angel and not fallen—and though I happened to be related to him, I still couldn't say I knew a whole lot about them. But what I did know was they messed with people's lives. Cole was now a seeker and my mom was dead—a byproduct of their interference. So I wasn't a fan of them, even if they were supposed to be the embodiment of good.

My phone rang and I hit the button for speakerphone. "Hi Cole," I said.

"Please tell me you're not driving and talking on the phone."

I rolled my eyes. Sometimes Cole could be a pain in the rear. "Why did you call me if you didn't want me to answer?"

"Are you driving?"

"Don't worry, Mr. Worrywart. I've got you on speaker."

"Hey," he said sharply. "It's *Sir* Worrywart."

That earned him an even bigger eye roll. He could probably see it wherever he was calling from, most likely his apartment. If he was really concerned about my paying attention to the road, he should stop making comments that deserved exaggerated eye rolls. Just sayin'.

I heard a clanging in the background and frowned. "Are you still working?" Despite being only twenty, Cole was Bill's number one mechanic.

"Yeah, we had a transmission rebuild come in this afternoon, so I thought I'd get started on it."

Something was up. Cole wasn't the type to chitchat on the phone, and he especially wasn't one to stop working to call unless he had something to say.

"Did you want something?" I asked, not sure I wanted to know the answer.

"My mom agreed to Kyle coming down for a visit."

"Really." It came out as a statement rather than as a question. I was in disbelief. Cole's goal ever since I'd known him was to graduate high school and take custody of his fifteen-year-old brother. Even though his mom was a deadbeat druggie, she was reluctant to sign the papers for whatever reason. So this was a big step.

"Yeah." He sounded troubled, like he suspected she was up to something. She probably was. I didn't have much faith in her, but for Cole's sake I tried to be positive.

"Well, that's good, right?"

"I have to go pick him up. I thought about putting him on a bus or something, but..."

He didn't have to finish that thought. Knowing Kyle, he might take off to God knew where. Kyle wasn't a bad kid necessarily, just sorely misguided. If he wasn't getting mixed up with gangs or picked up for shoplifting, he was doing something else equally stupid.

The funny thing was Cole said Kyle reminded him of himself at that age. I couldn't picture the steady Cole I knew doing any of those things.

Although he had stolen a few cars, come to think of it. There were extenuating circumstances though and when we abandoned them, we made sure they were locked tight so they wouldn't get robbed.

"Plus," Cole added, "I think it would be a sign of good faith if I made the effort to get him myself."

"I understand," I said, a sick feeling filling my stomach. If I was successful in talking to Shenice tonight—and I *would* be successful—then I would be leaving soon, hopefully in a matter of days. Cole's trip to northern Virginia could cut my time short with him.

Could cut *all* of my time with him.

But he didn't know my plans, so I couldn't tell him that.

"Anyway, I was thinking you might want to go with me."

Our last road trip signaled the start of our complicated relationship. The Reapers were after him because I'd turned in his name as a pure soul. His soul had been white but unnaturally so. My angel ancestor, Areli, made it that way, hoping Cole could become my guardian angel. See why I wasn't so keen on angels? That was just one of many reasons. Probably the biggest was that it was Areli's fault I was a seeker to begin with.

But that's a whole other story.

"I don't know..." I said, even though I wanted to scream *yes*. I didn't want to intrude on their brotherly bonding time.

"I don't like leaving you."

I felt like I'd had this conversation before. In fact, I knew I had. The last time Cole went up to see his brother, the you-know-what hit the fan, so I could understand why he was reluctant to leave me.

"I know, but I have work."

"Shenice will let you off."

That was true. Shenice was the best boss ever. If I asked for time off, she'd shoo me out the door without even asking why.

"I'll think about it," I said.

"It's not like you have school," Cole pointed out. That

was also true. And what he didn't know was I would never have school again thanks to my freshly earned GED. Although it wasn't a diploma, I was still proud of it. It sucked that I couldn't celebrate the achievement with anyone.

Although Bill had been appointed my temporary guardian when my mom died, that only lasted a short time since I just turned eighteen. So I had no parental authority to answer to. But Bill would let me go, anyway. He was just as understanding of a guardian as Shenice was a boss.

There was no reason I shouldn't go with Cole, other than the fact that the more time I spent with him, the harder it would be to leave. I'd tried distancing myself in anticipation of my fleeing the coop, but that hadn't worked out so well. I couldn't make myself stay away.

Maybe this could be our last hurrah before I said good-bye.

"I'll think about it," I said again. I didn't want to commit until after I'd talked to Shenice. I needed to keep my priorities in line. And my first priority was fulfilling the promise I'd made to myself that I would do everything in my power to help Cole live a normal life and not that of a seeker.

Shenice's apartment was a block over from the complex where my mom and I once lived, so I had no trouble finding it. Parking, though, was another matter. The lot was packed and on top of that, the spaces were tiny. Bill had just fixed up this car—*my* car—and I didn't want to risk damaging it again. He'd done it as a surprise for my eighteenth birthday and had also presented me with the title. He was such a good man—better than I deserved. It would break his heart when I left.

But I couldn't think about that now.

I trudged up to Shenice's third floor apartment, bypassing the second floor which smelled suspiciously of weed and chocolate chip cookies. It only took her a few moments to open the door.

"What are you doing here?" she asked, surprise written on her face.

"Can I come in?" I tucked my hands in my pockets.

"Yeah, sorry." She opened the door wide so I could enter, then locked the deadbolt behind me.

I took a moment to look around. Her apartment was small and it reminded me of the apartment in those old *Friends* reruns. Everything was mismatched, but it somehow blended together perfectly. It was shabby chic. If I had put it together, it would probably have turned out more "cheap yard sale."

We all had our strengths, I guessed. Though lately, I was doubting what mine were. Or if I even had any at all.

"So," Shenice prompted, crossing her arms over her chest in a defensive posture as if she knew what I wanted to talk about would be something she wouldn't like. She was perceptive like that.

But she'd already agreed to this. I just needed to remind her of that fact.

"I want to go find other seekers," I blurted out. I wanted to face palm myself. So much for being smooth and easing into the discussion.

She dropped her arms and scrunched up her face. "What?"

"Do you remember when—"

"Yes, I remember," she said with a touch of attitude. "But you're not out of high school yet. That was the agreement."

She didn't mention the other part of the agreement was I had to be eighteen. I'd already fulfilled that end of the deal. She hadn't realized I was only weeks away from turning eighteen when she made that stipulation. Perhaps she should have looked closer at my employment documents.

I pulled my phone out of my pocket and pulled up the email from the GED office. Wordlessly, I handed it to her. She quickly scanned it, then pounded on it with her finger, trying to scroll to see...what, I didn't know. She held my phone out to me so I could see the screen, but I didn't look at it. I already knew what it said.

"What is this supposed to be?"

"I'm done with high school," I stated, though that should have been obvious since she'd read the email.

"No, ma'am." She shook her head vigorously, her micro braids shaking from the exertion. "You were supposed to graduate."

I shrugged. "I believe the exact term of the agreement was I had to be done with school." I gestured to the phone, which had gone blank. "I'm done."

She shook her head again, more gently this time. "Ava, why did you do that? You know your mama would have wanted you to graduate properly with a diploma."

"My mother isn't here," I said sharply, turning away.

Shenice's gasp was audible. She might have been shocked by my harsh delivery of the blunt statement, but it was true. Even before my mom died, I'd had time to come to terms with it. My mom had had grand aspirations for me. She'd wanted me to go to college and build a better life than she was able to build for herself.

But if she'd been honest with herself, she would have realized that was never going to happen.

"Look," I said, making eye contact with Shenice. "I was dealt a pretty shitty hand of cards for my life, and I'm trying to make the most of it."

"I don't understand why you're hell bent on finding other seekers." Her eyes pleaded with me to help her understand. "What do you hope to accomplish?"

The truth was I didn't exactly know. But I needed to learn more about what I was. Xena once told me I was a small piece of a much larger puzzle. It was time I met some of the other pieces and learned about this supposed puzzle.

Also, I couldn't stay here. If I was going to protect Cole from the life of a seeker, then I needed to get far away from him—and *stay* far away.

And though I considered myself somewhat of a loner, I knew myself enough to know I would be lonely.

"I need to do this," I said quietly. "If you knew there were other people like you out there, wouldn't you want to find them?"

Shenice was a sensitive and the only one of her kind. Instead of seeing and communicating with ghosts, she saw angels who were normally masked from human sight.

Seekers looked like regular humans and my mom and I kept our seeker abilities hidden, so if I sought out to find other seekers on my own, I'd likely come up empty. But Shenice would be able to find handlers because they were fallen angels. And where there were handlers, there were bound to be seekers.

As soon as Shenice found them for me, she could return to her regularly scheduled life. I didn't intend to disrupt it any more than necessary. Though I couldn't expect a normal life, Shenice could. I didn't want to strip that from her.

"Ava, I don't know. I don't see how this is going to end well."

I stepped closer to her and squeezed her hand. "Please."

Looking into her eyes, I thought for a moment she was going to renege on her promise and my stomach tied itself into knots. She *had* to agree. I didn't have a back-up plan.

She sighed. "Okay. But we can't leave right away. I have some ends I need to tie up first."

"Of course," I said. I'd expected as much and truthfully, I was glad. It gave me that many more days with Cole.

But no number of days would ever be enough to prepare me to say good-bye.

CHAPTER 2

"I HAVE A SURPRISE FOR you," Cole said, speaking loudly to be heard over the whirling of the fan and the humming of the window unit air conditioner. Despite both of those and the fact I was wearing tiny shorts and a tank top, I was sweating. His apartment over Bill's shop was not the most insulated.

I pushed aside my e-reader. I used to read all the time before things got crazy. Lord knew I could use the escape, but it was too freaking hot to focus on the words.

"What?" I asked with trepidation. I wasn't keen on surprises these days.

"If I told you, it wouldn't be a surprise," he said blandly.

I shot him a look. "Then why bother to tell me you have a surprise if you don't want me to ask about it? Why not just...*surprise* me?"

He smirked. "Because you're fun to tease."

I punched him lightly on the shoulder and he grabbed my wrist, pulling me against him.

"Hey," I protested, but he pressed his lips to mine and my eyes closed and my objections ceased.

His mouth was magic—applying just the right amount of pressure to make my toes curl and my heart pitter-patter. When his tongue slipped into my mouth, I fisted one hand on his shirt and wrapped my other arm around his neck.

I was working on pure instinct, and it was like my subconscious knew to pull him close and not let go.

Because I would have to very soon.

I pushed that thought out of my mind, letting myself get caught up in the feel of him. He moved to my neck, trailing kisses there and his hand slipped under my shirt. I shifted so he lay on top of me on the couch, then wriggled to free my leg and hook it around his, drawing him even closer. I loved the feel of his body aligned with mine.

It was hot, sweaty, and well...*hot*.

I was plain, ordinary. I didn't have any right to have a boyfriend as mouthwatering as Cole, but someone on Cupid's payroll must have screwed up. And I wasn't complaining.

Groaning, Cole pulled away from me. "If we're going to get to your surprise, we need to get going."

I stared at him. "Really? *Now?*"

He stood. "I hate to say it, but yeah. We should go."

"I'm revoking your man card."

He frowned. "It doesn't work that way. You have to be a man to take away a man card."

"Well, whatever," I huffed. Cole definitely deserved to lose his.

"Trust me. You'll like the surprise."

"I'd better," I muttered.

WHEN COLE PULLED INTO THE Dick's Sporting Goods parking lot to unveil my surprise, I was confused. I wasn't exactly what you'd call athletic.

I looked over at him and the skepticism must have shown on my face. He'd made us leave the apartment for *this*?

Laughing, he guided the Rustinator into a parking

space. "Don't worry, we're not going there." He pointed at a sign adjoining the sporting goods sign. "We're going there."

Field and Stream.

Huh. I wasn't exactly an outdoorsy type, either. Then it dawned on me. "We're buying a gun?" I asked excitedly.

I'd been wanting one, but those suckers weren't cheap and I'd been saving my meager paychecks for when Shenice and I hit the road. Of course with Xavier still potentially on the loose, I'd need some way to defend myself.

There had been no sign of him, but after my mom shot him, Xena had assured me he was still alive. She'd been right about every other thing, so I didn't doubt her now.

Last week, I'd even gone to a local pawn shop to check out some used guns, but the place was sketchy and frankly, it weirded me out to get a used gun—one that could have been used to kill someone. I knew it was an irrational concern, especially when money was tight, but it was there.

Cole reached into his pocket and produced an envelope. "Your birth certificate. You'll need it for the background check."

For a brief second, my good mood dampened. Bill must have given it to him. Before my mom passed, she'd given Bill all our important documents, but everything else had been left in the room she'd stayed in at Bill's. Seeing the birth certificate reminded me I still needed to clean it out and I was running out of time. I wasn't going to leave that for Bill to handle.

"You have your license, right?" Cole asked.

I realized he thought my change in attitude meant I didn't have the other part I needed to purchase the gun.

That wasn't the only thing we needed though. I didn't know why I was so excited to be here—I still didn't want to spend a lot of money. Sometime this week I'd have to suck it up and revisit that pawn shop.

"I can't afford it," I said. "But we can look." I put on a happy face, not wanting him to think I didn't appreciate the surprise he'd lined up for me.

"Happy belated birthday. I'm buying you the gun as the second part of your present."

My hand went up to finger the silver pendant he'd already given me. It was angel wings. We both appreciated the irony of the necklace.

"That's a lot of money, Cole."

"Don't worry about it."

"But—"

"I said don't worry about it. You know me," he reasoned, "and you know I wouldn't spend the money if I couldn't afford it. Let me do this for you."

I looked over at him and saw the love in his eyes. Most girls would get excited over flowers or a fancy dinner or jewelry—and don't get me wrong, I loved the necklace— but he understood me. He understood that the greatest thing he could do for me was give me a way to defend myself against my greatest fear—Xavier. The fact that he wanted me to have a gun showed me he believed in me.

I'd take that over diamonds any day.

He waited a beat. "Are we going in or what?"

I grinned. "Yes."

We got out of the car and walked toward the front of the store hand-in-hand. We entered on the sporting goods side and right away, I noticed a cluster of girls playing with a volleyball. I recognized them—they were on the varsity team at our school. When they saw us, one of them nudged her friend and nodded in our direction.

They stared us down and I scooted a little closer to Cole as we neared them.

"Hi Cole," the tallest one said in a sugary sweet voice. Her name was Danielle. She had the face and body of a Victoria's Secret model. She was in my grade, and the last I'd heard she was first in line to be valedictorian of our class. She was also nice—everyone liked her. She was the type of girl who made me wonder how someone could come out on top in all areas of the gene pool lottery.

"Hey Danielle," Cole said, slowing down a tad.

What the hell? Why weren't we breezing past them?

She smiled, obviously pleased he knew her name. "And Eva, right?"

"No, actually it's Ava." Cole stopped so I was forced to as well. Damn.

"Sorry about that." Her friends silently stood behind her, making a V-shaped formation. It made me feel like I was starring in a made-for-TV version of *Mean Girls*.

Except Danielle was way too pretty to be a B-rated actress.

"Anyway," she said to Cole. "I'm having a Thank-God-it's-still-summer party in a few weeks. I was going to call you."

I looked up at Cole, and he didn't seem surprised by her declaration. Wait...she had his phone number? How the hell did she get that?

The green-eyed monster known as jealousy reared its ugly head, wanting to claw her eyeballs out.

But seriously, what the hell? Was she asking him out right in front of me?

"You can come too," Danielle said to me, as an obvious afterthought.

I narrowed my eyes at her. Suddenly she didn't seem so nice anymore.

Slowly and carefully, I lowered my guards to check her aura. It had been so long since I looked at any that the brightness caught me off guard and I flinched.

There were swirls of pink and silver—sweet and glamorous.

She reached out and touched my arm. "Are you okay?"

I slammed my guards back into place and looked at her. Her concern was genuine and I was suddenly embarrassed, wondering how I had just looked from her perspective. Probably like a grade-A weirdo.

My cheeks flushed. "Yeah, I'm, um, fine."

Cole glanced down at me, then turned to the girls. "We need to get going."

I could have kissed him right there. *Get me out of this awkward situation.*

Danielle took a step back. "Sure thing. I'll text you the invite."

Cole ushered me away, me still clinging to his hand. I was grateful he didn't look back at her even though I could feel her gaze boring into the backs of our heads.

"What was that about?" he asked.

"What do you mean?" I tried to look innocent, but Cole was having none of it. He rolled his eyes.

"You were totally weird with Dani back there. And were you checking out her aura?"

Damn. I was hoping he hadn't noticed that.

"Dani? I thought her name was Danielle?"

He rubbed his neck. "She goes by Dani sometimes."

"Oh." I hated how jealous I sounded—like a damn jealous girlfriend.

But that's kind of what I was. Since when did Cole have friends who were girls? Or any friends for that matter? Between school and the shop and well, me, he didn't have time. And anyway, I thought that was the way he preferred it. He was the ultimate loner.

But what did I know? Perhaps *Dani* knew him better than I did.

"Are you seriously sticking out your lower lip right now?"

I quickly sucked it in but not before earning myself a hearty laugh from Cole.

I got that tingle in my nose that told me tears weren't far behind. *Suck it up, Ava.* The last thing I wanted was to cry in public. This wasn't like me. I wasn't the jealous type. Besides that, Cole and I had been through so much together. There was no reason I should feel threatened.

For goodness' sake, we were at this store so he could spend hundreds of dollars buying me the thing at the top of my wish list.

But even though I knew all this to be true, I was not okay with that little interaction back there—both with how familiar *Dani* seemed with Cole and my reaction to it.

Cole scanned the area, then pulled me down the vacant skiing aisle. Pressing me up against a display, he caged me in with his arms. His nearness was intoxicating and overwhelming in an oh-so-good way. My heartbeat became a drum in my chest, beating a rhythm that sounded out his name. And just as his body had invaded my space, his presence invaded my mind. He was all I could think about.

"You're the only one I want." He kissed me, lightly sucking on my lower lip. "Got it?"

I nodded mutely, not able to form any words. He dipped his head again, coming in for another kiss, and I fisted my hands on his t-shirt, bringing him in closer.

His tongue delved into my mouth, exploring and claiming.

Whenever Cole kissed me, there was no doubt in my mind I was his.

And he was mine.

"Hey! You kids! You can't do that here!"

Cole shot the employee who'd interrupted us a nasty look, then stole one last kiss before leading me away.

THE SPORTING GOODS STORE WAS a bust as far as guns went. They didn't have anything I wanted at a price I was willing to let Cole pay. But he had another surprise up his sleeve, which was why he was so eager to leave his apartment. There was a gun show at the pavilion and that's where we headed next.

While Cole bought our tickets, I watched people go

through security. The security team used zip ties to render entrants' guns inoperable. I was amazed at the sheer number of people who were carrying. I mean, we *were* at a gun show, so I supposed I shouldn't have been that surprised.

More though, I think it was the type of people carrying. There were the ones I expected—men who looked like they had just gotten off their Harleys, men sporting tattoos that were probably gang related, men wearing camo. Basically, all your stereotypical gun owners.

It was the unassuming men and women that threw me for a loop. One lady looked like she should be teaching Sunday School instead of patronizing a gun show.

It just made me wonder how many people I passed on a daily basis that were armed and dangerous.

Although, Xavier was proof of the fact that one didn't need a weapon to be considered dangerous. He had that one covered with his freaky abilities.

The last few times I'd seen him, though, he hadn't displayed any of them. I couldn't believe I hadn't realized that before. Did it mean something? Or was it just a coincidence? I didn't know, but Cole returned with our wrist bands so I put it out of my mind.

He fastened one on my wrist. "Ready?"

We made our way through security, which didn't take long since we weren't carrying. I actually didn't know if Cole had a concealed carry permit. I needed to see about getting mine and quick. There were plenty of online classes I could take, which was kind of scary if you thought about it. How did staring at a computer screen for a few hours prepare someone not to accidentally blow their toes off? Or worse, someone else's toes?

Cole led me into the main showroom, and there were tables upon tables full of weapons—rifles, handguns, assault rifles, knives. If it was legal, it was here. It was a bit disconcerting, actually. My pulse spiked and I gulped.

Cole didn't seem to be having the trouble I was. He walked over to a table and picked up a ridiculously large revolver. For a moment, I was alarmed. Could anyone just pick up any weapon at any time? There were so many people—how could they be sure someone wouldn't run off with one? It was not like they did a background check to get in this place.

Then I realized there was a metal wire keeping the gun secure to the table, only allowing it to be moved about three feet. *Sheesh.* Of course there was proper security. I needed to chill out.

Cole turned to me and grinned, holding up the gun. "How about this one?"

I cocked my head and looked at it skeptically. "I'd have to start lifting weights just to carry the darn thing." It truly was comically large.

"True," Cole agreed. "You are kind of wimpy." I stuck my tongue out at him, which only made him grin wider. I swore one of his greatest pleasures in life was teasing me. He picked up a tiny pink semi-automatic. "This one is more your speed."

"I don't think so." Although Cole was on board with buying me a gun, if I left it up to him, he'd choose one adorned with sequins or lace or something equally ridiculous. He was perverse like that.

But honestly, I kind of liked that about him. It kept things interesting.

I stepped closer to the table so I could peruse the weapons for myself. Everything was either comically large or teeny tiny. Where were the normal weapons?

I strolled down to the next table and found it more to my liking. There was a great assortment of Sigs, Glocks, and Smith & Wessons. Luckily, I'd already done extensive research, so I was familiar with the different kinds of guns. I picked up a 9mm Glock, similar to the gun I'd borrowed from Bill, but winced when I saw the price tag. Yikes. No way was I letting Cole pay for that.

He came up beside me. "That one's nice."

I appreciated that he didn't imply I couldn't handle a 9mm, like he'd done when we first started at the gun range months ago. When he'd first told me he was taking me gun shopping, I was worried he'd insist I get a .22, but I wanted something with more bite.

It'd been a while since I'd held a gun in my hand. Since the night my mom shot Xavier, to be exact. The cold, smooth metal in my hand brought images to mind that I would be happy never reliving again.

The final shot—the one that hit him in the face—was brutal and bloody. It was like his face exploded. I didn't see the aftermath—Cole pulled me away before I could check on him.

It was probably better I didn't see.

Xena assured me Xavier survived. Apparently having his face blown off wasn't enough to kill him. But I wished it was. He killed my mom, and I wished she'd had the satisfaction of killing him.

Instead, I would have to pick up where she left off. It was a legacy I would gladly take, no matter how difficult.

But while Xena assured me Xavier was alive—just alive, not necessarily alive and well—she also assured me I wouldn't see him anytime soon. Though I still wasn't on speaking terms with her, she texted me every once in a while with pertinent information.

I never replied.

"Hey," Cole said, and I snapped out of it, putting the gun back on the table. He picked it up. "I've always wanted a Glock."

I honestly didn't care about the brand so much. I just wanted something solid and reliable.

Picking up a different one, I tested the weight in my hand, then wrapped my fingers around the hilt.

Watching me, Cole shook his head. "That one doesn't fit your hand well. It's too thick." He quickly scanned the table, then plucked one from the back. "Try this one."

He handed it to me and I glanced at it. "It's pink." What was up with Cole and the pink guns today?

"I know." He smirked. "It suits you."

I rolled my eyes. I was not a prissy pink wearing kind of girl. I didn't think I even owned any pink. But still, I obliged him, wrapping my hand around the gun and holding it up as if I were firing it.

Huh. It actually felt good in my hand, like it was an extension of my arm rather than a cold, metal device.

"This one might actually work," I said.

Cole started chatting with the vendor while I examined the gun more closely. I closed my eyes, feeling its weight in my hand and imagined using it to send a bullet into Xavier's heart. And then his brain. A couple of hundred times.

Morbid? Perhaps. A little sadistic? You betcha.

He'd killed my mom. Nothing I could do to him would ever be enough to make up for that fact.

But I was more than willing to try.

CHAPTER 3

ON OUR WAY BACK TO Cole's place, Shenice texted me with one word.

Thursday.

I gulped. Today was Saturday. In just a few short days, I would get what I wanted.

I glanced over at Cole. But somehow I also wouldn't.

I'd known this day was coming. I'd wanted it to come. Hell, I'd arranged it. But having the actual date set made it so much more real.

Would I really and truly be able to leave Cole?

I reached across the seat and snagged his hand. The thought of leaving him overwhelmed me, making me feel like my chest was being crushed and I couldn't breathe. Putting my hand over my heart, I inhaled deeply, willing my chest to stop hurting.

I had to do it. He would always be a seeker, but I could still save him from having to live like one.

Cole ran his thumb over the back of my hand. "So I was thinking of going tomorrow."

"Going where?" I asked automatically. My chest hurt so much I could barely breathe.

He gave me the side eye. "To get Kyle."

"Oh, right." I inhaled, holding the breath for a few seconds before exhaling. That seemed to help.

"Are you coming with me?"

I chewed on my cuticle, then yanked it out of my mouth. Shenice would have a fit if she saw me doing that. She'd been giving me free and regular manicures in the hope I'd like having nice nails and stop chewing them.

So far it hadn't worked. But I was trying. That had to count for something, right?

"When would we come back?"

"Monday. Tuesday at the latest." He looked over at me. "Come on. Shenice will give you the time off. The shop hasn't gotten any busier, right?"

"It's doing a *little* better," I muttered. Shenice had been about to go out of business when Xena gave her money to keep the shop open, hire me, and keep an eye on me. We'd had a slight upsurge in clientele, but not enough to keep the shop afloat. I wondered if Xena was still paying her. I wouldn't put it past her. Even though she kept her distance, I figured she was probably still meddling in my life. She didn't seem to be able to stop herself and I couldn't stop her, either, so I tried not to worry about it.

Now that Shenice had given me our leaving date, I didn't want to do anything to make her change her mind and decide not to go. But even if we got stuck in northern Virginia an extra day, I would still be back in time.

"And I know we haven't seen..." he trailed off, not wanting to say Xavier's name, but I knew exactly who he was talking about. We had an unspoken agreement not to talk about him, effectively ignoring the situation until it became an active threat. "But if what Xena says is true..."

He trailed off again, and again I knew exactly what he was talking about. Xavier was out there somewhere. Now that my mom was gone, I didn't know if he'd come after us again since he no longer had the leverage he needed to force me to do things for him. But he was unpredictable. I didn't pretend to understand what went on in that warped mind of his.

The best I could figure, Xavier didn't have any quarrel

with Cole. His fight had always been with me. My mom and Cole were innocent casualties. It was yet another reason I needed to leave. If Xavier decided to come after me, I didn't want Cole getting caught in the fray again, especially if his brother was going to be in the picture.

I looked at Cole, studying his profile. He wore his Aviator sunglasses, which I loved. He'd gotten his hair cut recently—probably because of how freaking hot it had been—so his hair wasn't overgrown like it normally was. Instead of being a slightly messy badass sexy Cole, he was a well-groomed badass sexy Cole.

I'd take him any way I could get him, for as long as I could have him.

Screw it. Why was I hesitating? I had less than a week left. I didn't want to spend it with him in northern Virginia and me down here.

"I'll go."

I SAT AT THE KITCHEN table with Bill, spooning Cheerios in my mouth double time. Despite setting an alarm, I still managed to get up late. It was a special skill of mine. Cole would be here any minute.

Bill tapped his thumb on the table and his other hand clutched a coffee mug. I could tell he wanted to say something, but in true Bill fashion, he was holding it in.

"Spill it," I said between mouthfuls.

He sighed. "I know you're eighteen and that legally makes you an adult, but I don't know if I should try to stop you from going on this trip with Cole."

I wanted to snort. As if he could stop me. I could count on one hand the number of days I had left with Cole.

But because it was Bill and I loved him and all he'd done for me this past year, I held in my snarky retort. And I honestly appreciated how hard he tried to do right by me. He'd lost his own daughter nearly twenty years ago when she was seventeen, and he never fully recovered, not that one ever could recover from something like that. I knew I'd never recover from losing my mom. I was learning to deal with it, but that wasn't the same as recovering.

"It's fine," I said gently. "You trust him."

"Yes, but you're both young and hormones—" Bill turned bright red and cleared his throat, looking at the cabinets, the refrigerator, the stove—basically at anything but me. "I want to do the right thing. What your mama would do if she were here."

Bill finally looked at me, and his gaze was filled with fatherly love. A piece of my heart broke. It was going to destroy Bill when he found out I was gone. Not as much as the death of his daughter of course, but it would hurt him.

Damn. I'd planned to leave him a note so he wouldn't worry, but I was kidding myself if I thought a note would be sufficient. Bill took me and my mom in when we had nowhere to turn and became like a father to me, especially during the time my mom was sick and since she'd died.

I put my hand on his hand. "She would let me go."

I didn't know if that was true. It probably was. Cole had become an extended member of our family. You didn't go through some of the shit we'd gone through together without forming a close bond.

I didn't say it so Bill would "let" me go. We both knew he couldn't stop me. I said it to assuage any guilt he felt about whether or not he was doing the right thing.

I heard Cole's car out in the driveway, so I hurriedly shoved the last few bites of cereal in my mouth and chugged my orange juice. I was just putting my dishes in the dishwasher when Cole let himself in.

He stood in the kitchen doorway, his hands shoved in his pockets.

"Hey," he said.

Ever since Cole stayed the night after the last incident with Xavier and Bill had a stern talking with him before he was allowed in my bedroom, Cole had been weird around

Bill and me. I'd seen him at the shop with Bill when he didn't know I was watching and he was fine then. And he was obviously fine when it was just me. But put the three of us together and it turned into weird mania. That talk must have scarred him or something. He'd barely even hold my hand in Bill's presence.

Our situation was a little odd in that Bill acted as a father figure to both of us, even though Cole had recently turned twenty. His real father had never been present. He didn't talk about it much, but it had to bother him on some level.

I'd never met my father, either. He hadn't even known my mom was pregnant. When I was growing up, I never thought about him. My normal was me and my mom. Now that she was gone, though, I'd become more curious about the man who fathered me. But I didn't know his last name and he wasn't listed on my birth certificate, so the chances of finding him were slim. And I had more pressing issues to worry about.

"I'm ready," I said as I closed the dishwasher.

"There's no rush," Cole replied. "They're not expecting us until dinner."

I slipped on my flip-flops. "Dinner?"

Cole shuffled his feet, pushing his hands deeper into his pockets and looking at the ground. "Yeah. My mom invited us over." He looked up at me, his eyes full of trepidation. "Don't expect a lot. She probably—"

"Cole." I walked to him and kissed him on the cheek. "It'll be great. I'm glad I get to meet her."

He visibly relaxed, then tensed up again, looking over at Bill and checking for his reaction over my PDA. I rolled my eyes. But far be it for me to tell my boyfriend to stop respecting his elders.

Cole's mom was a piece of work. The only reason she became a mother—not once, but twice—was because she hadn't been careful or smart enough to keep herself from getting pregnant. From what Cole had told me, she had no maternal instincts whatsoever.

But as someone who recently lost a mother, I was glad she was making the effort. Perhaps it was a step in the right direction. I wasn't naive or optimistic enough to think she'd suddenly turn into a devoted parent, but her showing any sort of interest in Cole was an improvement.

"You kids drive carefully," Bill said.

His concern was laughable. Cole drove like an old man unless he had to do otherwise. We'd been in a few harrowing situations involving a high speed chase and a mini-van trying to push us off the road, and he'd handled both like a pro.

I wish I was as cool, calm, and collected as he was in stressful situations. I'd gotten better, but I still had my freak-out moments.

It didn't take me long to fall asleep in the car. There was nothing like the lull of a moving vehicle to make me nod off.

I woke to the sound of a motorcycle by my window. My pulse spiked as adrenaline flowed through my body. I peered out the window and as the bike passed, I saw a stream of long blond hair flowing out from the helmet.

Not him.

The last I knew, Xavier's means of transportation was a motorcycle similar to that one. Every time I saw or heard the whirring of a bike, I had a visceral reaction. I'd never noticed how many motorcycles were on the road until recently, and I can tell you it was more than you would think. I was having heart palpitations left and right. It was surely taking years off my life.

Cole glanced over at me, then grinned. "You've got a little something." He pointed to his chin.

My fingers flew to my face, wiping furiously as I blushed. I totally had drool running down my chin. How had I not felt that? Smooth was not my middle name. Luckily, I wasn't trying to impress Cole. I'd never been able to, but he loved me anyway.

"Where are we?" I asked.

"Almost to Fredericksburg. Your phone has been going off like crazy. I'm surprised it didn't wake you up."

I leaned down to fish my phone out of the bag at my feet. Nine missed texts. What...the...hell? Did I end up on some sort of texting telemarketing list?

Nope. It was Xena, times nine.

My teeth clenched together in a grinding motion that was sure to ruin them. I made a conscious effort to relax my jaw. I didn't have dental insurance—or medical for that matter—so I wouldn't be going to the dentist any time soon.

Taking a deep breath, I opened the first message.

Where are you?

My answer? *None of your business.* But I didn't bother responding. She knew where she stood with me.

Seriously, where are you?

The texts went on like that, getting slightly more desperate with each one. I would have liked to see Xena frantically tapping the messages out on her phone.

Because we shared an ancestor somewhere back in our gene pool, she could find me like I had a homing beacon shoved up my nether region. Frankly, the thought of telling her I was leaving hadn't even occurred to me. I didn't care if she'd made a deal with my angel ancestor, Areli, to protect me. She should have thought of that before she'd failed to divulge the fact that Xavier was also in her gene pool.

That's right—she was related to both me and Xavier. Maybe I could have overlooked that, but I couldn't overlook the fact that she'd lied about it. It made me wonder what else she might have lied about.

Or still was.

She was going to lose her shit when I left for good. But once again, I didn't care. My conscience was clear...at least where she was concerned. And anyway, Shenice would probably let her know what the deal was. As far as I knew, the two of them still communicated, but I didn't ask. I wanted to stay on good terms with Shenice and a conversation about Xena would not end well. Shenice disapproved of my cutting Xena out of my life. I generally respected her opinion, but on this we'd had to agree to disagree.

"Is everything okay?" Cole asked.

"Yeah. It was just Xena freaking out because I'm out of range."

Cole didn't comment. He was smart like that.

I think he was one step closer to forgiving her than I was, but he hadn't said as much. Cole could be a total hardass about some things, but now that he'd come to terms with being a seeker, he'd become a lot more Zen. I was still getting used to it.

I yawned. "What time is dinner?"

"Not until six."

I checked the time. It wasn't even noon yet. We would have quite a bit of time to kill. But knowing Cole, he'd want some time to settle himself before facing his family. He didn't say that—wouldn't want to disrupt the tough guy vibe he had going on—but these visits wore on him. I hoped my company would help.

My eyes grew heavy again and I didn't fight it, letting sleep overtake me again.

I DIDN'T WAKE UP UNTIL we were parked in front of a hotel. This time, I discreetly wiped my chin before Cole could comment on the drool on my face. Although this time, my face was clean. *Figures.*

This hotel was much nicer than the one we'd stayed in last time we'd taken this trek. Of course, then we'd been on the run from the Reapers and were low on cash, so we didn't have many options. I hoped this hotel had a continental breakfast with one of those waffle machines with the timer on them. Those were the best.

I stretched and Cole looked over at me, shaking his head. "One of these days, you're going to drive and *I'm* going to sleep."

I snorted so hard I almost choked on my own snot. The few times Cole had ridden with me, he'd clutched his knees so hard his knuckles turned white. I didn't know why. I was actually a good driver. So, okay, there was that one incident with the bush. But I swear it came out of nowhere.

Despite how creaky and rusty and old his car was, Cole would never again let me drive the Rustinator unless it was life and death. And even then it'd probably be a toss-up for him—*death or let Ava drive?*

I'd like to think he'd make the right decision, but he was a dude and dudes were weird about their cars. Or at least this one was. I didn't know many others, so my frame of reference was a bit lacking.

As soon as we got out of the car, the heat smacked me in the face, making it hard to breathe. The humidity made my skin damp and my tank top cling. *Ugh.* This summer had been one of the most brutal I could remember.

We grabbed our bags out of the trunk so we could escape into the air conditioning.

"Hey, a pool!" I exclaimed, seeing the wet oasis behind a fence to the side of the hotel. Except *damn it*, I hadn't thought to bring a bathing suit.

Judging by Cole's expression, he hadn't brought one, either.

Cole and I had been equally busy with work since summer started—and I had my GED class—so I could count on one finger the number of times I'd been in a bathing suit. For once, our schedules had aligned and Cole took me to the beach where we'd sweltered and pretended to have fun for a few hours before we finally called it. The heat index was one-hundred and ten, so even frequent dips in the ocean hadn't helped.

He flashed me a wicked grin and I immediately knew what he was thinking. "You know after hours, we could jump the fence and—"

"No. Uh-unh. Not going to happen." No way was I getting arrested for public nudity. Someday Cole and I could skinny dip, but that day was not today. "But there's probably a Target nearby. We could buy suits."

I hated to dip into my stash of cash, but I was just that desperate for relief from the heat. Plus, it would be nice to splash around with Cole for a few hours.

I was collecting memories these days. Soon, they'd be all I had.

CHAPTER 4

COLE AND I SPLASHED AROUND in the pool like we were little kids, even going so far as playing Marco Polo. When he accidentally grabbed my boob, we got dirty looks from the other guests, effectively ending that game.

Though, I couldn't say for sure it was an accident.

We left after that, needing to get ready to head over to Cole's mom's house. When I came out of the bathroom after doing my makeup, I was surprised to see him in a collared shirt and dark jeans. Other than my mom's funeral, this was the most dressed up I'd seen him since I hadn't attended his graduation. Neither he nor Bill thought to take any pictures, so I could only assume he'd dressed appropriately.

He looked delicious, and I was tempted to try to convince him to blow off dinner and stay here at the hotel. Dinner might feed my stomach, but one-on-one time with Cole fed my soul.

I wouldn't do that, though. This was too important to him.

He sat on the end of the bed, staring at the TV but not really watching it. His knee bobbed up and down and he chomped on a wad of gum. I could smell the peppermint from across the room.

I'd never be able to smell peppermint again without

being reminded of kissing Cole. He had a peppermint addiction, and I kind of liked it. Kissing him was like licking a candy cane. Only much, much yummier.

"If we leave in twenty minutes, we should get there about ten minutes early," he said.

I sat next to him and his knee-bobbing shook the entire bed. I was tempted to put my hand on it to stop it. "Okay."

"Unless you think we should stop and pick something up. Like, shit, I don't know. Flowers? Or a pie or something?"

"I don't think that's necessary," I said, but when his other knee started bobbing up and down, I amended my statement. "But it would be a nice gesture."

He jumped up and I knew I'd made the right call. Flowers would be a nice gesture, but more importantly, they would give him something to focus on until we got there.

"Let's go," he said. "There's a store on the way."

In the car, he'd traded in the knee bobbing for thumb tapping on the steering wheel. At a red light, I reached over and closed my hand around his fingers to stop it.

"Relax," I said. "You're starting to make me nervous."

It was true, but that wasn't why I said it. I didn't want to spout false assurances I couldn't guarantee. I couldn't say whether or not dinner would go well, but either way, it would be okay. *Cole* would be okay because he was strong, stronger than any shit his mother could throw at him.

"I just want to make a good first impression, you know?"

I cocked my head at him. I did know, sort-of. But this was his mother, the woman who'd birthed him. He'd spent more than half his life with her. The time for first impressions was long gone.

I reconsidered. He wasn't the same person he was when he'd lived in northern Virginia with her. I hadn't known him them, but from what he'd told me, he'd done a complete one-eighty. Maybe he was getting a second chance at a first impression.

I smoothed down the edge of his collar, which had turned up. "You look great. You're successful in your job. You're charming...when you want to be." That earned me a grin. "You got this."

"Thanks." He seemed to relax and I gave myself a mental pat on the back for a job well done.

In the flower section of the store, though, it was like the pep talk never happened. He stared at the selection of flowers, obviously overwhelmed. It made me wonder if he'd ever bought flowers for anyone before. He'd never gotten me any.

Finally he picked up a dozen long-stem roses. "How about this?"

"Um, those might be a little much," I said, picking up a bouquet of brightly colored flowers that screamed summer to me. "How about these?"

"Okay, yeah. Those look good." He shoved the roses back into the display and took the bright ones from me. "Should we pick up a dessert or something?" He frowned as he looked at the flowers. He seemed like he was double-guessing the choice, which was not like him. He always knew what he wanted and had no problem taking action.

His anxiety was killing me. I wanted to put him at ease, but I didn't know how to do that. Apparently my forte wasn't my pep talks that stuck.

"Do you know what's on the dinner menu?" I asked.

He shook his head.

"We should probably forgo dessert then. We don't know what would go with dinner and anyway, she might have something planned already."

He nodded. "Good point."

He paid for the flowers and once back out at the car, laid them carefully in the backseat, like they were worth hundreds of dollars instead of the twelve bucks he'd paid. But he was noticeably more relaxed. Buying the flowers seemed to have put him at ease.

The closer we got, the more anxious I became. This could either go wonderfully right or terribly, horribly wrong. My gut told me there would be no in-between.

Cole found street parking right in front of his mom's townhouse, a good omen. As I looked at the overrun lawn, the duct tape on the front window, and the rusty awning, I tried not to judge. If my mom and I had lived in a house instead of an apartment, the exterior of our home might have looked like that. My mom worked crazy hours, and I didn't know anything about home maintenance.

Somehow, though, I knew my mom would have figured something out. She would have worked herself to the bone before allowing our home to crumble around us.

Cole's eyes narrowed at the house, zeroing in on an old tire sitting on the sidewalk. Trying to think optimistically—there could be a perfectly good explanation why she wasn't keeping up with the exterior of the home—I took his hand as we started up the walk.

He let go of my hand to press the doorbell, since he held the flowers in his other hand. No one answered so he pressed it again and knocked on the door as well, loud enough to wake the dead.

Still nothing.

My heart sank.

He passed me the flowers and opened the door. "Mom?" he called out. He walked in and I followed.

The room was hot and stank like dirty laundry and rotten food. Trash littered the floor. A sofa with one missing cushion lined the wall, but that was the only furniture other than a coffee table.

In the middle of the coffee table were a supply of needles, a spoon, a lighter, and a baggie filled with white powder.

"*Fuck.*"

That one word summed it up perfectly.

I turned to Cole, wanting to comfort him, but his

demeanor suggested he wouldn't welcome it. Not right now.

Then I watched as the last minuscule piece of hope he'd been holding out died in his eyes.

I hated her. I hated this woman I'd never met. I hated her for standing in the way of Cole helping his brother. I hated her for failing Cole again and again when he was growing up. But most of all, I hated her for making him feel like he was worthless when he was anything but.

He was everything.

I heard a scuffle on the stairs and turned to see a woman stumbling down them. She wore panties and a dirty white tank top that was so threadbare I could see right through it. Hair that was so dirty and greasy I couldn't determine the color completed the look.

Her face was expressionless and her eyes vacant. When they landed on Cole, the edges of her mouth tilted up slightly.

When there had been no answer, I'd thought she wasn't home. That had been bad enough. This was much, much worse.

My gut was right. There was no in between.

She stumbled toward him, nearly falling when her feet got tangled in a plastic bag. "What are you doing here?"

"Dinner, Mom. Remember?" His hands curled into fists, and for a moment I thought he was going to lay one on her. Instead he took a step back.

Good! I wanted to cheer. *Put some distance—literally and figuratively—between you and that bitch.* I edged closer to him.

"I'm starved." She flopped on the couch. "Did you bring food?"

"When you invite someone to dinner, you generally provide the food," he said tersely.

"Did someone invite you?" She frowned. "Oh, was that today?"

"Fuck this," Cole spat. "Where's Kyle?"

"Not here."

"No shit. Where is he?"

"Juvie, I think. Someone came and got him."

Cole stilled. "*What?*"

"Yesterday. Or maybe Friday. I don't remember."

"Why the hell didn't you call me?" He started to pace in front of her, repeatedly running his hands over his head. Cole was losing his shit. Gone was the Zen.

"Hey," she said sharply, looking up at him. "I'm your mother. Don't talk to me like that." She slurred the last few words as her gaze landed on the coffee table. With shaking hands, she reached for the baggie. Her fingers fumbled as she tried to open it.

Cole snatched it out of her hands.

"Hey!" She stood on wobbly legs, reaching for the baggie, but Cole held it out of her reach.

She stared at him, the fire in her eyes the first sign of emotion I'd seen since she appeared. Then she hauled off and slapped Cole across the face.

I gasped, putting my hand over my mouth.

It wasn't a hard slap, but it was enough to turn his cheek. I didn't think it was possible, but my heart broke even more for him and the fact that this sorry excuse for a human being was his mother.

I wanted to end that bitch. I had a lot of pent-up aggression from the last year, and I would be more than happy to take it out on her.

"Ava, please wait in the car." He didn't turn as he spoke and his voice was eerily calm—*the calm before the storm.*

Shit, shit, shit. I didn't know what to do.

I took a step toward him. "Cole..." I didn't have an end to that sentence, but I knew I didn't want to leave him alone. There was no way this situation could end well.

"Please." His voice was ragged, desperate. And it was that desperation that prompted me to heed his request. I looked at him one last time, willing him to look at me so I'd know he'd be okay in here and so he'd know I had his back if he needed me. But he didn't turn.

I let myself out, still clutching the happy-looking flowers in my hand.

CHAPTER 5

IT ONLY TOOK TEN MINUTES for Cole to reappear, and I scrambled up from the curb where I'd been sitting. The car had been locked but no way was I going back inside to ask him for the key. Besides that, it would have been hot as hell in there—the car, not the house. Though inside the house was definitely another version of hell.

He tossed me the keys. "Drive," he growled. I blinked, looking at the keys I now held in my hand.

Shit, shit, shit.

Now I really wanted to march back in there and kill that woman. If Cole had already taken care of it, then I'd kill her a second time.

Wordlessly, I got into the driver's seat and started the car. I pulled away from the curb, eager to get away from this hellhole. I drove more carefully than I ever had before. I feared Cole would break if one more bad thing happened, and I didn't want that bad thing to be me wrecking his beloved Rustinator.

The only problem was I didn't know where I was going. I glanced over at Cole. He stared straight ahead, his face an impenetrable shield to how he was feeling.

I didn't want to bother him with asking for directions so I fumbled around in my purse for my phone, wanting to use the navigation. Except I didn't know the address of the hotel offhand. *Damn*.

"Left," Cole said, his voice mechanical and devoid of emotion. It was just like him—he was hurting, yet he still noticed I needed help. After I made the turn, he instructed me to get in the right lane, using the same tone.

"What happened in there?" I asked cautiously, not really expecting him to answer. But I was dying to know. At his core, Cole was a good person, but I feared his bitch of a mother might push him too far, might push him to do things he wouldn't forgive himself for.

"Turn right." He was silent for a moment. "I flushed her stash."

"That's it?"

"That's it," he said with finality, signaling the discussion was closed. I exhaled, grateful Cole had been strong enough not to let her get the better of him.

I eased to a stop at a red light and looked over at him. It was then I noticed the claw marks on his arms—angry scratches inflicted by that bitch of a mother.

And then I knew he was definitely telling the truth. He hadn't done anything but dispose of the drug she'd made herself a slave to, but she'd done everything in her power to stop him. She was bony and disoriented and he easily could have knocked her away, but more than likely he hadn't wanted to raise a hand to her for fear he might hurt her.

She didn't deserve the consideration. One of her sons had been picked up by the cops, and she couldn't even remember the details. She'd assaulted her other son when he'd spent an hour agonizing over bringing her flowers.

Rage boiled within me. I wanted to make a U-turn and punch that bitch in her face. Cole might not be willing to hit her, but I sure as hell was.

We made it back to the hotel and silently I followed Cole inside. I wanted to hold his hand, but they were shoved in his pockets. I almost thought he'd forgotten I was with him until he held open the hotel door for me. I closed it and locked it, then leaned against it.

"I'm sorry," I whispered. It was insufficient, but there was nothing else to say. His mother was horrible. She was a slave to her addiction, and any goodness she may have had as a person was sucked up into it.

I'd heard you should hate the addiction, not the person, but I wasn't big enough to do that. Not right now. Not while Cole was hurting right in front of me.

He sank down onto the bed and put his head in his hands. I waited. Cole wasn't a big talker in times like these, but I'd wait him out. We had all night.

I sat behind him and wrapped my arms around him, resting my cheek against his shoulder blade. We sat there a long time.

"I saw her aura." Cole's voice was shaking in a way I'd never heard before. Not when I'd been hurt, not when he'd learned he was a seeker, *never*.

I scooted to sit beside him. "What do you mean?"

"I saw it."

I shook my head. "You must be mistaken. She's way too old for that."

Seekers could only see the auras of those in their general age range. I'd never figured out exactly how wide the span was, but Cole definitely should not have been able to see the aura of someone twenty years older.

"I'm telling you—I saw it." He was insistent. I wanted to believe him, but it was impossible.

Wasn't it?

"Okay," I said slowly. "What did you see?"

"It was black." He hung his head. "A pure black mist."

"Oh, Cole." I wrapped my arms around him again. I didn't know what to believe. Maybe the shadows were playing tricks on him. Maybe in his anger, he hallucinated it.

Or maybe he really did see it.

That possibility scared the shit out of me. I didn't know exactly what it meant, but I knew that made him special among seekers and in this case, being special was not a good thing.

All the more reason to keep handlers away from him.

THE NEXT MORNING COLE STARTED making phone calls at exactly eight a.m. when city hall opened. I was still in bed.

It took a while, but he was eventually able to locate his brother. Unfortunately, they wouldn't allow Cole to speak with him. Parents and guardians only. It was total bullshit. If they only knew what type of parent Kyle had.

Except, didn't they? Cole hadn't mentioned anything about social services lately, but they'd opened a case on his mother. I could kick myself for not keeping in the loop on that. Talk about being selfish. Granted, I'd had a lot going on, but still. I was a shitty girlfriend.

"Is social services still investigating your mother?" I asked.

He threw his phone down on the bed in disgust. "The case is *pending*. That's all anyone will tell me."

So at least I didn't miss anything. Anyway, he would've told me if there had been any news.

He sighed, dropping down on the bed beside me. "They won't say it, but I think his case is low priority. He's not really young and he's in trouble with the law himself, so I get it. It's not like he's a helpless little kid who can't fend for himself."

What he said was true, but what he didn't say was that at one point, both he and his brother had been helpless children at the mercy of their druggie mother. How long had she managed to keep it somewhat together until she'd descended into what she was now?

I didn't ask. After he'd told me about seeing his mother's aura last night, he clammed up, not saying anything else. He was processing it in his own way. As much as I wanted to help him, I knew him well enough to give him space.

"Get dressed," he said. "We should get on the road."

"Are you sure you don't want to stick around longer to see if you can make more progress on Kyle?"

"No," he said with finality. "There's nothing I can do that I can't do from home. There's no point hanging around, and frankly, I'm ready to get away from here."

Get away from his mom was what he meant.

I jumped out of bed and walked toward the bathroom. "Okay. Just give me twenty minutes to shower and get dressed."

Exactly twenty-two minutes later, we were in the Rustinator on the way back to reality. Or at least, a different reality. With every mile of asphalt we covered, my stomach tied itself up tighter. As long as I was away from home, I could pretend my departure date wasn't looming.

And this trip hadn't exactly turned out to be the joyous last hurrah I had hoped.

"I'm sorry," he said, breaking the silence and interrupting my thoughts.

I glanced over at him, but he remained facing forward. "What do you mean?"

"I'm sorry you had to witness that."

"Cole," I said his name forcefully, so he'd look over at me. I wanted him to see my face when I said this. "It's not your fault."

He returned his gaze to the road. "No, but I know what she's like. I should have known better. That part is on me."

"*No*," I said firmly. "That part is not on you. No one can blame you for wanting to believe the best of your mother."

He laughed bitterly. "Even if she's never given me any reason to?"

"Even then. *Especially* then." I paused. "You can be irritating as shit, but you're a good person, Cole.

Everything I saw in the last twenty-four hours just makes me believe it more."

Then the air conditioner sputtered. I looked at it in horror. *Please, no.* It ignored my plea and quit.

Cole pounded on the dash a few times with his fist, but his sophisticated solution to the dilemma did no good. It only took seconds for the temperature in the car to rise.

I rolled down the window and was blasted with a wave of hot air that did little to cool me off. I glanced over at Cole and he shook his head. "Don't say it."

I had a line of insults primed and ready to go, but I choked them down. "You're lucky I'm taking pity on you right now."

Cole grinned. This was probably the only time he would ever accept my pity. The thing was I didn't pity him. Not really. Only his obsessive love for this stupid car.

I crossed my arms and sank down in my seat, the sweat already gathering on my thighs. "You're lucky," I said again for good measure.

WHEN WE GOT BACK, COLE decided to put some time in at the shop even though he wasn't scheduled. I think he still needed to take his mind off things. Nice Beauty was closed on Mondays, so I didn't have anywhere to be. I positioned a fan to blow directly on me and hopped up on my usual stool, turning on my e-reader.

The book was good—some kind of epic fantasy time travel story—but I couldn't focus on it. I liked watching Cole work. It was a guilty pleasure, and I planned to indulge the rest of the afternoon.

I was not a grease monkey groupie by any stretch, but it was enticing to watch Cole work. He knew what he was doing and wasn't afraid to work hard, often putting in long hours and being covered in grease before he called it quits. His work ethic was something to be proud of.

But that wasn't why I watched. It was just hot, and I wasn't talking about the scorching temperature. Like right now, his muscles strained as he fought to loosen an old bolt. Or when he was doing something more intricate, his eyes focused intently on the task. Sometimes he looked at me with that same intensity. It was enough to send my heart racing around in circles in my chest.

Bill emerged from his office, smiling when he saw me. "I didn't realize you were coming back today."

I ducked my head, feeling guilty. "Sorry." I should have texted him. Though I tried not to take him for granted, I totally did. Bill was solid and dependable, and he'd never once scolded me for pulling a jerk move, which I seemed to do frequently.

"Sorry," Cole echoed.

"Where's Kyle?" Bill asked, and the air in the room thickened.

"Things didn't go as planned." Cole's voice was flat. Bill knew him well enough not to ask any questions, at least not right now. Cole concentrated on the engine in front of him. After he lost himself in work for a while, maybe he'd open up to Bill.

I hopped off the stool. "Why don't I make dinner tonight?"

Bill wasn't much of a cook. After my mom and I had lived with him for a while, we learned he subsisted mainly on frozen meals and canned soup. A few months ago he tried to cook me dinner, and it took hours with the windows open to air the smell out. I wasn't the best cook either, but I could manage simple things, so when I was around, I tried to make the meals. The trouble was I usually worked during dinner hours and if I wasn't, then I was at Cole's place. So I'd managed to cook maybe once every other week.

Tonight would be the perfect night for a little family dinner, especially since I was running out of opportunities. But I was trying not to think about that.

"We don't have much in the house," Bill said.

"No problem. I'll stop at the store."

"Make sure to use the card."

Bill had given me a credit card several months ago, telling me to use it for whatever I needed. When I didn't use it at all the first month, he'd asked me if there was something wrong with it. Since then, I'd been using it for gas and groceries. I used it once to buy some clothes since mine were getting ratty, but even though everything was on sale and I got a great deal, I still felt guilty. Having the card meant I'd been able to save my money from Nice Beauty for my upcoming adventure, which simply added to the guilt. Bill didn't realize his generosity was enabling me.

I squeezed Cole's arm and gave him a peck on the cheek and then I was off. I had no idea what I planned to make for dinner. Probably some kind of Italian dish. I'd learned that as long as you didn't overcook the pasta, it was hard to mess up. The secret was adding lots of extra sauce and mozzarella. And usually the pasta boxes conveniently had recipes printed right on them, which made it easy.

Once at the store, I went straight to the pasta aisle, deciding on stuffed shells. It didn't take me long to gather what I needed and head to Bill's.

I pulled into the driveway and slammed on the breaks.

What...in...the...hell?

Xena sat on the hood of my mom's car, looking pristine—as usual—like she was in some shady air-conditioned spa rather than baking on the metal hood of a car. I was rocking pit stains just from hefting the groceries out to my car.

Another reason to hate Xena.

Okay, so maybe *hate* was too strong a word. I didn't *hate* her exactly, but I sure as hell didn't trust her. Which really sucked because I depended on her for information.

I eased onto the gas again, parking in my usual space and taking my time to get out of the car. Xena had kept her distance for months, so why was she here now?

I didn't like it.

I shoved my hands into my pockets and walked over to her. "What do you want?" Part of me cringed at my surly tone because I knew my mom would reprimand me for being rude, but I didn't have it in me to be polite.

"You should have told me you were leaving." Her expression was neutral, like it always was. She was a master at masking emotions, if she even had them.

Fallen angels were odd. They weren't human, but they looked and sounded it. They once were human, but when they became angels, what changed? When they lost their humanity, did they lose their feelings?

I didn't think so because Areli, my angel ancestor, had been visibly distraught when he talked about his lost love. But Xena and Xavier—the only two fallen angels I knew—were aloof and detached.

Of course, perhaps that was just in their DNA since they were related.

Can you tell I wasn't quite over that yet?

Soon, I'd know more about fallen angels when Shenice helped me find other seekers. Or so I hoped anyway.

"I don't report to you," I said.

"Fair enough. But let me tell you who you should be reporting to—Elizabeth, your new handler. I've managed to pull some strings and delay her arrival." Xena paused. "You're welcome, by the way."

"Thanks," I muttered, kicking at the grass.

"Don't mention it," she said dryly. "But I can't keep her away much longer, so you need to figure out how you're going to keep Cole's secret."

Oh, I had it figured out already, but she wasn't going to like it. No one was, but I didn't see any way around it. If the handler observed Cole too much, she'd figure out what he was. It was inevitable.

It was Xena who first informed me that Cole was off the radar and if we could keep him that way, he could live a normal life. Though I was grateful for this information and the fact that I could save Cole from the life of a seeker, I also kind of hated her for it. It was that news that was prompting me to leave him.

I begrudgingly had to admit Xena was kind of damned if she did and damned if she didn't when it came to me. But the bottom line was she never should have deceived me about her connection to Xavier.

And why was she here now, anyway? Didn't we have an unspoken agreement she would keep her distance? There was no reason she couldn't have just texted me.

"Do you need anything else?" I was being a total bitch, but I couldn't help it. My mom's death wasn't Xena's fault. If anything, it was my fault. But it was Xavier who inflicted the mortal damage. And Xena was his great-great-whatever-granddaughter. How could I really know where her loyalties lay?

A nagging voice inside me told me I should know because she'd never done anything to help Xavier that I knew of. Everything she'd done had been either for my benefit or to help the mysterious cause I still didn't understand.

I mentally told the voice to shut the heck up.

She looked at me for a moment, then hopped off the car. "Nope."

I crossed my arms and fixed my gaze on the grass at my feet. When I looked up after a few seconds, Xena was gone. *Poof!*

I stared at the spot on the hood of the car she'd just vacated. Before my mom died, she put the car into my name so it wouldn't get tied up in her estate. But I'd barely looked at it. Too many memories. We'd spent a lot of time together in that car between the moves and life in general. It was also in that car Xavier hurt my mom for the first time, nearly killing her by blocking her airway.

Turning away from the car, I scowled. Xena's presence had reminded me of things better forgotten.

CHAPTER 6

ON TUESDAY AFTERNOON, I WHISKED past Cole in the shop, the handles of the eight plastic bags I carried cutting into my wrists.

He looked up from where he was elbow-deep in oil. "What's all that?"

"Nothing!" I called out in a sing-song voice, climbing the stairs to his apartment.

I was turning into a domestic goddess. After making dinner last night, I'd washed everything in Bill's house—towels, blankets, sheets...if it fit in the washer, I washed it. It was a parting gift to Bill.

I wasn't about to do Cole's laundry, though. That was a little *too* domestic.

But I was going to make him dinner, and I was veering outside my comfort zone with a recipe for beef stroganoff I'd found on Pinterest. It called for about a hundred ingredients but I had two hours. I could figure it out by then, right?

As I stood in Cole's kitchen with the bags at my feet, I realized I might have overestimated not only my abilities, but the functionality of Cole's kitchen. It was more like a kitchenette, like you'd find at a hotel.

My confidence faltered, and I considered throwing in the towel before I'd even started and ordering pizza instead.

"No," I told myself firmly. "You can do this."

Cole didn't know it, but our days together were numbered. I'd put it out of my mind—that was the only way I was able to function normally. Because as soon as I thought about it, tears filled my eyes and my hands began to shake. I'd already been forced to play it off in front of Cole once. I wouldn't be able to manage that a second time.

I organized my ingredients and pulled the recipe up on my phone.

"Okay," I said, staring at everything. "Step one." I picked up my phone and read the first step. "Cut beef across grain."

That was it. That was all it said. What the heck did across the grain mean? Way back in middle school domestic science class when we sewed an apron, the teacher said something about cutting across the grain, but I couldn't remember exactly what the heck that meant. Something about cutting in the same direction of the threads in the fabric. The concept was probably the same, though, right?

I dug around in Cole's cabinet until I found a cutting board. It was tiny, but it would have to do. I unwrapped the hunk of beef and slapped it on the board. A drop of blood went flying, landing on my arm.

My stomach heaved and my vision blurred. I turned so my back was to the cabinet and slowly sank down to my butt. Sticking my head between my knees, I breathed deeply.

But it was no good. I could still smell the blood.

Bile rose in my throat and I scrambled to my feet and ran for the bathroom, barely making it before I lost my lunch in the toilet.

Why did I think I could do this? I should have known better. It wasn't even the fact that I had no idea what half the steps of the recipe meant. It was the blood I couldn't handle.

Ever since we'd had to inject Xavier's blood into my mom to keep her alive, the sight and especially the smell of blood made me dizzy and nauseated.

I rinsed my mouth out and splashed cold water on my face. Then I took a deep breath and gave myself a quick pep talk.

You can do this. It's just cooking. Suck it up and get it done.

I squared my shoulders and flung open the bathroom door. The smell of the meat wafted into the bathroom, and I slammed the door as I gagged.

The heat in the apartment was making the smell much worse.

God, I was so freaking stupid. I'd spent a lot of money I didn't have on those groceries, and now they were going to rot out there in the hot kitchen because I couldn't keep my shit together.

I was a flaming idiot. Not because I'd wasted money I couldn't afford to lose and underestimated my aversion to blood, but because I somehow thought making a nice dinner would make up for leaving.

I kicked the cabinet and screamed in frustration as tears blinded my vision.

I was doing the right thing. I knew I was, but damn it, why did it have to be so hard? I choked on a sob and slid to the floor. I'd once spent the night in this bathroom on the floor with Cole when he'd been super sick from coming into his ability of seeing auras.

I thought he'd hated me then. How would he feel once I disappeared?

I guessed it wouldn't matter because I'd be gone.

The front door opened, followed by the sound of Cole's footsteps. I'd recognize them anywhere. He paused outside the bathroom door for a moment before knocking.

"Ava?" he asked. "Is everything okay?"

"I was going to make you dinner, but..." I trailed off,

embarrassed to admit I'd let a hunk of beef beat me.

"I can't hear you."

"The meat," I said loudly. "In the kitchen. The blood."

Cole's footsteps went in the direction of the kitchen and a few moments later I heard the fridge open and close. I peeked out. The smell lingered, but it wasn't nearly as strong.

I stepped out of the bathroom, walking sheepishly toward the kitchen. I hovered in the doorway as Cole rinsed the cutting board, erasing all traces of the blood.

"Better?" he asked, wiping his hands on a towel.

I nodded. "I'm sorry. I was going to surprise you with dinner. I didn't realize—" My lower lip quivered and I turned away, not wanting to cry in front of him.

Cole grabbed me by the waist and spun me around to face him. "Hey," he said, and the peppermint scent on his breath mixed with the motor oil smell from his clothes, drowned out the last trace of blood from my senses. "I appreciate what you tried to do, but don't get upset over it. It's no big deal."

"It is a big deal." I pounded my fists on his chest. "I can't...It's just..."

He held me at arm's length so he could look in my eyes. "What's this about? And don't tell me it's the dinner."

"I..." It was there on the edge of my tongue to tell him what Xena had told me yesterday—that the new handler was on her way and if Cole had any hope of living a normal life and being there for Kyle like he wanted to, then I couldn't be in his life.

But I swallowed down the confession. He was worth it to me. I'd sacrifice anything to give him back what was stolen from him the night I made the decision for Areli to bring him back to life.

Cole looked at me expectantly and I cast my eyes downward. "I'm just stressed."

I used to be a horrible liar, but these days, I was getting so much better at it.

WE ENDED UP ORDERING PIZZA after all. Part of me was glad. I didn't even know if I liked beef stroganoff. I just thought I'd heard Cole say he liked it.

After we finished eating, we lay on the couch with our overstuffed bellies, watching a golf tournament because neither of us had the motivation to walk the four feet to get the remote from the table. And neither one of us even liked golf.

"I think I ate too much," Cole said.

I arched an eyebrow. "Seriously?" Cole could eat like no one I'd ever seen. Even with my fast seeker metabolism, if I ate the way he did, I would be a blimp.

Although, come to think of it, now that Cole was also a seeker, I supposed his metabolism was on overdrive as well. I hadn't paid attention to whether or not he was eating more than he normally did.

"Maybe we should go for a walk or something," I suggested, still not moving.

"Nah," Cole said. "It's too hot for that."

I agreed. Even though it was nearly eight, it was still humid and hot as hell. Literally—Xena had once told me hell didn't exist and the closest thing to it was life on Earth. Cheery thought, right?

Cole hefted himself off the couch, making the four foot trek to retrieve the remote. He flopped back down next to me.

"I heard from the lawyer earlier," he said, fiddling with the remote but not changing the channel.

"Oh yeah?" It was a crappy thing for him to have to deal with, but my heart swelled that he'd brought it up himself. I used to have to pry every little piece of information out of him. We'd come a long way that he now confided in me of his own accord. He was just so used to only depending on himself.

I hoped my leaving didn't shatter his faith in people.

"They're going to hold him for a while. Trying to scare him straight. But most likely he'll end up with community service."

"That's good, right?"

Cole shrugged. "Sort of. He'll be stuck up there until he completes the hours."

Damn. I hadn't thought of that. "How many?"

"The lawyer wasn't sure."

I picked at a thread on the couch cushion. "Have you ever considered moving back up there? That would make it easier for you to be in Kyle's life."

Cole was silent for a moment, and I could tell he'd also given the subject some thought.

"It's no good for me up there."

"Why not?" I asked. "Now that you're done with school, you could get a job there. There are so many freaking cars in northern Virginia. There's got to be a ton of auto shops, right?"

"It's really expensive," he said. "And besides that, I need to get him away from the bad element he's involved in. Otherwise he'll just keep getting sucked back in. That's what happened to me."

It seemed like he knew what he was talking about. At times like these, it was difficult to picture Cole as he used to be—a thug who stripped cars and sold the parts. The Cole I knew was so clear-headed.

"Anyway," Cole said, one side of his mouth quirking up in a sexy half-smile that made me swoon every single freaking time, "you're here."

My heart turned over, performing gymnastic feats I didn't know it was capable of.

"But Kyle should come first," I whispered. "He should be your priority."

Cole's smile turned into a scowl. "Sometimes it gets old putting someone first when they don't even give a shit." He scrubbed a hand over his face. "I'm just frustrated. Kyle doesn't make it easy. I know deep down he's a decent kid, but damn he's been a real asshole lately."

"Then it's even more important he has you," I said. "He needs someone who can see past the asshole part."

Maybe once I was gone and Cole realized I wasn't coming back, he'd change his mind. Maybe he would move back home to be near Kyle. He'd have one less reason to stay here.

"I guess," Cole said. "I don't want to talk about him anymore."

His phone dinged and he handed me the remote, then picked it up.

I wasn't trying to be nosy or anything, but I glanced over in that direction and I couldn't help but notice the name on the text: *Dani*.

My teeth started grinding and I seethed. I'd managed to forget about her, but now here she was intruding on my time with Cole.

"It's Danielle," he said, and the jealous girlfriend side of me was relieved at the nonchalance in his voice. "She sent the info for her party. You're invited, too. I'll forward it to you."

"No, that's okay," I said quickly. It made no sense, but I didn't want her text on my phone.

Cole shrugged and put his phone down. I wanted to ask him if he planned to go to the party. Or if because I wasn't interested, he wouldn't go either. I wasn't sure what the protocol was for this type of thing.

But of course, it didn't even matter. I'd be long gone by then.

"You know what we should do tomorrow?" Cole asked. "We should go to the gun range. You haven't even tried out your new gun."

That was true and because of the mess with Kyle, I'd forgotten all about it. It was shoved under my bed with the trigger lock on it. But Cole remembered.

"I love you," I blurted out and true to form, it was neither eloquent nor charming. But by God, it was honest.

He reached over and tweaked my nose the way a big brother might, but the look in his eyes was anything but brotherly. "I love you, too, Ava."

I knew his words to be true. In spite of my sometimes awkward nature, my lack of sophistication, and all the trouble that came along with my being a seeker, he really and truly did love me. Or perhaps he didn't love me *in spite* of those things. Perhaps he loved me *because* of those things.

I ran my fingers along his cheek, my gaze following their path as I sought to memorize his face. Then I pressed my lips to his gently and though desire burned in my belly, that wasn't what this was about.

This was about me wanting to give myself to Cole in every way possible. I wanted to share everything with him.

He returned my kiss in the same slow, tender manner, seeming to realize that was what I needed right now.

I pulled him toward me using his white tank top undershirt, and part of me wanted to grip it and rip it off him, Hulk-style. But that would have been ridiculous, so instead I pulled it over his head. Then I pulled my own shirt off.

His gaze raked over my body, and I paused, letting him get his fill and feeling bold. I was so glad I'd worn my lacy bra today.

I came back to him, kissing him more, trying to get enough to last me a lifetime, as if that were possible.

Mint...I'd never be able to smell it again without remembering the feel of his lips on mine.

I ran my hands over the muscles of his shoulders, feeling them slick with sweat from the heat and humidity in his apartment. I was sweaty too, but I didn't care. The only thing I cared about was being with him.

I hooked my fingers on the elastic of his athletic shorts and he gripped my hands, pulling away.

"Whoa," he said, surprise in his eyes. He'd made his position on us going farther very clear—he didn't want to take advantage of me and do something he thought I'd regret. Plus, he was freaked out by the fact he was nineteen and I was seventeen.

But we'd both had our birthdays. Now he was twenty and I was eighteen—a legal adult. That part of his argument was moot.

And it wasn't taking advantage of me if I was the one initiating. More importantly, I knew I wouldn't regret it. I wanted him to be my first.

"Cole." I looked into his eyes, making sure he knew I was serious. "I'm ready. I want to take the next step."

He rubbed the back of his neck, which I'd always thought of as his bashful look. "I don't know—"

"Don't you want me?"

His eyes snapped up to mine. "Hell, yes. That's not what this is about."

"Then what is it?" I prodded. "I'm eighteen now, so don't tell me I'm too young. This isn't a decision I've made lightly."

"Ava, it's so freaking hard keeping myself in check, but I don't want you to regret anything with me. You can only lose your virginity once. There's no going back."

"I know. I want it to be you." I leaned forward and pulled his lower lip into my mouth, nipping at it lightly.

Cole tore himself away, holding me at arm's length while his eyes searched my face. I knew what he was doing—he was examining me to see if I was serious, if I truly understood what I was asking for.

His expression told me he was battling with himself. So I would end the fight for him.

"I'm sure," I said.

He blew out a breath, and I closed my eyes, inhaling the minty scent.

"Okay," he said quietly. "But—"

I put my finger to his mouth. "There are no buts. I'm one hundred and ten percent sure."

The edge of his lips quirked up in a sexy half-grin.

"Are you sure you passed trig last year? One hundred and ten percent sure isn't really a thing."

"Shut up."

He laughed, then stole one more kiss before pulling me to my feet. Taking my hand, he led me into the bedroom.

CHAPTER 7

I STAYED THE NIGHT.

I'd slept overnight with Cole before, but never like this. Things were different.

But in a totally wonderful way.

He'd been so tender with me last night, taking his time to make sure it didn't hurt too much and I wasn't uncomfortable. And then he'd held me until I fell asleep.

At some point in the night, we must have separated because when I woke, we were both sprawled face down on the bed and our only point of contact was his hand on my butt.

I giggled, then slapped a hand over my mouth, not wanting to wake him up.

As I watched his eyelids begin to flutter, my heart felt like it would burst from my chest. I'd never felt so close to another human being before.

He blinked, his eyes slowly focusing on me. His mouth formed a lazy grin. "Good morning."

"Hey," I said softly. I was worried it would be awkward between us this morning, but nope. We were still just Cole and Ava, only a much closer Cole and Ava.

He tried to pull me forward for a kiss, but I squirmed out of his reach. "Morning breath!" I said with a hand over my mouth. I jumped out of bed and rushed into the bathroom to brush my teeth.

I stared into the mirror as I brushed and it hit me—*I can't do it.*

How did I ever think I'd be able to leave him? For months I'd been telling myself I would start to back away...tomorrow. Always tomorrow.

And now, tomorrow was literally *tomorrow.* I was supposed to leave with Shenice.

Supposed to...as soon as that phrase played across my mind I knew I'd have to call her and tell her it was off.

Cole and I had been through so much together. Our entire relationship consisted of one crappy roller coaster ride after the next, and still we somehow managed to get through it stronger than ever. We'd just have to find some way around this. Somehow, we'd have to figure out how to keep his status as a seeker a secret from whoever my new handler was.

Heck, Cole had come back from the dead. Surely we could manage this.

And maybe I might have to ease up on Xena. I didn't want to think I was using her, but she would be able to help us with this. Cole was more important than any grudge I held against her.

I spat one last time in the sink and wiped my mouth with the back of my hand. My mind was clearer than it'd been in months and my soul felt at peace. Maybe that was why I'd felt so conflicted about leaving—because it was the wrong thing to do.

I came out of the bathroom, passing Cole as he went in. I quickly got dressed and sat on the bed with my knees hugged to my chest, waiting for him to emerge. He came out with his toothbrush hanging out of his mouth.

"So," he said, his speech garbled. "I need to work for a few hours this morning, so I thought we'd go to the gun range this afternoon." He walked back into the bathroom to spit.

"Can you take the hours?" I asked.

He came back out and the sunlight danced across his bare chest. I nearly blushed and looked away, but instead I forced myself to hold steady. If Cole and I could have sex, then I could certainly admire him without feeling embarrassed.

Well, I gave it a valiant effort, anyway.

Last night hadn't been about the physical for me. Sure, that part was nice, but it was about connecting with him in a way I'd never connected with anyone else before. And I think he felt that, too.

"Sure." He walked over to me and trailed a fingertip along my cheek. "Are you okay this morning?"

Now I really did blush, but I maintained eye contact. "I'm great."

He leaned down to claim the kiss he'd wanted earlier and I was really—and truly—great.

I LEFT COLE SO HE could focus on work without me gawking at him.

And to be truthful, I didn't want to be around both him and Bill. Not yet. I felt like I had a sign on my forehead: *Cole and I DID IT!!!*

Hopefully I would get a handle on that. I just felt different. So different it seemed like anyone would be able to tell just by looking at me.

Even though it was early, the sun was shining brightly overheard. It was going to be another hot one. As I sat at a red light, I watched joggers go by. Hats off to them. My lungs would give me the big middle finger if I tried to run in this humidity.

As the light turned green, my passenger door opened and slammed closed. I jumped, my hands flying to my chest.

"Damn it, Xena." Once upon a time, I'd gotten used to her dramatic entries—and exits—but it had been a while, so I guessed I was out of practice.

"I thought you'd never leave," she said, clutching a cup of coffee. I don't know how she could drink hot coffee in this heat.

Behind me, an impatient driver honked his horn. Oh, right, the light was green. I put my hand up in a "sorry" wave and put my foot on the gas.

"What do you want?" I asked Xena, remembering my earlier vow to move past my thing with her and trying my best to keep a neutral tone. It was hard.

"I talked to Shenice and she's ready to go. You should leave today."

"*What? Why?* And why were you talking to her about me?" I suddenly felt like it was months ago when I'd first met Xena and she had the habit of saying things that demanded explanations, but then she wouldn't answer any of my questions.

This better not be one of those times.

She gave me a bland stare, one that gave me the impression she thought I was an idiot. And maybe I was, at least partially. She and Shenice had always talked about me, so that wasn't new. I was sort of a joint project for them.

"It's only one day early. You should go," Xena repeated. True to form, she hadn't answered any of my questions.

"About that," I said slowly, keeping my eyes on the road and not bothering to ask why she was suddenly so okay with me leaving. "I think I want to stay here. There's got to be a way to keep Cole's identity a secret."

"There isn't," Xena said bluntly. My heart started to sink, but I paused its descent. This was worth fighting for. *Cole and I* were worth fighting for.

"*No.* There has got to be a way. What's the new handler's name again? Elizabeth? And wait a second," I said slowly, the details of our last conversation coming back to me. That was the trouble with these chats with

Xena. She usually blindsided me, making it hard for me to organize my thoughts. "You were pissed I left for a few days and now you're telling me to leave for good? What the heck? Did you talk Shenice into letting you come with us?"

She wasn't even supposed to know about my plans to leave. Considering how pissed she was about my little trip, she should be angry I had planned to leave for good, not encouraging me.

This could not be good.

But no matter what scheme Xena had going on, I still planned to stay. That hadn't changed.

She sighed, a sign I was wearing her down. Maybe I'd get some answers after all.

"Elizabeth is no longer your new handler."

"What? Why not?"

And why did I even care? I hadn't met her. I didn't know her from the lady at the store who rang up my groceries. But if I didn't ask questions, then I'd never get any info from Xena, or at least, not the good stuff, anyway. She worked on a need-to-know basis, but her idea of what was need to know was completely different than mine.

"She was assigned to a different case," Xena said, as if that should have been obvious. I rolled my eyes and wished I weren't driving so I could walk away from her. I didn't care what Elizabeth was doing. I only wanted to know why it mattered that she'd been assigned to another case. What did it mean for me? Because Xena wouldn't be here if it didn't have implications.

"Just tell me what the hell is going on," I said. "I don't have the patience for your games."

I was getting pissed off. I'd had a perfectly wonderful morning, and Xena was quickly ruining it.

"Linda has been assigned to you." She emphasized the name *Linda* in a way that implied it wasn't a good thing. But then she didn't say anything else.

I banged my fist against the steering wheel. "Why do

we have to do this? *Just tell me what I need to know.*"

"Fine." She huffed, like I was inconveniencing her when *she* was a hitchhiker in *my* car. "Linda is a hard ass. And remember when I told you there was a divide about whether we should even use seekers? Recently, Linda has been leading the charge for either employing more seekers or making the ones we already have turn in more names."

So what she was telling me was that Linda was possibly the worst possible handler I could get. *Great.*

Except that wasn't quite true. Xavier still deserved that title. Which reminded me—

"Any news on Xavier?"

She shook her head. "Nothing."

"Are you sure he's alive?"

"Yes," she said stiffly. "I would know if he died."

"How?"

"I just would." She crossed her arms, ending the discussion. She was touchy about divulging handler secrets and everything to do with her relation to Xavier. I wasn't going to get anything else, so I dropped it.

"So back to Linda," I said as I pulled in Bill's driveway. But whatever question I had been about to ask left my brain because there was a woman standing on Bill's porch.

She looked like freaking Mary Poppins.

"Shit," Xena muttered. "She wasn't supposed to show up this soon."

"*Quick*," I said as Linda narrowed her eyes at me through the windshield. "Tell me what I need to know."

"Just go along with whatever she says right now. And *don't* say anything about Cole."

Duh...that was a given. Sometimes I swore Xena thought I was a raving idiot.

I got out of the car slowly to give myself time to size up this new handler. She wore a long sleeve blouse and a black skirt that fell to her calves even though it was supposed to be in the upper nineties today. Her hair was pulled tight away from her face and her complexion was pallid, like she hadn't been out in the sun in the last decade. Her expression, though, that was what made me change my opinion about her looking like Mary Poppins. She looked like she was sucking on a lemon and didn't have an ounce of cheeriness in her.

All handlers were fallen angels, which meant that at some point, they'd been the embodiment of good. Between Xavier and now this woman, I was starting to doubt that.

She looked me up and down, and the look of disgust on her face had me slowing my approach even more. She didn't exude evil—not like Xavier—but she wasn't warm and fuzzy, either.

But since I'd decided to stick around, I wanted to try to make a good first impression. This woman had the power to make my life miserable.

I pasted a smile on my face. "Hi, I'm—"

"What are you doing here?" She'd turned her attention to Xena, ignoring me.

My nostrils flared. What a bitch.

Xena returned her stare, not flinching. Though I was still at odds with Xena, I was definitely on her side in this situation.

"Aren't you supposed to be—" Linda waved her hand to show how superfluous she thought it was, "working on your special assignment?"

I cocked my head at her. Though she'd tried to mask it with disdain, her voice was laced with jealousy. And now I was dying to know what the special assignment was.

Though if this woman wanted the task, it couldn't be anything good.

Xena smirked as she walked up the stairs toward Linda. "I believe that's classified information."

Linda's face twisted into a snarl. "I don't think anyone will care about classified if I bring him in."

Xena stood toe to toe with her, not backing down even though she was at least a head shorter than the other woman.

What the hell was Xena doing? So much for going along with whatever Linda said. I guessed that only applied to me.

I slipped past them to unlock the front door. "Does anyone want to go inside?" I asked in a cheerful voice. "It's awful hot out here."

"You can go," Linda said to Xena. "This is my territory now."

Xena brushed past her to enter the house in front of me, heading for the stairs. "I'll leave when I'm ready to leave."

Linda looked after Xena with a murderous look in her eyes, but she did nothing to try to stop her.

I had no idea what the hell I just witnessed. As usual, I was left with a million questions.

"Would you like to come in?" I asked Linda, trying to salvage the whole "going along with whatever she said" thing.

Linda tilted her nose in the air as she walked past, like she smelled something foul. I had news for her—she was the only foul thing here.

Except her scent wasn't foul. Not really. I couldn't place it, but she smelled like Thanksgiving to me. Was it pumpkin pie? I didn't actually like pumpkin pie, so I couldn't tell you what spice was in it, but Linda definitely had an eau-de-weird-spice-scent going on.

I followed her inside and closed the door behind me. Linda made herself at home on the couch.

"Would you like something to drink?" I asked. I had no idea what Xena was doing upstairs, and I wanted to stall the conversation with Linda as long as I could so maybe I could figure out what the heck was going on.

Who was I kidding? Fat chance of that. I was flying blind. This was why I hated handlers. That and the whole *they made me give them names for reaping* thing.

"No," Linda said. "My name is Linda and I'm your new handler since Xena failed spectacularly in that endeavor."

The way she said it made me think she considered it an insult to be assigned to me. And that perhaps the fact that Xena got that special assignment instead of her was even more of an insult.

Whatever. I didn't want to deal with her any more than she wanted to deal with me.

"I'm—"

"I know who you are, silly girl."

Right. "Okay," I said, clenching my teeth as I smiled at her. I wasn't going to be able to keep up the good girl routine much longer. "What can I help you with?"

"You were given a reprieve since the death of your mother, but that reprieve is now over. I need a name in one week. And then we will be moving to a new location."

Oh, no. I'd conveniently forgotten about the fact that handlers made us move every few months. I'd been here nearly a year, the longest I'd been in one place that I could remember.

I didn't know how to respond. Xena had said to go along with her, but now I was torn about that. If I was going to stick around here, then Linda and I would need to come to an understanding. Wouldn't it be better to start that conversation sooner rather than later?

Although, she couldn't force me. What was she going to do? Tie me up and physically move me? The image was laughable, just as laughable as the power handlers thought they had over seekers. *They* needed *us*, not the other way around.

I wasn't even going to broach the topic of my vow to never seek again. That definitely fell into the *later* category.

I threw my head back. "Actually, I'd like to stay here a while. It's not good to switch schools before my senior year. You know, because of applying for college and everything." I smiled sweetly. Even though I had my GED, I could now finish my senior year properly.

Linda laughed, but the sound wasn't funny. Not at all. It was mean-spirited and hateful.

"My dear, college is *not* in your future."

Finally, an adult who agreed with me about that and it totally worked against me. *Figures.*

She looked around the living room, taking in the surroundings. "So, this man Bill? He's like a father to you now?" She cocked her head as she asked the question.

And there it was. There was the power she had over me. I might be willing to be tortured to avoid turning in a name, but could I sacrifice Bill? Or God forbid if she learned about my relationship to Cole, could I sacrifice him?

The answer was a big fat resounding *no.* She had me right where she wanted me. *Check mate.* A huge chunk of my optimism fell into the abyss.

She stood. "One week. Any questions?"

"Nope."

I had nothing else to say. I had one week to figure out how I was going to handle this nightmare of a woman.

She gave me the once over one more time before striding toward the front door. The sound of it closing behind her was welcome.

I rested my elbows on my knees and put my head in my hands.

Well, that turned an already complicated situation into a big fat cluster. How the heck was I going to work my way through this one?

Because I had to figure it out. I just *had* to. Twenty-four hours ago I was hell bent on leaving. And now I was a hundred times more hell bent on staying.

Xena came back down, my suitcase thumping on the stairs after her.

"What are you doing?" I asked.

"I thought she would never leave," Xena said. "I packed for you. Shenice is on her way."

I stood and yanked the suitcase away from her. "I'm

not leaving. That was a mistake. I don't want to leave Cole and Bill."

Xena pinched the bridge of her nose. "If Elizabeth was your handler, I'd agree with you. But Linda changes things."

"What is it between you two? What's the special assignment she mentioned?"

She removed her hand from her nose and looked me in the eyes. And that was how I knew it was bad—she wore the same expression she did when she told me my mom's life depended on Xavier.

"I've been assigned to track down the seeker who can see all auras." She paused, taking a deep breath. "Which means I've been assigned to track down Cole."

CHAPTER 8

THE BLOOD DRAINED FROM MY body and pooled in my toes, making me light headed.

"What do you mean?"

"Someone knows," Xena said. "I don't know how, but someone found out about Areli changing a man into a seeker. And word is spreading that this seeker has no limits."

"But Cole..." I faltered. "He has limits. Remember how sick he got when he came into his abilities? And he still hasn't perfected blocking out the auras."

She shook her head. "That's not what I mean. Look, I don't know everything either."

I guessed handlers or fallen angels or whoever was in charge of disseminating information was about as forthcoming as Xena. Perhaps she came by it honestly.

"But no one knows it's him," I said.

"Not yet, but it won't stay a secret forever. And even though it's not her job, Linda is hell bent on finding him."

"Is that why she was assigned to me? Did she ask for the assignment because she suspects something?" Perhaps I had been wrong about her disgust in working with me. Perhaps it was an elaborate ruse.

Fear filled me. It was bad enough when I thought I'd have to keep Cole a secret from a normal handler. But now

I had to hide him from Linda, a handler who was specifically looking for him. And at what point would the powers that be realize Xena was failing at her task? When she didn't turn him in, eventually they'd put someone else on the case.

Xena shook her head. "That was just dumb luck on her part. She fought for the assignment to find Cole and even though she didn't get it, she's still going to look for him. She doesn't even realize how close she is."

No, but she probably already knew I was Areli's descendant and if she didn't, it was only a matter of time. If I were looking for someone Areli helped, that's where I'd start my search. Xena said it was dumb luck she was assigned to me, but I wasn't so sure.

I closed my eyes as the last of my optimism committed suicide. All of the good feelings I had left inside me evaporated as I realized what I had to do.

"I have to lead her away from Cole."

IT FELT LIKE A METAL claw was reaching into my chest and squeezing everything—my stomach, my lungs, but most of all, my heart.

Now that I knew one hundred percent I had to leave, I realized I'd never made my peace with it. Sure, I'd made all the necessary arrangements, but I'd been lying to myself the whole time, telling myself I'd be okay

I was most certainly not okay.

"I'm sorry," Xena said.

"How long ago did you get your special assignment?" I asked.

"About a week ago."

I couldn't even be mad at her that she hadn't told me. I'd been gone for part of that time and anyway, I wasn't very nice to her. I'd cut off my nose to spite my face.

But even if I'd had this information sooner, what

could I have done? Nothing. If Cole didn't have Kyle to worry about, then perhaps the two of us could go on the run together. Even still, I wouldn't want that kind of life for him. I didn't want it for myself, but I had no choice now.

"Are you going to tell Cole about it?"

Xena shrugged. "I haven't decided. Sometimes it's better not knowing things."

"Maybe," I said, "but I'd want to know. And he would, too."

Xena reached over and squeezed my hand, the gesture startling me. She didn't do affection. That was the most I'd ever gotten from her.

"I'll talk to him."

As I looked in her eyes, I knew that was her promise to me—her promise to keep Cole safe and look after him. It was also her way of asking forgiveness.

The sound of a car crunching gravel in the driveway destroyed the moment, and Xena dropped my hand.

"Be safe," she said simply.

I nodded dumbly, shuffling with my suitcase out the front door. Shenice waited in her car. When she saw me, she popped the trunk. I had my suitcase halfway in before I remembered I had wanted to drive so that once we found other seekers, Shenice could hop on a bus or a plane, depending on how far we got, and return home.

I pulled my bag back out and walked to my car.

"What are you doing?" Shenice asked.

"I want to drive."

She took one look at me and shook her head. "Uh-unh. You're in no state to get behind the wheel."

I guessed I must have looked as wrecked as I felt. Just an hour ago, I was lying in bed with Cole and now this.

Shit. I hadn't even gotten to say good-bye to him or Bill. I hadn't yet decided how I wanted to handle that. I was thinking a letter or something, but there was no time.

"I need to drive," I insisted.

Xena stomped down the porch steps. "What the heck is taking so long? You guys need to get down the road before someone realizes you're gone."

"Wait, can Linda track me like you can?" I asked.

"No, she doesn't have a strong enough connection to you yet. The more time she spends with you though, the deeper that connection will get." She paused. "And before you ask, the answer is no, she can't find Cole that way, either. Forming a connection is a conscious thing. It doesn't happen just by proximity. Now get out of here."

"Why are you being so nice to me?" I asked softly. I'd been such a bitch to her and she never retaliated. I didn't know how much she was risking in helping me keep Cole's secret, but that was no small transgression. She could probably end up in a lot of trouble.

"We all have things to atone for," she said simply. "Now go."

I shot a defiant look at Shenice, who'd gotten out of her car. She threw her hands up.

"Fine." She tossed her keys to Xena then stalked to her trunk to pull out her things. "We can take your car, but I'm driving."

That was probably for the best. I was numb.

I climbed into the passenger seat and buckled my seatbelt on auto-pilot.

Shenice got into the driver's seat and wordlessly, I handed her the keys.

"Where do you want..." she trailed off, seeming to know I wasn't capable of answering the question.

I pressed my forehead against the warm glass of the window and counted to sixty, over and over again, each minute representing another mile separating me from Cole.

WE DROVE NORTH, WHICH WAS as good a direction as any

considering we didn't know exactly who we were looking for. Just days ago, I'd traveled this same path with Cole. As we passed the exit to get to his hometown, my throat seized up and I had trouble breathing.

"Are you okay?" Shenice asked, glancing over at me and then at the exit sign, like she was wondering if she needed to pull off.

"Keep going," I rasped out.

We drove for another hour until we were just outside of Baltimore.

"I'm starving," Shenice said. "Are you hungry?"

I should have been. I hadn't eaten since last night, but my appetite was gone.

"Sure," I said anyway.

Shenice pulled off at the next exit. "Wendy's or Taco Bell?"

"Taco Bell," I said quickly. I wasn't particularly in the mood for tacos, but I definitely wasn't in the mood to sit in a Wendy's. Cole and I always seemed to end up there. It was his fast food restaurant of choice.

After using the facilities, we stood in line for food. The longer we stood there, the more the smell of food overwhelmed me, and I realized I wouldn't be able to eat. So when Shenice looked back at me after placing her own order, I shook my head. She sighed and ordered me two tacos and a drink anyway.

I took the cup she handed me and filled it with soda, then found an isolated table in the corner of the restaurant. Shenice sat across from me and laid our food out on the table.

"Girl, I want you to eat," she said. "The way you're acting, you'd think this road trip wasn't your idea."

There was no malice in her voice, but it was still a punch to the gut. Shenice hadn't even wanted to go on this trip, but she was doing it anyway—totally disrupting her life for me, and a day early with no forewarning, no less.

"Thank you," I said. "And I'm sorry. This is a lot

harder than I expected."

Soon, Cole would get off work and get ready to go to the gun range. What would he think when I didn't show?

I held the power button on my phone, turning it off. I couldn't deal with the calls and texts from Bill and Cole when they realized I was gone. Hopefully Xena would let them know not to worry.

At face value, leaving like I did was a really bitchy move. They wouldn't understand I'd had no choice, and it was better this way.

And there was no way they *could* understand because I couldn't tell them why I left. If I did, they'd no doubt insist on somehow trying to fix the problem. Having such loyal people in my life was a double-edged sword.

"I understand," Shenice said.

"I hope it wasn't too hard for you to get away a day early."

She shrugged. "It's no biggie."

Even if it was, I doubted she'd tell me. As I looked at her, I noticed her braids were gone and she now sported a super short haircut and her hair was dyed the red color of cherries. How the heck had I not noticed that before? It was majorly different.

"I like your hair," I said.

Her hand went to her head, like what usually happened when someone commented on a person's hair. "Thanks. I wanted a change."

I took a deep breath and picked up the taco I'd been ignoring. The recent turn of events totally sucked, but I needed to snap out of it.

For one thing, it wasn't safe to be in a fog, not paying attention to my surroundings. If I hadn't even noticed Shenice's hair, then could I be counted on to notice something important, like if Xavier or Linda showed up?

I hadn't forgotten about Xavier and repaying him for what he'd done to my mom. I'd grown up a little bit in the past few months though, realizing it was a waste of time to try to find him. But he was like a damn cockroach, and like the stupid bug, he'd show up again sooner or later.

I needed to be ready for him.

Except—*damn it*—my gun was still shoved under my bed. I hadn't packed it because I hadn't packed *anything*. Xena did.

Maybe if I tried harder I could make even more of a mess of this situation.

ONCE BACK IN THE CAR, we continued up I-95 and I tried to stay more alert and be a better co-pilot. I probably should have offered to drive, but when we walked out of Taco Bell, Shenice went straight to the driver's seat, eager to get on the road.

"Where do you want to go?" she asked.

I had to think about it for a moment. In my infinite wisdom, when I concocted the crazy scheme of leaving, I hadn't actually decided where to go. My focus had been on simply getting away.

The past few years, my mom and I had stuck to more rural, less populated areas. I couldn't believe that all seekers would do that, though. Wouldn't it be easier to blend in in more populated areas? Also, since there were more people, the deaths of a few wouldn't be as noticeable, which meant seekers could potentially stay in one place longer.

So maybe New York City? We were relatively close and there were tons of people. I'd never been there though, and the thought of venturing into the big city intimidated me. Also, it was expensive there, and I didn't have tons of money.

"Do you have a preference?" I asked. "Or do you know of anywhere more likely to have angels?"

"I have cousins in Philadelphia," she replied. "I haven't seen them in years. I wouldn't mind visiting them for a day or two. Angels can be anywhere, so why not there?"

I hesitated. Since I didn't have any connections of my own, I hadn't considered that Shenice might want to go somewhere where she did. That idea made me leery. Could someone track us there?

Xena was the only one who knew Shenice was with me. It would take Cole and Bill at least a couple days to notice the coincidence that Shenice had gone MIA at the same time I did. So we should be okay for a couple days.

"All right," I said. "That's as good a place as any."

"Good." Shenice sounded happy, making me glad I agreed. Since she was disrupting her life to go on this trip, at least she would get something out of it. It wasn't like my company had been a sparkling fountain of joy so far.

She reached into her purse sitting on the center console and pulled out her phone. Keeping one eye on the road, she skimmed through it. Hadn't she ever heard it wasn't safe to be on her phone while driving?

Staring out the window, I tuned her out as she chatted. As a group of motorcycles crept up on my side, my heart pounded, which was stupid. Xavier would never travel in a group. But I could see him inserting himself into one while on the interstate to blend in.

My paranoia was starting to run on overdrive. But I had to focus on something in order to keep my mind off Cole. That was the only way I would be able to function.

God, I just hoped Xavier wasn't still around back home. Cole was on guard—and let's face it, that was just how he lived his life—but I worried about Bill. I'd have to trust Xena would look out for him because there was nothing I could do.

"They're excited we're coming," Shenice said. "They actually live just outside Philly, on the Jersey side."

"Who are 'they'?" I asked, wanting to know more about the people we'd be staying with. I kind of wished we were staying in a hotel so I wouldn't be forced to socialize.

I was not in the mood to put on a happy face.

"It's my cousin Dante and his wife Tina. They have two kids, a boy and a girl. I can't remember exactly how old they are. Maybe eight and ten? They're nice. You'll like them."

"Are they sensitives like you?"

"No." Shenice shot me a look. "Dante is my cousin on my daddy's side, and they don't know about that. I'd like to keep it that way."

"Of course." I knew better than anyone how to keep a secret.

Shenice's cousin lived in a nice middle-class neighborhood in a cul-de-sac. Tina greeted us on the porch when we arrived and pulled Shenice into a hug.

"It's been way too long," Tina said as she released Shenice. "What have you been up to?"

"All work and no play."

"Don't I know it." Tina turned to me. "You must be Ava."

"Yes," I said, holding out my hand. "Nice to—"

She pulled me into a hug, catching me off-guard. "I'm a hugger, not a hand shaker."

I closed my eyes, giving into the warmth of her embrace for a moment. The open show of affection brought tears to my eyes, and I hastily blinked them away.

"Come in," Tina said. "We've been having a heat wave."

The temperature was significantly lower than it had been in Virginia, and the humidity was all but non-existent. If this was a heat wave, then the normal summer weather must be pure heaven.

But what was really heavenly was the smell as soon as we walked into the house. My appetite actually woke up and paid attention.

"Girl, what are you cooking?" Shenice asked.

"You picked a good day to come," Tina said. "I have a pork loin in the slow cooker. It's a new recipe."

"Tina runs her own catering business," Shenice explained.

"What kinds of things do you cook?" I asked.

"Everything. If it's edible, I can make it."

"She's really good," Shenice said. "Last year she even got featured on a cooking show based out of Philly."

"Oh, stop." Tina waved her hand as the front door opened and two kids—a boy and a girl—walked in.

"Mom, Brian got in trouble on the bus!" The little girl squealed. She smirked at her brother.

He shoved her. "Shut up! No, I didn't."

"Yes, he did! Miss Wanda made him sit up front right behind her."

Tina sighed and crossed her arms. "What did I tell you about this?"

"But—"

"No," she said with a firmness only mothers could master. "Go straight to the kitchen and start your homework. And you—" she pointed at her daughter "—what did I tell you last night about your room? There are still dirty clothes everywhere. You have five minutes to take care of it or you're grounded this weekend. That means no TV, no iPad, nothing."

The little girl's eyes opened wide and she dropped her backpack to the ground, making a beeline for the stairs. The boy huffed and stalked off in what I assumed was the direction of the kitchen.

Tina sighed and picked up the backpack. "Heathens. Both of them. You'd think their parents taught them no manners."

Shenice shot her a sly look. "Didn't they?"

Tina grinned. "Apparently not. They didn't even say hi to either of you."

"Are they in summer school?" Shenice asked.

"It's an enrichment program thing. And thank God for it. I needed the two weeks of silence, but unfortunately, it's about to come to an end. That's the thing about working from home—I get to be with the kids all summer. It's a blessing and a curse." Tina headed in the direction her son went. "Come sit with me in the kitchen while I finish dinner."

"Actually, I'm tired," I said with an apologetic smile. "Do you mind if I rest for a bit?"

"Sure," Tina said. "Make yourself at home. You'll be sleeping on the couch downstairs, so if you want, you can go ahead and make yourself comfortable there."

"Thanks."

Downstairs was actually the basement, but it was finished. Still, it creeped me out a little to think I would be sleeping underground. I couldn't help but think about some of the funerals I went to and the caskets being lowered into the ground. I shivered, both from that thought and the chill in the air.

I pulled a blanket off the top of the couch and cuddled up. I'd been wide awake the entire drive, which was unusual for me. I'd been too numb to do anything, even sleep.

Now everything from the past twenty-four hours flooded my mind, including my time with Cole. But even though it made my heart hurt, I didn't regret it.

CHAPTER 9

DURING DINNER DANTE INVITED US to go see The Linc, which was where the Eagles played. He was in charge of ground maintenance, and they were gearing up for the first pre-season game, so most of his time was spent at work these days.

The next morning, Shenice drove again because she was more familiar with the roads. It still felt weird being a passenger in my own car.

The Linc was huge, but then again I had no real point of comparison. The biggest stadium I'd ever been in was the one at my high school. As I stared up at the massive structure, I couldn't help but think how much Cole would have liked this. He wasn't particularly into sports, but he was a guy and he still would have appreciated it. Bill, too, for that matter.

It made me sad to have this experience without them.

Dante was waiting for us at the entrance with a big grin on his face. He spread his arms wide. "Welcome to my home."

Shenice chuckled. "What would Tina have to say about that?"

"She knows I bleed green." He cleared his throat and the cocky expression fell off his face. "All the same, don't tell her I said that, okay?"

My first thought was to take my phone out and start taking pictures like a tourist, but then I remembered—my phone was back at their house. It was still turned off and I had no plans to change that anytime soon, so I figured there was no point in carrying it around.

Since I'd napped yesterday, it had taken me a while to fall asleep last night. I'd left a light on in the bathroom but closed the door, and the glow from the crack under the door cast a spotlight on my phone as it sat on the table, tempting me. I had been so close to being selfish and saying *screw it*. But if I called Cole, he'd want me to come home. I could hear him in my head, telling me how stupid I was being in an exasperated tone. If I refused to listen to him, he might try to come to me. Or at least, I hoped he'd want to.

My gut—and my heart—told me he would.

No, the way I'd left was best. It was a clean break or a quick rip of the Band-Aid. It hurt like hell, but if I was honest with myself, I never would have been able to leave otherwise.

"Come on," Dante said. "I'll show you where the owner and other VIPs watch the games, and then we'll go down to the field."

We followed him inside the stadium, which was eerily quiet. I couldn't imagine how loud it must get on game days when it was filled to its capacity of nearly seventy thousand. And I couldn't help but wonder if a place like this would have made it easier to seek. With that many people in one place, surely I'd have no problem finding a pure soul.

But that didn't matter anymore because I wasn't putting any more deaths on my conscience.

On the second level, there was more activity as workers pushed carts overflowing with boxes of supplies.

"Hey Ava, can you take our picture?" Shenice said, handing me her phone. I took it and waited while she and Dante posed under an Eagles emblem. "How's my hair?"

she asked.

"Good," I said, not really checking. Her hair always looked great. "Smile."

I took three pictures, then handed the phone back to her. She and Dante peered at them and then started to argue about which one to send to their parents. I tuned them out and turned away. It was a good thing I did. I jumped to the side, narrowly avoiding being creamed by a huge cart of paper cups stacked so high whoever was pushing the cart couldn't see over them.

I shook my head, watching the disaster waiting to happen continue down the walkway.

"Hey," someone said in a low urgent voice. A few feet away, a painter worked on touching up the walls. He was old, his leathery skin lined with wrinkles, and his back was hunched. His hair was jet black and thick, though.

I looked over my shoulder to see if he was talking to Dante, but Dante and Shenice were still engaged in the pictures.

"Hey, *you*." The man pointed at me this time, leaving no question about who he was talking to. Even still, I raised my eyebrows and pointed to my chest, the universal unspoken language for "who, me?"

"Yeah." His voice was gravelly, like he'd smoked too many cigarettes.

I looked over my shoulder again, then took a step closer, wondering what the hell this was about. We were out in the open, but I was still feeling the "stranger danger" vibe.

He sidled up to me. "This is my territory, you got that?" His breath was foul, and I knew I was right about him smoking too many cigarettes. I nearly gagged.

"Um...sure." I had no idea what he was talking about and quite frankly, he was creeping me out. I started to walk away.

He grabbed my arm, jerking me backward. "I mean it, girlie. I got dibs on all the souls around here. Don't even think about it."

My jaw dropped open, and I gaped at him for a moment before wresting my arm out of his grasp. For an old man, he had a tight grip. I rubbed at where his fingers had dug in.

"Ava, is everything okay?" Dante walked over, a frown on his face. "Is Reggie bothering you?"

Reggie scowled but said nothing.

My eyes shifted to my arm where he had grabbed me. "I'm fine. Everything is fine."

Dante narrowed his eyes at Reggie for a moment before putting his hand on the small of my back to lead me away.

I looked back at the man, and I couldn't help but think he resembled Xavier.

THE MAN'S WORDS ECHOED IN my mind—*"I got dibs on all the souls around here."*

It had totally taken me off guard. I was so used to concealing my seeker status I didn't process what his words meant until we were nearly to the stairs.

He knew. Somehow that man—Reggie—knew I was a seeker. That was the only explanation. There was no way it was a coincidence he had spouted off about souls.

And what he said...*"I got dibs..."* That meant he must be a seeker, too. I stopped in my tracks and Shenice nearly slammed into me.

"Sorry," I muttered. "I just need to..." I pointed behind me.

"Ava, honey, are you okay?" Shenice asked. My clever on-the-fly explanation hadn't fooled her.

"Fine. I just need to go back. I forgot something."

She put her hands on her hips and looked me up and down, and I tried to look as innocent as possible. But I hadn't been innocent for a long time.

"We can wait," Dante said, but he glanced at his watch as he said it. That was all the opening I needed.

"No, go ahead," I said. "You're going to the owner's box, right? I can meet you there."

"Do you know where it is?" Shenice asked blandly, poking a hole in my plan.

I had no idea, but I needed to get back to talk to Reggie. "Top floor?"

Dante nodded. "Just ask anyone and they can point you in the right direction."

"Great!" I called over my shoulder, taking off at a jog back toward where we'd left Reggie. When I got there, he wasn't there. Someone else had taken over his job of slathering paint on the walls.

"Where did the other guy go?" I asked, slightly out of breath. Even though I'd vowed to start exercising after I'd had to chase Xavier through a parking garage, I hadn't followed through. I was still woefully out of shape.

"He's on break."

Damn. He couldn't have gotten very far, though. "Which way did he go?"

The guy shrugged. "Dunno. But the break room is thataway." He pointed and I took off running again, my flip-flops slapping the concrete. I'd be lucky if I didn't break my neck.

As I turned the corner, I spotted him. "Reggie!"

He turned, his eyes widening at the sight of me. Then he took off in a hobbled run.

"Wait!" I yelled. "I just want to talk to you."

It seemed he had a bad knee, so despite my ineptness at running, I easily gained on him. I had almost caught up when he took a turn too close to a trash can, hitting it with his knee. He went down with a yell, groaning and clasping at his knee as he lay on the ground.

I skidded to a halt next to him. "Are you okay?"

"What does it bloody look like?" he grunted.

"Sir, I just want to talk to you." I knelt next to him to

try to help him up, but he swatted my hands away, so I gave him space.

"I already said everything I'm gonna say." He shifted to his hands and knees, but when he tried to stand, his knee buckled and he sprawled on the ground again. I winced. It looked like it had hurt.

But it was his own dumb fault. He shouldn't have run from me. He initiated the contact, so if he didn't want to talk, he should have left well enough alone. I never would have noticed him on my own.

I hesitated for a second, then put my hands under his arms to help him. This time he didn't swat me away, but I thought I heard something that sounded eerily like a growl emanate from his chest. The man was a jerk, but whatever. I'd take partial responsibility for his accident. He wouldn't have fallen if I hadn't been chasing him, so I was going to help him whether he liked it or not.

Of course, if he just would have stopped and had a simple conversation with me, neither of us would have been running, so there was that.

But now that he was injured, he wouldn't be able to get away from me. Problem solved.

"Do you know me?" I asked cautiously.

He snorted, giving me a look that told me he thought my question was idiotic. "I ain't never seen you before."

I gritted my teeth, resisting the urge to correct his double negative. And to fuss at him for grabbing me since he admitted he didn't know me. Someone needed to teach him some manners. Hadn't he ever heard you caught more flies with honey than with vinegar? He was so old he was probably too set in his ways to change now.

"Yes, but why did you say what you did?" I asked, not wanting to repeat his words in case I was wrong and they were only the ravings of a madman.

He snorted and stared at me incredulously. Then he blinked a few times, his surly expression fading. "You don't know, do you?"

I shook my head because I had no idea what he was talking about, so how could I possibly *know* anything?

"What the hell rock have you been living under?" He shook his head. "It ain't my job to teach you. But I mean what I said. This is my territory."

"I'm just visiting," I said, trying to reassure him. Maybe if he didn't feel threatened he would open up more. "I'm not trying to take over."

He squinted at me, like he was trying to ascertain whether I was telling the truth. I didn't understand his concern, anyway. He and I wouldn't be seeking the same souls because he was at least forty years older than me.

"Good," he said finally. "See that you don't." He started to hobble away.

"But sir," I called after him, not bothering to catch up with him. "How did you know who—*what*—I am?"

He turned. "How do you not know? Give it time. You'll figure it out."

And with that cryptic piece of advice, he left and this time, I didn't try to stop him.

CHAPTER 10

THE REST OF THE TOUR passed in a blur, and I couldn't even enjoy it. I had to force a smile when Shenice pretended to spike a touchdown in the end zone and enacted an elaborate victory dance. Dante laughed, telling her she would have earned herself a penalty for excessive celebration.

I couldn't stop thinking about my strange conversation with Reggie. I didn't know what I expected, but it wasn't him. He was a grizzled, grumpy old man with no social skills. But the more I thought about it, it made sense. Seekers were isolated, or at least my mom and I were, so he probably lost his social skills long ago. And decades of seeking was enough to make anyone bitter and miserable.

Somehow he'd known I was a seeker just by looking at me. But how was that possible? If he hadn't spoken to me, I never would've noticed him, much less considered he might be a seeker.

It was bizarre. There had to be something about me that tipped him off, but what? He didn't seem surprised in the least I was a seeker, so that must mean he'd met others before.

With a start, I realized he was the first seeker I'd ever met besides my mom and Cole. And I'd been too shocked to get any information out of him. Shenice, Dante, and I were currently in my car driving away from the stadium. I'd missed my shot.

Dante gave directions while Shenice drove. He was taking us to a hole-in-the-wall restaurant that served Philly cheese steaks that were so good a line formed around the block every day by noon, which was why we were heading there now at ten-thirty. It was a little early for lunch for my tastes, but whatever. I didn't want to wait in line for two hours for some meat and cheese on a roll, no matter how good it was. Food had never been one of my priorities.

The plan was for Shenice to drop Dante back at the stadium after lunch, and she and I would continue on to look for seekers somewhere. As usual, our plan was vague. I hadn't gotten a chance to talk to her alone, so she didn't know I'd already found one.

To be more exact, he'd found me.

I could slap myself right now. Why hadn't I demanded he tell me how he recognized me? Perhaps it was the fact he was an old man who'd gotten injured by my exuberant need to talk to him. But why had he run? Why was he trying to avoid me after he'd approached me?

I didn't understand and I never would because unless a miracle occurred, it was unlikely I'd see Reggie again. The Linc wasn't an establishment any old person could walk into.

Although, my encounter with him did make me hopeful. If he could recognize me that easily, then that had to mean he'd seen others before, so maybe they wouldn't be as hard to find as I feared. Since he recognized me as a seeker, perhaps other seekers would be able to do the same. Maybe I didn't have to find them. Maybe I just had to let them find me.

The idea was a little unsettling. It made me feel like I was putting myself out there as bait or something, which was a ludicrous analogy. I *wanted* to be found.

As Dante promised, the restaurant wasn't busy and we got our food quickly and found a table. But as he'd also promised, by eleven it started to get busy and every table in the small room was occupied. By the time we left, I had sweat dripping down my back from the heat caused by the hot grill and the number of bodies packed in the small space.

I had to admit, though—the food was delicious. Not worth a two hour wait, but I'd eat it at ten-thirty again.

We dropped Dante off at the stadium, and I stared up at the huge structure, so angry at myself that I'd failed so miserably in my first encounter with another seeker. To be fair, Reggie was surly and uncooperative. I hoped any other seekers we found would be friendlier.

Shenice turned to me as we idled in the parking lot. "Where do you want to go?" she asked.

I had no idea, so I went with my old standby. I wasn't seeking souls, but this was a sort of seeking. "A public place with lots of people."

She pursed her lips for a moment, then smiled, putting the car in gear. "I know just the place."

The place turned out to be the King of Prussia mall, which was huge. Shenice told me it was the biggest mall in America, even bigger than the Mall of America, which I'd thought was the biggest since it had a roller coaster in it. Turned out I was wrong.

We parked in a parking garage and made our way inside. There was a bounce to my step as I had high hopes. I'd gotten lucky this morning, so maybe I'd get lucky again.

It wasn't all that busy, though, which immediately dashed my hopes. It helped that it was summer, so kids were out of school, which meant there were more here than there normally would be at noon on a weekday. In fact, a lot of the employees at the stores and restaurants were teenagers. This would have been the perfect place for seeking.

But I definitely wasn't seeking souls. I didn't want to

say I never would again because I'd learned the hard way that as soon as you drew your line in the sand about not doing something, inevitably circumstances would arise that would make you eat your words.

But my mom had sacrificed herself so I wouldn't have to do it anymore. If I turned in another name, it would be a slap to her face. No, I wouldn't dishonor her memory like that.

Shenice and I wandered to the food court and she treated me to a smoothie, which I sipped as we continued to lap around the mall.

"See any angels?" I asked hopefully.

Shenice glanced around for good measure, then went back to poking her straw into her cup to break up the frozen bits. "Nope."

I sighed, the last of my optimism fleeing. This morning could have been a fluke. I was back to relying on Shenice's angel detection ability, but I doubted handlers would hang out at the mall with their seekers. My mom and I had never gone to a mall with Xavier. Perhaps I might have ended up at one with Xena at some point, but my relationship with her was not the typical handler-seeker relationship. Or at least that's what I assumed. How the heck would I know?

"Shenice, do I look different to you?" I asked.

She glanced over at me. "You seem depressed lately. And you don't smile much."

"No." I sighed again. "That's not what I mean. I mean, do I look different than everyone else? Different than a regular person?"

Shenice gave me a look, then guided me to a bench. "Hon, you are a regular person. I asked the same questions when I was your age. Just because you have an ability, you're still a human being. You're still normal."

Technically, I was part angel. A small part since Areli was several generations back in my line, but it was still there.

"No, that's not what I mean, either," I said. "Back at the Linc, that man—the painter—he knew I'm a seeker."

Shenice dropped her chin down to her chest and stared at me. "What?"

I looked down at my nails, which were chewed as far as they would go without bleeding. The past twenty-four hours had been hell for my poor fingers.

And the rest of me for that matter.

"He told me to stay out of his territory, that all the souls were his. He was worried about me poaching or something, which doesn't make sense. He's a lot older than me, so we can't see the same auras anyway."

Shenice's mouth dropped open. "He *knew*? How did he know?"

Damn. So much for getting info. I needed to remember that Shenice was not Xena. Although, Xena was so cagey with information, it might not have mattered.

"That's what I was hoping you could tell me," I said. "I have no idea."

"Maybe we should call Xena. She prob—"

"*No.*" I shook my head to make my point clear. I'd immediately thought of Xena as well, but we were *not* calling her. "We can't call anyone from back home."

"Xena's not from home. Not exactly."

If I didn't like Shenice so much, I would have rolled my eyes at her. Instead, I shot her a look to let her know what I thought of her clarification.

She put her hands up. "I'm just saying, Xena usually knows this kind of thing."

I shook my head again. "No, not this time. I don't want to involve her and it's not why you think. I can't rely on her anymore. If I'm going to make it on my own, then I need to figure things out."

That was definitely a big part of it. I also didn't want her to have to lie to Cole about my whereabouts. Plus, I wasn't entirely sure she would keep my secret. I was ninety-nine percent sure, but I could never tell with Xena.

She was unpredictable sometimes.

That seemed to be a common theme for handlers.

I wished I knew more about Linda. Would she try to hunt me down? Did she have the resources to do it? If I never saw that woman again it would be too soon.

"But you're not on your own," Shenice said, tapping my knee gently. "You've got me."

I opened my mouth to respond but thought better of it. Then I dropped my gaze to the ground, not wanting to look her in the eyes. Surely she couldn't think I expected her to stay with me forever. And surely she realized I wasn't going back. So what did she think was going to happen?

"Come on." I stood. "Let's keep walking around."

I wasn't ready to have that conversation yet.

WE WINDOW SHOPPED THE ENTIRE afternoon, coming up empty. No angels. No seekers.

Meeting Reggie right away had skewed my expectations. Because what were the odds? Of all the places I could have ended up twenty-four hours after setting out on this adventure, I managed to land in the path of another seeker and one who outed himself to me, no less. It was effortless on my part.

Well, aside from the whole leaving behind the two people I cared about most in the world. That was no small effort.

I asked Shenice if we could go back to the stadium to try to find Reggie, but she nixed that idea, as expected. She didn't like how he grabbed me and went all mama bear with me. I wasn't wild about that either, but he was a seeker and we knew where he was. However, Shenice was convinced we'd find seekers soon. She seemed to think there were lots of them.

I didn't know how to feel about that. On one hand, it

was nice to think I wasn't alone. But if there really were a lot, then why hadn't I met any before now? On the other hand, how many names was that? I couldn't get on board with tipping the scales to cause someone's death before their time. I couldn't get on board with people playing God, even if we were guided by handlers.

Maybe because of that.

Because...Xavier.

The last Xena told me, at least one of the souls he collected was unaccounted for. The woman in question died, but what happened to her soul? Did Xavier somehow do something with it? Were the Reapers still involved? Or did he circumvent them all together?

I didn't know much about the Reapers. I'd never had a desire to meet one. They creeped me out. While most angels were once human, Reapers never were. And they not only collected souls—they also caused death. At least, the ones I dealt with did.

When I thought of Reapers, I pictured them like the dementors from the *Harry Potter* movies, sucking the souls out of people.

But that wasn't all they did. They'd also saved both me and my mom before. Once when I was almost hit by a car, and once when my mom tried to kill herself. Apparently seekers' lives were too valuable for us to take them in our own hands.

But if there were lots of us, then why?

So many questions and not any answers. The more questions I came up with, the more I became convinced Reggie wouldn't be any help anyway. He didn't strike me as an all-knowing kind of guy. He was more of a *keep your head down and don't get noticed* type.

So it was irritating that in spite of this, he knew how to recognize other seekers while I didn't.

Something else I wondered about was whether Shenice would really be able to help me. So we find an angel. Then what? If the angel happened to be a handler, what were we supposed to do? Force him to tell us where his assigned seekers were? Yeah, right. So our other option would be to spy on and follow the handler until he happened to meet with seekers. A double *yeah, right* to that.

The more I thought about everything, the more frustrated I became. I'd thought I'd learned from past mistakes. I'd thought I'd learned not to jump into things but apparently not. I didn't think this through.

However, I was still sure I'd done the right thing. No matter what, Cole needed the opportunity to live a normal life. It just sucked that meant I couldn't be in it.

CHAPTER 11

THOUGH I TRIED MY BEST to be a pleasant guest, I excused myself as soon as possible after dinner that night. I had a lot of thinking to do. I should have thought everything through before insisting Shenice take me away, but it seemed I was incapable of thinking more than one step ahead. All my costly mistakes over the last year were because I'd failed to consider all the repercussions of my actions. But had I learned?

Nope. Apparently not. Because I was still doing the same stupid thing. Different mistakes, same foolish thinking. Or *not* thinking.

Shenice would not be able to stay with me forever. It wasn't fair to her. Somehow, I needed to carve out a life for myself. I had hoped to surround myself with other seekers and then go from there, but I was no longer confidant about that plan. Being a seeker was enough to make anyone bitter. What if they were all like Reggie?

I tossed and turned for I didn't know how long and when I finally fell asleep, I had fitful dreams of mingling with dozens and dozens of Reggies. They were all different heights and weights and had different hair colors and styles, but they all had his face, transfixed in a scowling expression. It was freaky.

A scream woke me, jarring me from the dream, which

might have been welcome except I almost fell off the couch as my arms and legs flailed.

I jumped up, my sleepy eyes wide, looking for the threat. A quick scan of the room told me it was empty except for a little girl screaming and pointing at me.

I blinked and looked over my shoulder once more, expecting to see a boogie man or something, but nope. She was definitely screaming because of me. Or *at* me.

"Shh..." I said. "It's okay." I stepped closer to her with open arms, wanting to comfort her. But that only made her shriek more.

I gaped at her, not sure what to do. I didn't understand why she was freaking out. She'd had dinner with me twice now and had barely paid me any notice.

Feet pounded on the stairs and Tina, Brian, and Shenice appeared, the three of them nearly colliding at the bottom. Shenice was still in her pajamas and judging by her disoriented expression, the screaming had woken her up, too.

"Mom! Something's wrong with her!" The little girl's voice was terrified, and she continued to stare at me with wide eyes. I looked down, scanning my body for some sort of "wrongness" I had somehow missed. No injuries, no blood, nothing. Just plain old Ava.

"What do you mean?" Tina asked, looking back and forth between me and her daughter. I shrugged my shoulders and put my palms up to show I had no clue what this was about.

"She was *glowing*. Like a monster or a witch or something."

Oh, shit. My eyes widened and my nostrils flared. Apparently I'd pulled my magic glowing act.

I could project my aura, but I didn't have much control over it and it usually happened when I slept. The stress of the last two days probably brought it on. And now this poor kid thought I was a monster.

Tina sighed and crossed her arms. "I told your father

not to let you watch *Ghostbusters*."

"But Mom—"

"Stop telling stories."

"But—"

"And I can't believe how rude you're being to our guest." Tina shot me an apologetic look. "You need to apologize."

"But—"

"*Right now*, young lady."

I breathed slowly as guilt crept in. Sarah was telling the truth, and she was about to get in trouble for it. Then on top of that, she was scared and possibly even traumatized. But what could I do?

Excuse me, Tina, but she isn't lying. I'm actually a freak of nature.

That wasn't going to happen. I was starting to care less and less about myself these days, but explaining about seekers opened the door to a discussion about Shenice's ability and that wasn't my secret to divulge. Plus, there was an unknown number of seekers who I assumed also kept their identities secret. It wouldn't be fair to jeopardize them.

I'd watched several TV shows and read a few books about vampires and other supernaturals "coming out of the closet." It was an interesting concept, and it made me wonder what would happen if seekers outed ourselves. Would anyone believe us? I was sure some people would, and it would be relatively easy to prove we were legit. Just hand over the name of a pure soul for a seeker and wait for the person to die. I was sure after that happened a handful of times people would start to believe us.

That thought made me sick.

So then what would happen? Who would people blame? Not the Reapers because no one could see them. And handlers could mask themselves, so who knew if they'd stand with us or let us take the fall. I was betting on them feeding seekers to the wolves. I wasn't impressed with the integrity of the few handlers I knew. Xena was okay for the most part, aside from her tendency to lie and keep secrets, but Xavier and Linda were scummy. They'd stand by and watch as a mob attacked us.

Yeah, it was best to keep the world of seekers under wraps.

Sarah's eyes shifted to me and she visibly flinched while looking at me. I wrapped my arms around myself, feeling vulnerable and exposed, but mostly guilty. I wanted to explain to her so she'd know she wasn't crazy, so she wouldn't end up with nightmares.

"Sorry," she whispered.

"It's okay," I said softly. I wanted to let her know that even though I glowed, I wasn't a monster. I didn't want her to have lasting effects from this experience. But I stayed silent.

"The bus comes in five minutes," Tina said. "Get your backpack and get outside."

"Yes, ma'am," Sarah muttered. With one last glance at me, she scurried up the stairs, probably grateful to get away from me. I couldn't blame her.

"I'm sorry," Tina said to me. "She has an overactive imagination anyway, but her dad's been letting her watch—"

"No, it's okay," I said. "Really." I wanted this conversation to end. I really wanted this entire experience to be over.

Fat chance of that. I was a seeker for life. So if it wasn't this, it would surely be something else.

"Come on," Tina said to Brian. "You need to get to the bus stop, too." She went up the stairs and he followed. Shenice stayed with me, her arms crossed and a wary expression on her face.

I looked at her and grimaced. "I'm sorry," I whispered. "Sometimes I project my aura when I sleep. It hasn't happened in a while, so I didn't even think about it."

She stared at me for a moment before dropping her arms to her sides and sighing. It was one of those *I'm not mad at you, I'm disappointed* moments, which made me feel even worse. I'd rather she be mad at me.

"It's not your fault," Shenice said. "You can sleep in the bedroom tonight, though. It has a door. I'll stay down here."

"I'm sorry," I said again, knowing it was inadequate. Shenice had trusted me enough to bring me to visit her family, and I'd royally screwed up. I hadn't meant to and I couldn't have helped it, but the damage was done all the same.

"I'm going to shower." She trudged up the stairs, leaving me alone.

I sank down onto the couch and rested my head in my hands. Why could nothing be easy? I couldn't even sleep without it causing problems.

The last thing I wanted was to cause trouble for Shenice's cousin's family, especially when they'd been so welcoming to me. Would they question Shenice about it when I wasn't around? Or would they continue to assume Sarah had been making it up? Probably the second one. Dante and Tina were grounded. They didn't seem like the type to believe in ghosts and things that go bump in the night.

In a way I was relieved. But it wasn't right.

There was a series of doors opening and closing—Tina coming back in from the bus stop, Shenice shutting herself in the bathroom, and then Tina going back out again. After a moment, I heard her van back out of the driveway.

Now what?

I chewed on my cuticle, wrinkling my nose and pulling my hand away from my mouth when I tasted blood. Then without thinking too deeply, I quickly stripped off my pajamas and pulled on shorts and a t-shirt. Keeping an ear out for the sound of the running shower, I stuffed the rest of my things in my suitcase.

I scanned the room, looking for paper and pen. I'd left abruptly last time and hadn't gotten to say any kind of good-byes. I needed to do better this time. Shenice would probably be out of the bathroom in a few minutes, though.

Damn it. There was not a single piece of paper in sight. I remembered Brian did his homework in the kitchen yesterday. That meant there were probably school supplies there.

I rushed up the stairs, dragging my suitcase behind me. On the counter was a basket overflowing with crayons, glue, pencils, and a pack of notebook paper. I grabbed a pencil and a piece of paper.

But as I held the pen over the paper, I didn't know what to write. *Good-bye?* That somehow didn't seem sufficient. *Thanks for everything?*

I wrote that and paused again.

The water turned off in the shower, so I cursed and scrawled on the paper. *Sorry. I don't want to make a bigger mess of your life. I'll be fine.*

I stared at it for a moment, then added, *Love, Ava.*

It sucked. It wasn't enough, but I was out of time. I hoped she would understand I was trying to do the right thing. I was *always* trying to do the right thing. Let's hope I got it right this time.

I ran out to the car, not looking back.

I DIDN'T KNOW WHERE I was going. I just drove.

My phone was still turned off, so I couldn't consult navigation. Anyway, it wouldn't matter if I did. I had no destination in mind.

I was a mess. I hadn't showered or even brushed my teeth. And my stomach was growling. Eventually I would need to decide on a location and check into a hotel, but for now I was simply driving, wanting to put some distance between me and Shenice.

In addition to the hunger, guilt gnawed at my stomach. Shenice was going to be pissed, but there was no avoiding that. I wondered if I should have left her some money to cover her bus fare back home, but I was strapped for cash as it was. I could get by for a little while, but at some point, I would need to settle somewhere and get a job. Living in my car did not appeal to me.

Yet, I was not above doing it.

I'd wondered why my mom didn't try to fight the system, why she'd simply gone along with Xavier all those years. I understood a little more now. I couldn't imagine subjecting a kid to this kind of life. Our life had been hard enough as it was.

After driving about thirty minutes, I stopped at a Wawa to brush my teeth and grab something to eat. I also picked up a map—an old school paper monstrosity that unfolded to the size of the hood of my car. While I gassed up, I laid it out to consider my options. It really didn't matter where I went. Seekers could be anywhere.

So I might as well go somewhere nice, right?

I could go to Boston or somewhere else in New England. The weather should be pleasant this time of year. The farther away I got, the better. But dang, that would be a long drive. Perhaps I'd be better off starting somewhere closer.

Like the beach. Although I'd lived by Virginia Beach the past year, I hadn't spent much time there. Atlantic City wasn't too far and there would be plenty to keep me occupied. It was also a tourist destination, so I would blend in. I could relax with my toes in the sand, looking for seekers and trying to figure out my next move.

The ocean called to me because that was where my mom was. Maybe she'd had that in mind when she requested her ashes be scattered at sea. If she'd been buried in a cemetery, she'd be static. But now, she was part of the ocean, which meant she was everywhere.

Being in the ocean was the closest I could get to her.

Now more than ever I needed to feel her near me again.

My mind made up, I folded the map and as I did, a dot caught my eye. *Hershey*.

Yum. Chocolate. That sounded promising.

I loved chocolate as much as the next person, so why not? There was also an amusement park. I could go to look for seekers. There were bound to be lots of teenagers there. Although, I probably shouldn't spend the money on admission. But there would be people there. Lots of people.

I forgot all about Atlantic City for the time-being. Maybe I'd go there next.

I measured the distance on the map using my fingers and the little one-inch scale. Hershey was maybe one hundred miles, so two hours? It wasn't like it mattered. I didn't have anywhere to be.

It took longer than two hours, mostly because traffic was horrendous. Trying to get around Philly at rush hour made me feel bad for the poor people who had this commute on a daily basis. Since it was too early to check into a hotel, I swung by Hershey Park, just to make sure I could find it. A small part of me got excited as I looked at the roller coasters. I couldn't remember the last time I'd been to an amusement park. Probably in middle school on a field trip with my friend's church youth group. It was so fun running around the park by ourselves. I hadn't known the other kids very well, but I remembered feeling so grown up. It was the first time my mom had let me go on a trip like that.

As I stared at the parking lot filled with cars, I realized that if I did end up going to Hershey Park, it would be a much different experience. I wouldn't be there to have a good time. My agenda would be very different. And I would be alone.

I blinked, then squared my shoulders and focused on the road. I wasn't doing this. Yes, I was alone, but that was my choice. I was doing what needed to be done, and I wasn't going to lose myself to a pity party.

Time to get my priorities in order.

I decided to look for a hotel, even though it was still before noon. Maybe they'd let me check in early. Searching for the most rundown hotel I could find, I selected one on the edge of town. It was actually a motel with doors that opened to the outside, which made me uneasy from a security standpoint. But this had to be cheaper than the big national chains that were safer and cleaner.

After I parked, I sat in the car, staring at the building with trepidation. The roof was painted brown metal and the walls were mustard yellow. The doors to the individual rooms were dark green and most of them had huge Frisbee size patches of paint missing, revealing the metal underneath.

Maybe this was a bad idea. Maybe I should look around for a hotel that didn't put worry in my stomach.

I sat and scouted it out for another ten minutes, but nothing sketchy happened. I was being paranoid. Getting out of the car, I saw a "Free Breakfast" sign posted in the front window that I hadn't noticed. That settled it. Free breakfast was right up my alley. That would help with my finances.

The lobby was old but clean, which made me relax. The front desk was unmanned so I rang the bell. While I waited, I strolled over to the breakfast area. No waffle maker, but that was too much to expect in a place like this.

"Can I help you?"

I turned to the desk clerk, a girl who couldn't have been much older than me. Habit had me shoring up my guards against her aura.

"I need a room, please."

Her eyes shifted to the computer. "Is it just you?"

"Yes."

While she did her thing on the computer, I picked up a Hershey Park brochure sitting on the counter. My hopes sank when I saw the price of a day ticket. I couldn't spend nearly seventy dollars. That was more than I was paying for this hotel room.

Feeling defeated, I put the brochure on the counter and something on the back caught my eye. I picked it up again and looked closer. They had a nighttime admission special that got you in after four for half the price of a normal ticket.

Score! I could definitely swing that. I didn't need to spend hours and hours there, anyway.

"Is the second floor okay?" the clerk asked. "Check-in is technically not for four more hours, and those are the only rooms we have ready."

"That's perfect."

"Fill this out." She pushed a form across the desk toward me. "Can I have your credit card?"

"I'm paying cash."

She looked at me for a moment before rattling off the total. "I do need an ID, though."

Damn. So much for putting a fake name. It probably didn't make a difference. Bill and Cole weren't tracking me and even if they were, I didn't know how much of what I'd seen on TV was real, anyway. Surely putting my name on a paper form in a dinky hotel wouldn't be enough to give away my location.

The only one who might be able to find me was Xena and she was on my side. She'd practically shoved me out the door. And she'd hold up under any kind of interrogation.

If she wanted to.

I took my key card and got back in my car to repark on the side of the building where my room was. The only bad thing about being on the second floor was having to lug my suitcase up the stairs. I was a sweaty mess by the time I got there, which once again confirmed my conclusion that I was out of shape. Granted, the suitcase was pretty big, but still. My arms shouldn't be aching.

The room was small. The pattern on the carpet reminded me of caterpillars and the bedspread was cheap polyester. I could handle that, though. The worst part was the room smelled overwhelmingly like Axe body spray, like a thirteen-year-old boy had doused himself from head to toe. *Yuck.* I thought I'd left that smell behind in middle school.

Oh, well. I propped the door open to try to air it out. But it only took a minute to realize it was way too hot to leave the door hanging open. It was either roast or be assaulted by Axe. I mentally apologized to my nose as I closed and locked the door.

I pulled my phone out of my pocket and put it on the dresser. I sank down onto the bed, clasping my hands between my knees and staring at the metal and plastic device. How many texts and missed calls were waiting for me? Probably a lot.

Or worse...what if there were barely any?

I didn't want Cole and Bill to be hurting, but I selfishly couldn't bear the thought of them simply shrugging their shoulders and moving on, like my absence didn't affect them. Like they didn't care.

That was silly. Both of them loved me. Neither one would do that.

But what would they do to cope? Bill would probably throw himself into his work. And Cole? Probably the same.

Or perhaps he'd take *Dani* up on her party invitation. Perhaps she'd issue him an invitation for a private party. Images of her perfect body wrapped around him flooded my mind. Her stupid perfect personality, perfect brain, perfect *everything*. If anyone could make Cole forget about me, it was her.

I tore my gaze away from my phone and went into the bathroom.

I was the one who left *him*. So even if he did move on, I couldn't hold it against him.

No, not *if*. *When*. Because what did I expect him to

do? Pine over me forever?

As usual, I was being ridiculous. I never could think clearly where Cole was concerned. I would do anything for him, no matter how crazy. It clouded my judgment.

And when he touched me, half of my brain cells went into stasis, making coherent thought impossible. The last time he touched me—

Oh, God. What must he have thought when he realized I was missing? I went straight from his bed to just *poof!* I'd asked him to be my first, and he'd obliged and it was wonderful.

Then I left.

I'd never be with him again.

My lower lip quivered and tears spilled over. I hadn't allowed myself to think too deeply about it. At the time, I'd thought having the memory of us being together would bring me comfort. I couldn't have been more wrong.

It hurt so much.

Blinded by my tears, I reached for the shower knobs to start the water. Might as well get cleaned up.

As the steaming water washed over me, I imagined it was washing away everything—my problems, the memories, the hurt, *everything.* It helped for a few minutes, but as soon as I turned the water off, everything came rushing back.

I wished the water had washed *me* away.

CHAPTER 12

AS I LOOKED IN THE mirror and combed my wet hair, I made a vow to myself—no more looking back. Only looking forward.

Because really, what good did it do to wallow in the past? I needed to learn from my mistakes and move on. The only thing I could change was what was in front of me.

But first things first—food. I couldn't keep eating at fast food restaurants and picking up junk at gas stations. It wasn't healthy, but in addition to that, it was expensive.

I pulled clean clothes out of my suitcase, looking at my pile of dirty ones. That was something else I hadn't considered. Eventually I would need to do laundry. So I'd have to keep my eye out for a laundromat.

Before setting out in search of a grocery store, I shoved my phone in a dresser drawer, eliminating temptation. Sure, it would easier to get around if I could use the GPS, but I wasn't an idiot. I could find my way without it.

It only took ten minutes to find a grocery store. As I walked up and down the aisles, I realized I had another problem—no refrigerator. I supposed I could get a cooler and keep refilling it with ice, but that would be a pain. For now, I'd stick to non-perishables and try to get my fill of dairy and fresh food at breakfast.

Finding meals that didn't require refrigeration or a microwave was tougher than I'd expected. I ended up loading up on crackers and snacks. At the last minute I threw in a loaf of bread and some peanut butter. I remembered seeing individual jelly packets in the continental breakfast area at the hotel, so I could swipe some of those to make sandwiches. Far from ideal, but overall I was pleased. I could get by for almost a week on the twenty dollars I spent, especially if I ate a big breakfast every morning.

I headed back toward the hotel with my haul. There were still several hours to kill before I could purchase an evening admission to Hershey Park. So I binged on PB&J and chips and watched crappy reality television for a few hours. It was nice to lose myself in other people's problems for a while.

Although, I don't think I would consider my spray tan being too orange an "epic disaster." Of course, my skin was pasty all the time, so what did I know about being tan?

I set out for Hershey Park, giving myself more than enough time to park and be at the gate as soon as I could get in. Since I was only going for the evening, I wanted to make the most of my time.

I got a little turned around, so by the time I got parked and made it to the front gate, it was pushing four, which was perfect.

It didn't take long to purchase my ticket and get inside. My first thought was I was glad I'd already stuffed my face because chocolate signs were everywhere. There were even human-sized candy bars walking around. Was it weird that those made my mouth water? I knew there were people inside the costumes, but still. If they were real, they'd be bigger than I was and a chocolate bar that big was cause for excitement in my book.

Despite everything, the festive atmosphere put me in a good mood. I wandered around for a bit, pausing to watch the screaming riders on the roller coasters. I'd never been much of a thrill seeker, so I didn't mind not going on those. I was irritated that once again I missed a swimming opportunity. There was a whole water park area. I wouldn't have minded floating around in a tube for a while.

I completed my tour of the park and instead of backtracking, I stood for a moment. Now what?

What was my plan? I didn't have one. Not really. Other seekers would be able to recognize me, but they might not approach me. That was out of my control. All I could do was make myself visible and approachable.

Sooner rather than later, I'd have to make a decision about where I wanted to live so I could get a job. Seeing that the hotel clerk was near my age gave me hope that perhaps I'd be able to find a decent position that would pay more than minimum wage. I'd also have to see about getting an apartment or renting a room or something. I couldn't live in a hotel indefinitely.

One thing at a time. I'd just left Shenice this morning, so instead of rushing into something, I'd give it a few days to figure out the best course of action. This was me, trying to be all mature and stuff.

I was actually starting to get hungry since it was dinnertime, and I could have kicked myself for not bringing snacks. Like at all places like this, food was expensive. But I had to eat, so I sucked it up and bought a hot dog.

I found a bench in the shade and sat to eat. Across from me was a couple probably a year or two younger than me. She played with her hair and her gaze kept darting to the ground. He had his hands shoved in his pockets and a shy look on his face, though it was obvious he adored the girl. I came up with a story for them in my head—it was their first date, but he'd had a crush on her for years and only recently mustered the courage to ask her out. What he didn't know was that she'd actually started to notice him in the last few months, especially after her heart had been broken by another boy at school. They'd only just gotten here because she had to babysit her siblings, but she'd already decided she liked him. A lot. And she wanted him to kiss her.

As the fictional story unfolded in my mind, my fingers found the angel pendant on my necklace and played with it. The smooth metal was a tangible reminder of what I'd left behind. It was heavy around my neck, yet I couldn't take it off.

I tore my gaze away from the couple. Suddenly, making up a story about them didn't seem so fun anymore.

Balling up my trash, I stood, wanting to get away from here. I tossed my trash into a nearby trashcan and wrapped my arms around myself as I walked.

My festive mood from earlier was all but gone when someone knocked into me as he walked past. This wasn't a soft brush of shoulders. This was a hard hit, enough to make me cry out, "Ow!" and stumble.

"Asshole," I muttered as I looked ahead to see who had hit me. It had happened so fast all I saw was a blur of black clothing.

No one wearing dark clothing was anywhere near me. I squinted. Way up ahead was a man dressed in all black— long sleeves and pants, even in this heat. Weird. Black hair.

An icy feeling started in my heart and spread to the rest of my body.

It couldn't be.

But I'd said that before. I had to find out.

I became the asshole as I ran through the crowd, weaving and bobbing and jostling people as I tried to catch up. You'd think I would have learned not to wear flip-flops by now, but nope. My feet were sweating, causing them to slip and slide around on the cheap foam. I curled my toes in an effort to keep them on.

Screw it.

I stripped them off and ran barefoot, trying not to

think about all the disease-infected nastiness my skin was touching.

But in the seconds it took for me to take off my shoes, I'd taken my eyes off the man and now I didn't see him.

Impossible. How could he have gotten away so fast?

If it was Xavier, he wouldn't have to get away. He could have simply masked his presence. *Damn.* Now I really wished Shenice were here. He wouldn't be able to hide from her.

I stopped and put my hands on my hips, breathing hard and scanning the crowd, hoping to catch a glimpse of him. After a full minute passed, I had to admit it was pointless. I wasn't going to catch him.

It was like the stupid incident in the parking garage all over again. And that hadn't ended so well.

Don't jump to conclusions. I tried the thought on for size, but it didn't fit too well. Jumping to conclusions meant at least I would be somewhat prepared. So I'd have to assume Xavier was in the area and use caution.

Now I really wished I had my pink gun. But it wouldn't have helped me here since I doubted weapons were allowed in the park. Also, I never got my concealed carry permit, so I was nervous about carrying. I wasn't a one-hundred percent rule follower, but I definitely wasn't a law breaker. Not if I could help it, anyway.

I was just putting my flip-flops back on my feet when I heard a shriek from up ahead.

Aw, heck. That couldn't be a coincidence.

I jogged up to a small gathering of people. A little girl was in near hysterics while her mother tried to calm her down. A female park employee knelt next to them. The crowd cleared allowing me to get closer, and I saw the poor little girl's knees were torn and bloody.

I shifted so my view of her knees was obscured. Even so, I could feel myself pale at the sight of the blood. I was glad I wasn't close enough to see it well.

But *ouch.* That had to hurt. My sympathy went out to

the poor girl.

The mother was furious. "Who does that to a child?"

The employee—a girl about my age—shook her head. "I don't know."

"And I hate to say it," the mother said as she rubbed her daughter's back, "but the man looked like Freddy Krueger."

I gasped. I didn't know much about horror movies, but I knew who Freddy Krueger was. His face was a mangled mess, kind of like how you'd expect someone who'd been shot in the face to look.

If I wasn't convinced before, I was certainly convinced now. That was Xavier. I wouldn't put it past him to knock over a child and not think twice about it.

But why the heck would he knock into me and then run away? The last time he'd done that, he wanted me to know he'd left a vial of blood in my mom's hospital room. It was the first clue she needed him to survive.

Now, though, it didn't make any sense.

Sigh. Nothing ever did with him, not at first. But he never did anything without reason.

The employee shook her head, her mouth twisted in anger. "I know exactly who you're talking about. I've seen him lingering around here before. I'll alert security, but first let me help you to the first aid center."

"Honey, can you stand?" the mother asked.

The little girl shook her head and put her arms up. Her mother scooped her up under her knees and the little girl hugged her neck.

I wanted to talk to the girl more about Xavier to find out how long he'd been hanging around and exactly what he'd been doing, but I couldn't ask now while she was busy with damage control. I looked around, trying to figure out where the employee was stationed. But there was no empty vending carts or unattended rides. I'd have to follow them or I'd never find her again.

As I started to back away so it wouldn't be obvious

what I was doing, the girl stood and turned, her gaze landing on me.

Her eyes widened and her mouth fell open a little. As she gave me the once-over, her mouth stretched into a grin. I found myself looking over my shoulder to make sure she was indeed looking at me.

She stepped close and squeezed my hand. I was so surprised I nearly jerked it out of her grasp. "Stay here," she whispered. "I can't wait to talk to you."

With a final imploring and excited look, she ushered the woman and little girl away, leaving me staring after them.

CHAPTER 13

I PACED. THERE WAS A perfectly good vacant bench just to my left, but I couldn't sit because *what...the...heck?*

What just happened? That girl acted shocked to see me and then ridiculously happy, like she knew who I was, which she didn't. I had never seen her before in my life.

But she might know *what* I was.

I gasped, putting a hand over my now hanging open mouth. A few passersby cocked their heads at me and I shuffled over to the bench, sinking down onto it.

That girl had to be a seeker, just like Reggie from The Linc. This was exactly what I was hoping for, but I still couldn't stop my hands from shaking or from questioning whether that *really* just happened. Nothing ever went my way and I meant *nothing*. Except now. I'd wanted to find seekers and I found them. The ease of it made me suspicious.

How was it they could recognize me, but I wasn't able to recognize them? Was it a learned skill? It must be. Of course, I'd have had no way to hone it. Until Cole, the only seeker I'd known was my mom. I tried to think about her objectively to figure out if there was something different about her. A *tell* of some sort.

Memories of her flooded my mind—memories I'd worked so hard to lock away. Her taking me to the bus stop on my first day of school. Her attempting to make me an elaborate princess cake for my seventh birthday and failing miserably. The feel of her hand in mine as she took her last breath.

The pain of that moment was unreal, and I never wanted to feel anything like it again. It had felt like a metal claw was squeezing my heart, the emotional pain so intense it became physical, like a part of me was dying with her.

Even the memory was overwhelming.

My throat closed, making it hard to breathe. I put my head down between my knees and sucked in air, but that only made me more light-headed.

"Holy crap, are you okay?"

I sat up straight, the sudden motion making my head swim and my vision blur. I tried to inhale deeply, but that wasn't happening so I took a few short, shallow breaths instead, just trying to suck in any air I could. My vision cleared enough for me to see the girl from earlier standing in front of me. She must have realized what was happening because she held out a water bottle dripping with condensation. I pressed it up against my forehead for a second before twisting off the top and taking a big drink.

"Thanks," I said.

"No problem." She sat on the bench next to me and put one leg up, turning so she faced me. "Better now?"

"I think so." I fiddled with the water bottle, embarrassed. I'd barely even met this girl and I already came off like I was mental. "I think it was a pan—"

"A panic attack, yeah. I used to get them." She pushed her hair out of her face. "The putting your head between your knees thing didn't ever work for me, either."

"I don't usually get them." That was true, but I'd gotten them enough to recognize it for what it was.

She put her hands up. "I'm not judging." Even though she said that, her eyes assessed me. Her expression was still friendly, but it was definitely curious as well. It made me self-conscious. But my own curiosity won out.

"How do you know me?" I asked softly.

She cocked her head, an action that reminded me of Xena. However, that was where the resemblance ended. This girl had dirty blonde hair currently pulled up into a ponytail and blue eyes. She also had a tan and enviable curves. She was probably a contender for the most attractive superlative in her high school. But while she was attractive, she wasn't perfect, not like Danielle. This girl had a girl-next-door kind of beauty, making her less intimidating.

"I don't know you. Not yet, anyway." She stuck out her hand. "I'm Claire."

I shook her hand. "Ava."

She tucked her hands under her legs and looked at the people walking by. She'd said she wanted to talk to me, but so far she wasn't doing much talking. But for once, I was content to sit and wait. Part of my new *being mature* thing.

"So..." she said. "This is weird. I always wondered if Chase and I were the only teens. I didn't think we were, but it's still weird actually meeting you."

"Who's Chase?"

"Oh, my brother. Sorry."

"But what about your parents?"

She shook her head, indicating they weren't like us.

"But..." I trailed off. Maybe I totally misread the situation. Maybe she thought I was someone—or *something*—else all together. "You're a seeker, right?"

It made me a little nervous to put it out there like that, especially since I'd never talked to anyone about it. Well, other than Reggie. But I needed to confirm. If she wasn't actually a seeker, then she wouldn't have any idea what I was talking about. Heck, she might think I was some kind of freak talking about Quidditch or something. Because didn't people do that? Run around with pretend flying broomsticks and play that game?

"Duh." She scrunched up her nose. "Can't you tell?"

"No." My tone was a mix of blandness and frustration. It really sucked I'd finally managed to find people who I should fit in with unequivocally and I was still the odd woman out. It was my lot in life to fly solo in more ways than one.

"Oh. Well, that's weird." She curiously examined me again, probably looking for the defect that made me unlike all the other seekers.

I ignored her assessment, not caring if she thought I was weird among the weirdos. I just wanted answers. "How can you tell?"

"I don't know how to explain it." She twisted her lips to the side as she thought. "It's like we emit a certain kind of energy or something. Like you know how people have auras? Seekers have this energy instead of an aura."

"I have an aura." I frowned at her and lowered my guards just enough for her colors to come blazing through, then I slammed them back into place. "So do you."

Now she was the one who frowned. "But I can't see Chase's aura. Just the seeker energy."

We stared at one another for a moment, each of us trying to decide whether to believe the other. She looked away first, checking the sports watch strapped to her arm.

"Shit," she said. "I have to get back to work. But we still have a lot to talk about."

"Yes." That was one thing we agreed on.

"Chase works here too. We get off at ten. Can you meet us somewhere later tonight?"

I nodded. "Where?"

"Let's see. Most places will be closed by then. But there's a twenty-four hour diner not too far from here on Chocolate Avenue near the Staples."

"Okay." I tried to think where that was, but I didn't remember seeing a Staples. I'd have to consult my trusty map.

She pulled her phone out of her pocket. "Give me your

number."

"Um..." A blush spread to my cheeks. "I don't have a phone. I mean, I do, but I'm not using it right now."

She looked at me like I was crazy. Apparently I emitted a certain kind of energy that all seekers but me could detect and I could see auras even though no other seekers could, and it was my lack of a phone that affirmed my diagnosis as a crazy person.

"It's complicated," I muttered.

She stood and tucked her phone away. "Okay." Her tone was unsure, like she thought I was trying to run out on her.

"I promise I'll be there," I said. "You have no idea how much I want to talk to you."

My words must have convinced her because she smiled. "Great. We'll be there by ten-thirty, eleven at the latest. It depends on if my boss is being a dick tonight." She clapped her hand over her mouth guiltily and looked around to make sure said boss hadn't heard. With a quick wave, she walked away.

It was only then I realized I hadn't asked about the "Freddy Krueger" man. Dang.

Lately, taking care of Xavier had fallen to the back burner, not because avenging my mom's death wasn't important, but because it would be difficult—I still didn't know how to kill him. Regardless, I had to find him first. This was the first potential Xavier sighting since my mom shot him.

Suddenly I became nervous Claire and her brother wouldn't show, that I'd blown my chance.

I shook off the worry. Claire had approached me, not the other way around. They would show. And if they didn't, I knew exactly where to look for them.

I still had a lot of time in the park, but I was done, wanting to leave on a high note. I'd set out to find other seekers and not only had I found them, but I'd found ones who were my age. I closed my eyes and allowed a cheesy grin to spread on my face. I was beyond pumped.

As I neared the exit, a huge Hershey bar was posing for pictures with guests. What the heck? Might as well make a great night even better. I slipped into a gift shop, emerging five minutes later with the biggest chocolate bar I'd ever had.

CHAPTER 14

AT TEN ON THE DOT, I parked in the diner parking lot. As I stared up at the neon sign reading "Bev's Diner," the neurotic side of my brain went into overdrive. Was this the right place? Claire hadn't said the name of the restaurant, but I didn't see any other diners near Staples. This one was literally in Staples' parking lot.

Even though I wasn't carrying my phone, I should have taken her number. Earlier in the park, I'd been confident I'd be able to find her again if she didn't show, but dang it, that was still stupid. Sure, I knew where she and her brother worked—although I had no clue what her brother looked like—but if they didn't show, what was I supposed to do? Waste all my money on admission to Hershey Park in the hopes they happened to be working that day? And the park was big. It could take hours to find them.

I took a deep breath and exhaled slowly, letting the worry leave my body with the breath. There was no sense stressing about something I couldn't control—I couldn't make Claire and her brother show up.

So instead I shifted to worrying about the stuff I could control. Sort of. I couldn't go back and undo my actions, but I did have control over them. And though I'd vowed not to live in the past, sitting in the dark parking lot by myself, I couldn't stop the thoughts from flowing through my mind.

I wished I hadn't left things so poorly with Shenice. But heck, that sentiment could be applied to almost every relationship I had. Bill, Cole, Kaley...

Shit. I hadn't even considered her. She was busy with a babysitting job that took up most of her time, so I hadn't seen her much this summer. But I still felt bad. She was the first real friend I'd had since I came into my birthright, and I'd messed it up.

Not that it mattered much. I wasn't planning to return to Tidewater, so I'd never see her again anyway. Still, though, I hoped when she learned I'd cut and run, she wouldn't be too hurt. I'd been a crappy friend to her.

If I'd turn my dang cell phone on, I would probably know how she felt instead of having to guess. I could only guess at how many text messages were waiting for me.

I might be willing to kill Xavier if given the chance, but I was a coward.

Speaking of Xavier, I hadn't stopped thinking about him since the mother in the park had said that man looked like Freddy Krueger. And he'd been hanging around Claire. It *had* to be him. Maybe since he no longer had me to do his dirty work, he was trying to find other seekers. Though for what purpose, I had no clue. Nothing good.

While Xena said he was alive, she hadn't said anything about the extent of his injuries and I hadn't thought to ask. I hadn't cared. As long as he breathed, it was one breath too many, no matter what shape he was in. He'd taken a lot of hits when my mom shot him, so it made sense he might not heal fully.

He'd bled.

The image of the bullet exploding in his face in a mess of blood and flesh kept replaying in my mind. It was gory. Perhaps it was morbid to revisit that scene, but it gave me hope. If he could bleed, then he could die, right?

Xavier once said to me, *"Do you have any idea how*

much pain can be inflicted on someone who can't die?"
The memory of how sadistic his voice sounded always
gave me chills. Lately, I'd been thinking about that phrase
a lot. Because if Xavier couldn't die, then I might have to
find the answer to that question.

But no matter how much pain I inflicted upon him, it
would never be enough to make up for the tightening of
my heart every morning when I woke up and realized I was
starting another day without my mother. There was
always that split second when I first woke up that I forgot
and remembering was like reliving it over and over again.

I flipped on the radio, wanting something to distract
me from my thoughts. But as the minutes ticked by and it
got closer to eleven, no amount of music could take away
the unease in the pit of my stomach.

Eleven came and went. Then eleven-oh-five. Eleven-
ten. Eleven-fifteen.

They weren't coming.

Part of me was surprised because Claire had seemed
intent on us meeting. But really I shouldn't have been. It
was my normal pattern of two steps forward, one step
back. I'd have to seek her out.

Damn. I hit the steering wheel in frustration. I wasn't
above going to Hershey Park every day and turning myself
into a stalker, but that would devastate my wallet. I
couldn't just let this opportunity pass me by, though, no
matter what it cost.

I sighed, fishing around for my keys in the dark. No
sense sitting here any longer when there was a slightly
sketchy—and Axe scented—hotel room waiting for me.

Just as I turned the key in the ignition, a dirty white
mini-van pulled into the lot with a screech and parked a
few spaces down. Claire jumped out of the passenger side
and hurried toward the front door of the diner.

I couldn't help but smile. She must have figured I'd
given up waiting by now, and it was nice to see I wasn't
wrong about her—she was eager to meet me.

I turned off the car and got out. The sound of my door closing made Claire turn. When she saw me, a relieved look spread across her face.

"Sorry!" She trotted over. "My boss is such an ass. He never lets us go when he's supposed to. Schedules mean nothing to him."

I wouldn't know about having an asshole boss. Shenice was always so good to me. *Too* good. I was the asshole.

I shifted uncomfortably, putting that out of my mind. "I'm glad you came," I said. "I was about to leave."

"Sorry!" she said again, making me feel like more of a jerk. I hadn't meant to make her feel bad. She couldn't help it if her boss made her stay and it wasn't like she had any way to get in touch with me. What was she supposed to do? Call the diner and ask them to look for a rogue teenage girl?

"It's okay," I said hurriedly.

She flashed a smile, then looked over her shoulder at the van. "Chase! What the heck are you doing? Hurry up!"

A moment later, the driver's side door opened and her brother stepped out.

He was a male version of her, which made him gorgeous, but in a totally masculine way.

His dirty blond hair was on the long side and immediately made me think of a surfer, even though we were nowhere near a beach. And come to think of it, I didn't know if I'd ever actually met a surfer, so how would I know?

What I did know was Chase had the sun-kissed skin of a beach bum, great hair, and a figure that was enviable, though in a much different way than his sister's—in a way that made my mouth water and had me averting my eyes lest I continue gawking.

The only other time I openly gawked at a guy was when Cole pulled me out of traffic, saving my life. Of course, I learned later the Reapers would have saved me if he hadn't been there. I'd never been one to believe in knights in shining armor and damsels in distress, but I fit the stereotype that day.

And looking at Chase, I had to say I wouldn't mind him coming to my rescue.

Damn it! I was gawking again. I looked down, suddenly finding the chipped toenail polish on my big toe utterly fascinating.

My thoughts caught me off guard. I wasn't the boy-crazy type of girl, and I wasn't about to turn into one now. So while I would acknowledge Chase was good looking and I was attracted to him, that was where it ended.

I felt for the angel pendant and the feel of the smooth metal between my fingers snapped me out of it. Cole was the only one I wanted, but unfortunately, he was off limits.

"Hey," Chase said. Reflexively, I shifted my gaze to him as he spoke and found myself looking into the bluest eyes I'd ever seen. They were ocean blue, and not American ocean blue, but the color of the ocean in the Bahamas or the Caribbean or some other exotic place I'd never get to see in my lifetime. It made my earlier surfer comparison even stronger.

The only word I could use to describe his eyes was *dreamy.* I wanted to smack myself for that idiotic thought, but it fit.

Even though his eyes were brilliant, I didn't miss the skepticism in his gaze or his voice. I lifted my chin up a notch. Claire had approached me, not the other way around. He had no reason to be suspicious or distrusting.

Although, probably having lived the seeker life was enough of a reason. If he'd seen even a fraction of the stuff I had this past year, then I couldn't blame him for being suspicious. So I would cut him some slack.

I held my hand out politely. "I'm Ava."

His gaze flickered down to my hand for a moment, and I was about to retract it when he stepped forward to take it.

His grip was firm—almost challenging. I barely resisted the urge to roll my eyes as I took my hand back and wrapped my arms around myself. He could cut the macho stuff.

"I'm starved," Claire said, oblivious to the silent power struggle between me and her brother. "Let's get a table."

The diner had self-serve seating, so we found a booth in the corner that would give us a small level of privacy. Claire and Chase slid into one side and I sat across from them. It sent off a me vs. them vibe, but I was sure I was reading too much into it. Of course they would sit together. They actually knew one another, whereas I'd chatted with Claire for less than five minutes.

There was so much I wanted to ask them. However, before we could talk, Claire waved the server over.

"Double cheeseburger, no onions. And give me a double order of fries. Plus a Coke." Claire looked at us. "Do you guys want anything?"

"Um..." I reached for the menu tucked behind the napkin holder. Claire hadn't looked at it.

Chase glanced at me, then looked up at the waitress. "Can you give us a minute, please?"

She nodded and tucked her pad in her apron before turning to walk away.

"Put my order in!" Claire called after her.

Chase shot his sister an exasperated look.

"What?" She shrugged apologetically. "I'm really hungry. I didn't eat dinner."

She'd probably spent her dinner break talking to me instead of eating. It wasn't my fault, but I still felt bad.

I opened the menu and perused the selections, which were typical diner fare. I didn't want to spend the money after I'd already spent money on food at the park, but I felt like I needed to order something. I decided on an appetizer of cheese fries.

Chase hadn't picked up the menu.

"Are you ordering something?" I asked. Perhaps if he didn't order, then I could do the same.

He nodded. "I don't need the menu."

I realized he hadn't ordered because he was waiting for me to look at the menu. He was being polite. Although, it hadn't offended me that Claire had ordered without us. *When a girl's hungry, a girl's got to eat.* I totally understood.

"You can call the server back if you want," I said. "I'm ready."

Chase flicked his fingers in the air, and she appeared as if she were a genie. He ordered grilled chicken and veggies, no butter, and coffee. *Yuck* to all of that. I ordered water and greasy cheese fries, feeling very unhealthy, but at least my food would taste good.

"So what's your story?" Chase asked after the server walked away.

"What do you mean?" I ran my finger along a line on the table, using that as diversion from Chase's baby blues.

"You know, how long you've been a seeker, how you got that way. The usual." Chase put his forearms on the table and leaned forward, looking at me intently and making me feel like I was being interrogated.

"Stop grilling her." Claire swatted her brother's arm. "There's two of us and one of her. We'll go first so it doesn't seem like we're ganging up on her." She leaned forward. "We're not, by the way. Ganging up on you. We've just never met another seeker our age. How old are you anyway?"

"Eighteen," I replied. It still felt weird I was legally an adult. Though I was out on my own, I didn't feel like one.

Claire clapped a hand over her mouth. "Oops. I just said we weren't going to interrogate you, and then I go and ask another question. I'm eighteen. Chase is nineteen. We're almost exactly one year apart. My birthday is April 6 and his is April 14, so for eight days, we're actually the same age."

"Really?" I wanted to face palm myself. It was one of those stupid, obvious questions that didn't need to be asked. But she'd paused to catch her breath, so I felt the need to say something.

"Yup. When we were younger we used to tell people we were identical twins since we look alike. Or as alike as a guy and girl can look. Of course, that was when we were too young and stupid to realize that a boy and girl can't be identical twins because you know—boy and girl." She grinned.

I nodded, deciding to keep my mouth shut so no more idiotic things would could out. With Chase staring at me like he was, I was likely to start babbling. Kind of like Claire. But while she came across as cute and bubbly when she talked a lot, I seemed like a moron.

Chase wasn't much of a talker. I wondered if he ever got a word in when the two of them were little kids. Right now, he simply sat there with his arms crossed and his mouth pressed into a thin line. I didn't know why he was displeased. Didn't he want Claire to share? He needed to check himself if he thought this conversation would be a one-way street. I wasn't going to spill my life story and get nothing in return.

He was intimidating, but not nearly as intimidating as Cole could be. Chase's surfer appearance limited the intimidation factor, unlike Cole who had the total badass thing going on.

What would Cole think of Chase? I tried to picture the two of them interacting, but all I could imagine was each of them puffing his chest up like roosters in some sort of tough guy competition.

God, I missed Cole.

My eyes teared up at the thought and I quickly looked away, blinking rapidly.

"Anyway," Claire said, "our near-death happened when I was fourteen and Chase was fifteen. A car accident. Since we were minors, our mom had to agree. So that's our story. How about you?"

The server came with our drinks, giving me a moment to digest what she'd said. I didn't get it. It seemed like she'd left out a lot of details, assuming I'd be able to fill in the blanks, but if they weren't born seekers, then how did they get that way? Obviously, it had something to do with their near death experience.

Claire thirstily sucked at the straw, her big blue eyes focused on me. Chase didn't touch his coffee.

"I don't understand," I said slowly. "What do you mean your mom had to agree?"

Claire cocked her head. "When the handler came to ask if we would be seekers in exchange for our lives."

I closed my eyes for a moment, trying to take in and make sense of everything she was saying. "So just to clarify, you weren't born a seeker?" I asked, wanting to make sure I didn't misinterpret anything.

She shook her head. "Of course not. Have you met some like that? No seeker I've ever met was born that way."

Before, I'd jokingly said I was a freak among freaks and a weirdo among weirdos, and this confirmed it. *The one time I wouldn't mind being wrong.*

Chase studied me for a moment, but this time I didn't squirm under his scrutiny. "I think we just met one."

"Huh?" Claire asked. "What do you mean?"

"What's your story?" Chase asked quietly, even though I could tell he already knew.

I took a deep breath. "Until yesterday, the only other seeker I've ever met is my mother. I was born this way."

CHAPTER 15

CLAIRE'S MOUTH HUNG OPEN, HER soda forgotten. "How is that even possible?"

I jutted my chin out, getting a little tired of feeling like I needed to defend myself. "How is it possible that you *weren't* born a seeker?"

Suddenly, Claire gasped. "You're her. You're the one." Her eyes widened and she slowly reached her arm out to point at me, her one finger shaking.

This was the second time today someone had pointed at me like that. At least Claire wasn't shrieking in terror.

But dang it, I was not "the one" of anything. I wasn't freaking Neo in *The Matrix*. I was just Ava Parks, who had the misfortune of having an angel ancestor.

"Claire," Chase said, putting a hand on her arm. "Chill."

I shot him a grateful look.

She turned her head to look at her brother and when she did, her outstretched arm also moved, knocking over her soda. Both Chase and I jumped up as the brown liquid slid across the table. Since Claire was sitting on the inside, she wasn't so lucky. At least it fell next to her where Chase had just been sitting instead of directly in her lap.

"Sorry," Claire squeaked, rushing to drop napkins on the soda.

Chase and I stood close together. I shifted and my arm brushed his. I jumped away, my cheeks flushing. Then I looked up at him to see if he'd noticed. He hadn't. And when I said "looked up," I meant it. I hadn't realized how tall he was—at least as tall as Cole.

As tall as Cole.

That was the second time in the last twenty minutes I'd compared Chase to Cole. I needed to stop. What purpose did it serve? Why was I doing it in the first place? Was I doomed to compare every new guy I met to Cole?

Not that I thought about Chase that way.

Sighing, Chase pulled a bunch of napkins out of the holder and helped his sister mop up the mess. I stayed away. I didn't mean to be a jerk and not help, but the booth was small and I'd just be in the way. Our server noticed the commotion and came over with a damp rag, which worked much better than napkins anyway.

"Sorry," Claire said again, picking up the soggy napkins and dropping them on the server's tray.

"It's okay, honey." The waitress finished mopping up the mess, and Chase used another wad of napkins to dry the damp seats, both his and mine.

I slid back into the booth. "Thanks," I said, impressed with his gentlemanly act. He might put up a tough front, but he had good manners. He also genuinely cared for his sister, even if she did seem to vex him. At his core, he was probably a pretty good guy.

In that way, he also reminded me of—

Nope. I wasn't even going to finish that thought.

"Sorry," Claire said for the third time. "I can be clumsy sometimes. But I was so shocked to realize you're the one."

"What do you mean by that?" My tone was more angry than necessary and I didn't mean to come across like a bitch, but I was just so sick and tired of being the last to know things, especially things about me. Was I some sort of urban legend or something? A seeker myth?

"All she means is you're part of the original line," Chase said. "Areli's line."

I sighed, rubbing at my temple that was suddenly throbbing. The casual way he said it told me he'd had this information for a while, like it was no big deal. I'd only recently learned everything. Why did strangers seem to know more about my history than I did?

The server came with a fresh soda for Claire and our meals. Claire crammed a handful of fries into her mouth before the lady could even get the plate on the table.

"Thank God," Claire said through her chewing. She reached for the ketchup.

I picked at my cheese fries, but even though they smelled of greasy goodness, I didn't know if I'd be able to eat them. My stomach was in knots.

Chase unrolled the silverware and cut into his chicken, which looked bland as cardboard. Healthy, but bland. Out of all the side effects of being a seeker, having a fast metabolism was one of the few benefits. My mom never had to worry about her weight and I suspected I wouldn't, either. Since we had healing abilities, we never worried about our health much. So I could eat this entire plate of cheese fries and then some and not worry about clogged arteries.

I wondered if Chase and Claire had the same perks. It seemed they were a different breed of seekers.

I was at war with myself. I'd spent my entire life being secretive, so I was finding it difficult to lay everything out there. But here in front of me were the people I'd imagined meeting for the past six months. I didn't have to hide my identity from them. It was so weird.

But were they trustworthy? My gut told me yes, but this was new territory for me.

What the heck. If things went south, I'd simply find a new city to hole up in. There was nothing keeping me in Hershey.

"I've been kept in the dark about a lot of things my

whole life." My eyes focused on a piece of waxy cheese that I rolled around between my fingers. "So it would be helpful if you could tell me everything you know. Like how you became a seeker, about your handler, things like that."

I looked up at both of them and was surprised to see compassion in Claire's eyes. I couldn't read Chase's expression. While his sister wore her feelings, he kept his hidden.

"What don't you know?" Claire asked, then put her hand up to stop me from responding. "Stupid question. I'll tell you more about how we became seekers and then you can ask questions. Sound good?"

I nodded, happy Claire was willing to be so open. Judging by the scowl on Chase's face, he wasn't thrilled with the idea. But I didn't care. Once he spent more time with me, he'd realize I didn't have any ulterior motives. He didn't realize how lucky he was to have a partner in crime. I had no one.

So maybe I did have a motive—companionship. Was that so bad?

"We were in a car accident when I was fourteen and Chase was fifteen. A delivery truck t-boned us in the middle of an intersection. The damage was...*extensive.*" She paused for a moment, not seeming comfortable talking about the experience. She hadn't specified if the damage was to the car or the people inside. I guessed both. Chase's eyes focused on something behind me and his jaw worked as his sister told the story.

"It hit us on the driver's side," Claire continued. "Chase was driving and I was sitting behind him, so we were both hurt really bad. The paramedics were surprised we survived the trip to the hospital. We both had internal bleeding, broken bones, Chase had a collapsed lung—"

Chase cleared his throat and Claire spared him a glance. He had to be carrying around a load of guilt.

"Anyway," she said, "we almost died. My heart stopped at least once, but they were able to bring me back.

I don't remember all of it."

Something told me she didn't necessarily want to tell me everything she *did* remember, and I wasn't going to press the issue. I couldn't begin to imagine how traumatizing it must be to realize you'd died.

Like Cole.

I closed my eyes for a moment as feelings overwhelmed me. He and I had never really talked about when he'd died. He wasn't the sharing type. Instead, he kept things inside and dealt with them in his own way. Now, though, I wished I'd tried harder to get him to talk to me. Immediately following the incident, it was such a sensitive subject I hadn't wanted to bring it up.

I forced my thoughts back into a corner of my mind so that when I opened my eyes, I could focus on what Claire was saying.

"Handlers approached our mom. I don't know exactly what they said to her, but somehow they convinced her they were fallen angels and they could summon an angel to save us, but only if we would accept being seekers. Normally the person having the near-death has to agree, but since we were still kids, our mom made the decision."

"Wait," I said. "If the person is near death, like possibly unconscious, then how could they agree?"

"Usually the person has terminal cancer or something like that," Claire explained. "Normally the person is conscious. Turning kids into seekers is rare from what I understand. The youngest seeker we've met other than you was twenty-five."

"How does the process work?" I asked.

"I'm not sure exactly. We were unconscious." She wrinkled her nose. "But I'm pretty sure blood was involved somehow." She visibly shuddered and held out her arm, which was covered in goose bumps. "See? Even thinking about it grosses me out. I hate blood. I'm surprised I was able to handle it earlier in the park when that little girl was bleeding."

She wasn't the only one.

That reminded me.

"Tell me about the Freddy Krueger man."

"Who?" Chase asked, sitting up straight, his big brother protective mode going into overdrive.

"I haven't told you about him," Claire said. "He's just some creepy guy with a messed up face who's been hanging around the park. Today he knocked over a little girl and kept on going, not stopping to apologize or see if she was okay or anything. The way he was running, you'd have thought he was running away from someone."

Was he? If he was, I'd bet my life savings he was running from me. But why? Especially since he'd bumped into me. Otherwise I probably wouldn't have noticed him.

That thought made me queasy. Xavier had been that close, but I had been so busy making up stories in my head about perfect strangers I hadn't even been looking for him.

"Why are you asking about him?" Chase asked me, his eyes narrowing.

I fiddled with my straw while I tried to determine how much I wanted to tell them. I wouldn't mention Cole since the whole point of me leaving him was to keep his identity a secret. Somehow I would have to figure out if they'd heard of the seeker who had no limits that Xena was supposed to be looking for. I wondered how much their handler shared with them or if they were in the dark like I was.

But if Xavier was hanging around, I should warn them.

"I think he might be my former handler."

"Really?" Claire's eyes widened.

Chase leaned forward, his expression a cross between anger and suspicion. "You need to tell us what's going on. Why are you here all of a sudden? And why would your former handler be stalking my sister?"

"He's not *stalking* me," Claire said. "He's just been hanging around."

Chase flexed and unflexed his fist. "Damn it, Claire. You should have told me about him. You shouldn't always assume the best of people."

"And you shouldn't always assume the worst," she shot back. "I know there are bad people out there, but I still think most people are good at heart."

What she said reminded me of *Anne Frank's Diary*, which I read in middle school. I couldn't say that I agreed with her outlook. I fell more along Chase's line of thinking.

"Xavier isn't good at heart," I said quietly. "If he's hanging around, it's not for a good reason."

"Tell us about him," Chase said. His tone was business-like, and I could tell he would file all the details away in his mind.

"He was my mom's handler for her entire life. When I turned sixteen, I started seeking, so he became my handler as well. He started out normal. I thought of him like an honorary uncle or something. He always helped us move and even babysat me a few times. But he changed. The only word I can use to describe him is evil."

"Fallen angels can't be evil." Claire sounded adamant, like she refused to believe what I was telling her.

Chase and I exchanged a look, and I knew he not only believed me, but he'd figured it out for himself.

"Xavier killed my mom," I said, barely managing to swallow the lump in my throat. "And that's only part of what he did." I left it at that, not willing to talk about how I held Cole as he'd died.

Claire's lower lip quivered and then she gave her brother a little shove, signaling she wanted to get up. "Excuse me." She strode away from the table, her double cheeseburger forgotten.

Chase sighed.

"I'm sorry," I said. "I didn't mean to upset her, but she should know the truth."

"I agree," he said. "I'm sorry about your mom and if Claire wasn't so emotional, she would say the same. She's not normally so heartless. Our mom died about six months ago and Claire is still taking it hard. Part of her coping mechanism is blindly believing we're doing a good thing by seeking. Because making people angels has to be good, right?"

"But you don't agree."

"No." Chase scrubbed a hand over his face. "But since Mom signed us up for this, Claire refuses to acknowledge that what we're doing is wrong. It's like some kind of twisted loyalty to her or something. Deep down, Claire knows it's wrong. I just wish she'd admit it."

Chase and I were quiet for a moment, each of us lost in our own thoughts. I understood where Claire was coming from. I would have done anything to save my mom and this was Claire's way of keeping her mother's memory pure, of "saving" her memory of her.

"I'm sorry," I said. "For your mom, I mean."

"Yeah, it sucks. Breast cancer."

"I'm sorry," I said again. There was nothing else to say. I of all people knew "sorry" didn't mean much, though.

"It's okay."

"Will she be all right? Should I go after her?" I barely knew her, so I didn't know how much comfort I could provide, but I could definitely lend my shoulder if she needed to cry on it. Though Claire and I were the same age, in some ways, she seemed a lot younger than me. It was like I was haggard and bitter while she was optimistic and hopeful. I wondered if her aura reflected that. I wasn't going to look, though. Somehow looking at other seekers' auras seemed like an invasion of privacy.

"She'll be fine. Well, not really. But she won't talk about it so there's nothing we can do. She'll compose herself and be back in a few minutes." He leaned forward. "But while she's gone, tell me more about your old handler."

"Xavier is the worst hu—" I started to say *human*

being, but Xavier wasn't human. He was something else entirely. "The worst *being* I've ever met," I amended. "He has freaky abilities."

"Like what?"

"He can boil or freeze your blood. At least that's what it feels like. He also nearly suffocated my mom once, all without touching her."

Chase blinked a few times, like I'd totally caught him off guard. "Wow."

"I guess your handler can't do those things?"

He shook his head. "Not that I know of. Is that how he killed your mom?"

"I'm not sure exactly what he did to her. She had all kinds of weird symptoms." I didn't want to talk about those or I might have to join Claire in the ladies room with my own tear-streaked face. "He made it so she was dependent on his blood and refused to give it to her unless I provided him names."

"Since she died, I guess you refused." There was respect in Chase's voice, and I was oddly proud to have earned it. It also made me respect him more to know he approved of the decision to refuse Xavier. What Chase didn't know was that my mom had sacrificed herself to save me from Xavier's clutches. My mom was the one who deserved the respect, not me.

But again, I wasn't going to get into that.

"Sort of."

"And now he's hanging around here," Chase said, shaking his head.

I didn't understand it, either. "He's doing something with the souls. At least one is unaccounted for."

"How do you know that?"

"I got a new handler and she told me."

"Shit."

I nodded. His comment just about summed it up.

"Do you have any idea what he's doing?"

"No clue." I drummed my fingers on the table in an

angry rhythm. No one seemed to know what Xavier was up to. Shouldn't handlers have some sort of oversight? Especially sadistic psychotic ones like Xavier?

"So why is his face messed up?" Chase asked.

"I'm not entirely sure it was him," I clarified. "I didn't see him. But the last time I did see him, my mom shot him in the face." I paused. "Several times. So he probably looks like he belongs in a horror movie now."

Chase let out a low whistle. "Wow. I guess he couldn't heal fully from that."

I shook my head. "Nope."

Chase yawned, checking the watch on his wrist. I reflexively reached to my back pocket so I could check my phone for the time before I remembered I didn't have it with me. Perhaps I should get a cheap watch to go along with my cheap paper map. Who needed a phone anyway? Not this girl.

"What time is it?"

"Almost one," he said. "We should probably go. We worked ten hours today, and we have to work again tomorrow."

"Of course," I said, though I was disappointed. There was a lot more to talk about. And Claire still hadn't emerged from the ladies room. I was worried about her.

Chase signaled the waitress for our checks. "Does Claire have your number?"

I lowered my gaze to the table. "No. I don't have a phone right now. I can tell you where I'm staying, though. The hotel has a phone." Duh. Of course it did. What establishment didn't?

He pulled out his phone and swiped the screen. "What's the number?"

I felt like a complete idiot and the blush that spread to my cheeks only deepened the feeling. I didn't actually know the hotel's phone number. To add to my stupidity, I didn't even know the name of the place. Pine Cone Inn? Pure Cozy Inn? I had no idea. All I remembered was a P, a

C, and Inn.

"Sorry, I don't have it on me. It's the place out on..." I couldn't remember the name of the street, either. "Let me get my map and I'll tell you."

Chase had already put his phone away. "Don't bother. Do you want to meet up again tomorrow?"

I nodded. The waitress brought our check and Chase looked at it briefly before pulling some bills out of his pocket and dropping them on the table. I reached for the check so I could pay my share, but he pulled it away.

"I got it," he said.

"You don't have to buy my food," I protested.

"Too late." He stood, looking down at me in a way that challenged me to argue with him. I sighed. It wasn't worth the fight.

"Same time?" he asked "This place okay again?"

"Works for me."

"Great." He looked at me for a moment, like he wanted to say something else. Then he turned and walked toward the ladies room to retrieve his sister, calling, "See ya," over his shoulder.

It was only then I realized I hadn't thanked him for paying for my food.

CHAPTER 16

HAVING BEEN UP SO LATE the night before, I slept in and almost missed breakfast. When I woke and stared bleary-eyed at the clock, I only had ten minutes before the food was taken away, so I raced to the lobby in my pajamas with teeth and hair unbrushed and loaded up on fruit, yogurt, jelly packets, plastic utensils, and boxed cereal. I got a dirty look from the breakfast attendant for the five boxes of cereal I took, but whatever.

I took everything back to my room and watched mindless TV while I munched. Normally I wasn't a big TV watcher because I preferred reading, but my e-reader hadn't made it into my suitcase, which was a total bummer. I could read on my phone, but that would require turning it on, so yeah...wasn't going to happen.

I knew I was being silly about that, but avoidance was my coping mechanism of choice. Eventually I'd have to get over it and turn on my phone, but for now this was working for me, so I was going with it. I'd heard that society in general was addicted to technology, but I never gave it much thought. Now that I was going without a phone and computer, I understood. I thought I was doing well, though. Eventually I might have to do without a phone all together anyway. Bill took over my cell payments when my mom died and with me gone, I didn't know how long he would keep up with them.

It was all the more reason to figure out a long-term plan. My money wasn't going to last forever, no matter how well I managed it.

There was one thing I needed to spend money on—a weapon. I didn't have enough for a gun, so a knife would have to do. Though the thought of actually using it against someone made me queasy. A gun was more impersonal. For instance, I could shoot Xavier from across the room. But with a knife, I'd have to be up close and personal.

I never wanted to be that close to Xavier.

Part of me knew having a weapon would be ineffective, anyway. Xavier could use his freaky abilities on me before I even knew he was in my proximity. The fact that he hadn't snuck up on me and done that already told me he needed me for something. But what? I'd made it pretty clear I wasn't going to give him any more names. Yet there was nothing else I could think he would want from me.

And why me? I was obviously a difficult case for him, so why did he persist? Couldn't he find some other seeker to manipulate? Someone easier?

Unless he had a personal vendetta.

I quickly showered and dressed, then headed back to the lobby to ask for directions to either Walmart or a sporting goods store. It turned out Walmart wasn't too far, so I jotted down the address and directions on a scrap of paper.

I had no trouble finding it, which bolstered my confidence in getting around without GPS. It really wasn't that hard and it made my situational awareness sharper. Before I probably wouldn't have paid attention to where I was going, mindlessly following the GPS system's robotic voice. Since I knew I'd need to find my way back, I took note of my surroundings to make the return trip easier.

The sporting goods department at Walmart was disappointing. There were plenty of hunting rifles and pocket knives, but no big knives. I didn't know exactly what I was looking for, though. I couldn't exactly walk around with a Rambo knife. So on second thought, I picked up a medium-sized pocket knife that was small enough to actually fit in my pocket. Some of those suckers were big, like they were made for a giant's pockets.

Deep down, I knew I would be worthless in a fight with a knife, but it gave me piece of mind to have it, so that made it worth it.

As long as it didn't get turned against me. That was a sobering thought. Perhaps I'd have to practice wielding it, at least so it didn't feel so foreign in my hand.

Back at the hotel, I made myself a PB&J, then settled in to watch more TV while I practiced opening and closing the knife quickly without slicing off a finger. That thing was sharp, so that was something at least.

I'd seen signs for outlet shopping, and I wanted to go check it out, but that was a bad idea for two reasons—I didn't have any money to spend anyway, which led to the second reason, which was that it would waste gas driving out there. And gas wasn't cheap, so it all came down to money. Worrying about every cent I spent was stressful. Money had always been tight with me and my mom, especially after she got sick, but the pressure of it was nothing compared to now. Being alone intensified everything.

Even though I'd slept in, I dozed off in the afternoon. I made another PB&J for dinner, but I still had hours to kill before I met with Chase and Claire.

Sitting around twiddling my thumbs reaffirmed I needed to come up with a plan. I was still amazed I'd accomplished my primary goal of finding seekers, and ones my age, no less. I easily could have spent months or years searching with Shenice's help. So I was feeling pretty good about that.

I'd found them and soon I would learn everything they knew about handlers and seekers and souls and everything else.

But then what?

Right now a large part of me was filled with so much hatred toward Xavier and the system that had ruined my life. My soul had to be getting blacker with every vengeful thought. I didn't want to live like that. Somehow I needed to make peace with my lot in life so I could be happy. Or if not happy, then at least content.

But until my need for vengeance got worked out of my system, I had no hope of that.

I DIDN'T GO TO THE diner until ten-thirty because I figured there was no sense sitting in the parking lot waiting for an hour again. I was surprised to see Chase and Claire's mini-van already parked in the lot.

I hurried inside and found them sitting in the same booth as last night. Claire smiled and waved when she saw me.

That was a relief. I'd been worried about her, but she seemed to be back to her normal perky self.

I said that like I knew her, which I really didn't. But I'd gotten the impression she was always an optimistic glass half-full kind of person.

"Hi," I said. "Sorry I'm late."

Claire waved her hand to dismiss my apology. "No worries. We've only been here a few minutes. And I want to say I'm sorry for leaving so abruptly last night. I didn't even say good-bye. And I should have said something about you losing your mom."

"No worries," I said, repeating her phrase. "Trust me when I say I understand."

I nodded at Chase and though it had seemed we'd made a connection last night when Claire had been gone, he simply nodded back, his expression unyielding. I couldn't figure him out. Was he being stoic or simply an asshole?

"Did you see Xavier today?" I asked.

Claire shook her head. "No sign of him."

That was disappointing. I was hoping he'd show today. I was sick and tired of this cat and mouse game we were playing. I was ready for it to be over once and for all. Until it was, I'd never be able to fully move on.

They ordered food, but I stuck with water. I felt bad not being a paying customer at the server's table—that came from being the daughter of a woman who'd worked in the restaurant industry—but I needed to conserve my funds and I wasn't going to let Chase pay again.

Which reminded me I hadn't thanked him for covering the check last night, making me feel like a deadbeat. I opened my mouth do so, but his rigid expression stopped me. He didn't intimidate me, but I didn't want to engage in conversation with him while he was so grumpy.

Instead of jumping right into more seeker stuff, we chatted about normal stuff while they ate. I learned Chase played baseball in high school and would have probably ended up with a college scholarship except he quit when he became a seeker. Claire had played volleyball, but she wasn't a scholarship contender even though her team won a state championship. They still lived with their dad, but neither one seemed to want to say much about him. From what I could tell, they led relatively normal lives, which were only occasionally interrupted when they received a seeking assignment about once every six months. Their handler usually took them to a nearby town for that and tried to schedule them on school breaks.

How thoughtful.

Seriously, though, at least they didn't have to risk turning in one of their classmates or move around a lot. Why couldn't Xavier have come up with some sort of arrangement like that? Life would have been a lot more pleasant.

The more I thought about it, I realized that was probably why he did it. He didn't want things to be pleasant or easy for us. It was one way he kept control. If we didn't set down roots and develop a support system, we were less likely to rebel.

But I would never know for certain. Even if I asked Xavier, I doubted I could trust his answer. He never did or said anything that wouldn't benefit himself.

Of course, my mom never would have rebelled when I was younger because where would that have left me? She loved me, and that was something Xavier didn't understand. More than likely he *couldn't* understand. But it was probably better that he didn't. If he had, he might have used me as leverage against her.

Kind of like what he did to me.

When it was my turn to share, I told Chase and Claire about growing up seeing auras but not realizing what they meant until I was sixteen. I also told them about Bill and a little about Shenice and Xena.

I didn't mention Cole.

"What are your plans now?" Chase asked.

I wished I knew the answer to that question, but I tried to answer it as honestly as possible. "I need to find Xavier." I didn't say why, figuring it was implied. The look in Chase's eyes told me he understood.

And approved.

I squirmed under his intense gaze.

He cleared his throat and glanced at his sister before speaking. "I was thinking—"

"Chase, *no*." Claire shook her head empathetically. "We talked about this."

"You said you'd think about it."

"And I did. The answer is still no."

"Now there are three of us," Chase said, his eyes shifting over to me. "Don't you think Ava should have a say?"

I narrowed my eyes at Chase. Since when was he part

of a trio instead of just a duo? I wasn't aware I was included in their little group. What was he up to?

Claire crossed her arms and leaned back, her lips pursed.

"Our handler is due any day now," Chase said. "I want to leave so he can't find us."

"That's not a good idea," Claire said. I had thought she was going to stay silent, but apparently she couldn't stop herself from interjecting.

"Why not?" Chase asked. "Ava did it."

"Whoa," I said, putting my hands out. "Don't use my situation as an example." Things had gone terribly, horribly wrong when I'd tried to cheat the system. Cole had died.

Of course they didn't know that. And I wasn't going to tell them. But they needed to realize I wasn't a poster child for making the best decisions.

"It wasn't as easy as I might have made it sound," I said. Though come to think of it, I didn't think I made it sound easy at all. I hadn't really described what I'd gone through in the last few months. "I have a lot of regrets about how things went down."

Claire opened her mouth like she wanted to question me further, and I was glad when Chase spoke first.

"I can't keep doing this, Claire," he said quietly, his gaze fixed on the table. "It's going to break me."

My heart broke for Chase just then. When he looked up, there was raw pain in his eyes, the result of sending innocent people to their deaths and I believed his words—he was reaching the breaking point.

The two of us were more alike than I first realized.

Claire paled. "You know why we can't leave."

"Screw him," Chase said. "He made his choices. He can take responsibility for them."

I shifted uncomfortably, feeling this was a private conversation I was in the middle of and wondering if I should try to excuse myself.

"Chase," Claire pleaded. "You know we can't."

"What we're doing is not right, Claire. Deep down, you know this."

She crossed her arms and turned her head to the side, avoiding his gaze. Avoiding admitting the truth to herself.

Chase turned to me. "I want to leave. We can go to Penn State and sublet an apartment there. We'll blend in."

His idea wasn't half bad. A college campus would be a great place for teenagers to hide.

"Why doesn't Claire want to go?" I felt weird asking that right in front of her, but she still wasn't looking at us, and I needed to know all the details before I could offer my opinion.

"She's worried something will happen to our dad if we leave."

I didn't ask why Chase seemed okay with that.

"He's sick." Claire uncrossed her arms and leaned on the table. "He needs us."

"I wouldn't call being drunk every night sick," Chase muttered.

"Alcoholism is a disease," Claire said.

"It's a *choice*," Chase shot back, his voice laced with exasperation. This wasn't the first time they'd had this discussion. "*Cancer* is a disease."

"What about our contract as seekers?" Claire asked. "We'd be violating it. They aren't just going to let us go."

He shrugged. "They'll have to find us first. And I'd rather die than turn in another name."

Claire glared at him. "Don't talk like that."

"You know it's true." There was a gravity in his eyes that made me wonder what lengths he would go to. Did the same "you don't decide when you die" factor apply to them as well?

"You haven't thought this through," Claire said.

"I have. Look—" His voice softened. "Penn State is only less than two hours away, so the car ride wouldn't be long. You've been there before, so it will be familiar. We could stay there for a while and see how it goes. If we're not happy, we'll go somewhere else."

"Niles might get in trouble if we turn up missing."

"I can't do anything about that. But like Dad, he made his choice. Now we have to make ours."

I assumed Niles was their handler. I actually would like to meet him, to see if he was as eccentric as Xavier, Xena, and Linda. An extreme personality seemed to be a requirement for handlers.

Chase's plan was great, and I certainly didn't have a better one. I wouldn't mind living in a college town and experiencing the college lifestyle even if I wasn't actually a student. But while there was nothing keeping me in Hershey permanently, I wanted to stay here for a little while at least.

"I need to see if Xavier is going to show up again," I asked. "So I don't know how soon you want to leave, but I'd like to stick around for another week."

Chase rubbed his chin, his expression thoughtful. "Okay. That will give Claire time to come to terms with leaving and give us time to prepare."

I noticed he didn't say anything about her still needing to make a decision. He must assume she would fall in line. She didn't argue and in fact, she seemed resigned. I guessed he was right.

Claire wasn't very talkative after that, so they got their check and we called it a night. As we were walking out to the parking lot, Claire grabbed my arm.

"I almost forgot." She reached into her pocket and pulled out an envelope. "Here. Tickets to the park and a parking pass so you can visit us the next few days."

I looked down at the papers clutched in my hand and grinned. "Thanks, Claire, really."

She shrugged. "No problem. Park employees get a few perks. I'll be working at the merry-go-round the next few days. Chase will be at a vendor cart near the Ferris wheel. Come see us when you get there."

I hesitated for a moment, then pulled Claire into a hug. She was surprised for a moment but returned the gesture. I wasn't a big PDA person, especially with friends, but she seemed to need it.

Right before she got into the van, she smiled and waved one last time, seeming like her normal self.

CHAPTER 17

I WENT TO THE PARK after my trusty PB&J lunch and because it was Sunday it was packed. I wondered if it would have been better for me to just hang out in the hotel but honestly I didn't think I could take any more reality TV. Plus, if I was going to go away with Chase and Claire I wanted to get to know them a little better first. Spending time at the diner was fine, but they probably didn't want to do that every night after working all day.

I went to the merry-go-round first because that's where Claire said she would be. However the ride was swarmed with kids so I didn't want to distract her. I got her attention just long enough to give a quick wave so she'd know I was there. She held up four fingers and it took me a few seconds to realize that meant she had a break at four. That left me a few hours to kill, so I went in search of Chase.

He was exactly where Claire said he would be, manning a drink cart under a big green umbrella. I was surprised he wasn't overrun considering how warm it was. When he saw me I thought his lips quirked up into a small smile, but I couldn't be sure. Chase confused me. There were times he was perfectly friendly but other times he looked at me like he thought I was going to pull a knife on him or something. He could rest easy about that. My shiny new pocket knife was locked in the glove compartment of my car.

"Hi," I said, sitting on the curb behind him in the one spot where the shade reached. I figured he would have to stand at the cart but this way we could talk and I wouldn't be blocking potential customers.

"Hey," he replied, sparing me a glance before turning back around. That was it. Just "hey." No further conversation or details about our leaving. So I sat there feeling like an idiot wondering why the heck he included me in his escape plan if he didn't even want to talk to me. I didn't want to spend the next few hours staring at him and not talking.

Though from where I was sitting, I had to admit the view was nice—Chase was no hardship to look at. Despite no longer playing baseball, he still had an athletic physique. I'd be lying if I said I wasn't attracted to him.

The thought made me uncomfortable. It felt disloyal to Cole. But I supposed that since I left I'd given up claim to him, so in turn I didn't have to be loyal.

But I wanted to.

When I thought about him, the breath was sucked from my lungs and I felt light-headed. I missed him so much it hurt. I wondered how long I would or if I would ever get over him. Yet despite this, I was attracted to Chase. Was that a sign I was already starting to move on?

My fingers went to my angel pendant, feeling the smooth metal, and as I did, I closed my eyes, imagining Cole's arms around me, his lips caressing mine and his body hovering over me.

A slow heat formed in my belly and moved its way to my heart.

Nope, I was definitely not moving on. Nor did I want to.

I thought that in order for someone to move on from something, they had to forget it, at least a little bit. I didn't want to forget anything involving Cole.

Well, maybe the part where he'd died in my arms. That part was sucky.

"So Chase," I said, my tone demanding he pay attention to me. "Tell me more about your plan."

Of course it was at that moment customers appeared in front of his cart. He efficiently served them sodas, then leaned on the cart with his arm so he was facing me.

"There's not much to it. Just go somewhere else and live our lives."

I almost snorted. Did he really think it would be that simple? As I gazed up at him, I saw he did. Or at least he'd fooled himself into thinking that. Chase struck me as the practical sort, whereas Claire was somewhat flighty. So why didn't he understand seekers' lives were inherently more complicated? We'd never be able to just "live our lives" as long as the handler/seeker system existed.

"Are you sure you want me to go with you?" I asked instead of getting into the possible complications I foresaw.

"Sure," he replied easily. "Why not?"

I eyed him suspiciously but his question seemed genuine. Maybe he didn't realize he came off as a closed-off jerk sometimes. I was happy to enlighten him. We didn't have time to play games. "Sometimes I get the impression you don't like me very much."

He sighed, running his hands over his hair. Taking off his sunglasses, he sat next to me.

"I'd never planned to have anyone else with us, but Claire likes you. And I'll flat out admit it—I'm using you as bait to get her to agree to leave."

His candor startled me. However, I noticed he didn't exactly address my concern. Instead he reaffirmed something I already knew—Claire liked me.

"She barely knows me."

He shrugged. "She sees the best in people, even our asshole father."

"What's the deal with him?"

Chase rotated his sunglasses in his hands, staring at them. While he did that, I contemplated retracting my question, but if I was throwing my lot in with him and his sister, then I had a right to the full story so I would know exactly what I was getting into.

"He was in the passenger seat the night we got in the accident," Chase said, staring off into the distance, "but he walked away with nothing but a broken arm. We were at one of Claire's volleyball tournaments about an hour away. He'd brought a flask with him—possibly two, I don't really know. He was plastered by the time we left, so I drove. I didn't even have my learner's permit, but I figured we'd be better off with me driving instead of him. He actually passed out ten minutes into the drive. It was foggy and I didn't see the truck coming. The last I remembered was driving and trying to see through the fog. When I woke up in the hospital, I was totally confused. But by then, it was done. We were seekers."

I could understand why Chase would feel animosity toward his father. The accident was probably a fluke. If his dad had been driving, it probably wouldn't have made a difference, except then Chase wouldn't be saddled with guilt the rest of his life.

I didn't comment. What could I say? What had happened to them was horrible. Luckily, Chase didn't seem to expect me to say anything.

"Our dad is a piece of work," Chase said. "Kind of an asshole. He's a decent guy when he's sober, but that hasn't been in at least ten years. He barely keeps it together. If Claire didn't take care of him and cover for him, he would have lost his job a long time ago."

I didn't know my dad. The only thing I knew about him was his name was Michael. I didn't know his last name and I'd never even seen a picture. My mom had had a brief fling with him, and he was long gone by the time she realized she was pregnant. She'd never bothered to look for him.

I never thought of him much until recently because I'd been fine with it just being me and my mom. We were a unit. Now that my mom was gone, I'd thought about trying to find him, but quickly dismissed the idea. It would be impossible, anyway.

Now for the first time, I considered maybe it was better he'd never been in my life. Chase might think that about his father. For all I knew, my father could be a crackpot or a scam artist. I'd like to think my mom had better taste than that, but she'd been pretty wild in her younger days. Or so she'd told me.

"What about your mom?" I asked.

"She had several bouts of breast cancer. That's the only reason she stayed with my dad—because she was petrified of dying and leaving me and Claire with a stranger. She figured this way we'd have a relationship with him." Chase shook his head. "She was wrong about that. But another reason was she needed his medical insurance to pay for all her treatments. And that she was right about."

"I'm sorry." I hated myself as I said it. When I'd said it to him before when we talked about his mom, it wasn't enough. It still wasn't and it never would be.

"Yeah." Chase was quiet for a moment before he continued. "There's something you should know about Claire. She's not the same as she was before the accident."

"Of course not," I said. "That was a traumatic experience."

"It's more than that, though," Chase said. "I'm more or less the same. Probably more serious than I was before, especially since my mom was so sick and now gone. But Claire started having learning problems afterward. Memory problems, difficultly with math, stuff like that. Sometimes she'll flat out get confused, like she'll forget how to tie her shoes or something. She used to love math, like freakishly love it. She was even vice president of the stupid math club, but after the accident, she'd forget how to do the simplest equations. She barely earned enough math credits to graduate. Claire's heart stopped beating for almost five minutes. Brain damage can start after four minutes. It was like when her heart stopped, permanent damage was done. Becoming a seeker didn't fix it."

I thought about Cole and whether that applied to him. He was the same as he ever was and his heart had definitely stopped beating. But for how long I couldn't say.

"That's weird," I said. Perhaps I should have told him about Cole so we'd have a point of comparison, but Claire's situation wasn't the same as his. When Areli made him a seeker, Cole was already dead. Claire was still alive when she became one.

My heart went out to her. She got a complete and total bum deal as a result of the accident. Perhaps the process of turning people into seekers only cured the body and not the brain. Chase had told me people who agreed to be seekers were conscious, which meant they probably didn't have brain damage—only a physical malady.

"Niles let it slip that he'd never heard of someone being so far gone being asked to be a seeker, but then when I asked him about it, he clammed up. No matter how many times I pressed the issue, he wouldn't explain." Chase's voice was troubled.

I could only shrug to signal I didn't know either. All of this was new to me.

Xena would probably explain. Eventually. After I asked her half-a-million questions. I wished I could call her and get the information for Chase. Maybe someday down the line that would be a possibility. I doubted she'd stick around Tidewater permanently, so eventually I'd be able to have contact with her.

"Claire has always been too open-hearted for her own good," Chase, "so it's easy for people to take advantage of her. She's always been like that, but after the accident she became even more so. I can be a little overprotective of her. But that's my right."

He gave me a look that dared me to disagree with him.

"I think it's great she has someone looking out for her." I wouldn't have minded having an older sibling to have my back. Of course, Chase was the one urging Claire to buck the system, which was what got me in trouble in the first place. Except they weren't planning to buck the system. More like circumvent it.

And maybe it would work. Maybe if I hadn't taken the "go big or go home" approach, I wouldn't have screwed up so badly.

There was that saying that went something like "shoot for the moon, if you miss, you'll still end up among the stars." I had to call bullshit on that one. I shot for the moon and I sure as hell didn't end up in the stars. Although I have to say my ass definitely did get burned, so perhaps I did end up in the stars—directly on a fifty-thousand degree one.

Chase stood to greet and serve some customers. He remained standing when he was done but looked down at me. "Don't tell her I told you this stuff. She had a hard time when she went back to school because she felt like people pitied her. Her closest friends were nerdy geek types and once it became clear she couldn't keep up with them academically they drifted apart. Graduating and getting away from everyone who knows what happened is her chance at a fresh start."

"Chase, I adore your sister," I said. "I would never do anything to hurt her."

Chase hadn't said much about how his life had changed since the accident. Although he said he was more or less the same, I doubted the truth in that statement. Nobody came away from something like that unchanged.

We could all use a fresh start.

CHAPTER 18

THE NEXT FEW DAYS WERE uneventful. I dutifully went to the park and spent time with Chase and Claire on their breaks, but despite being at the park from nearly open to close every day, I saw no sign of Xavier. It was odd because the previous week Claire had seen him at least once a day. He'd knocked into me so I knew he'd seen me, which made me wonder if he was avoiding me. But if this was the case, then why make his presence known at all?

I didn't begin to try to guess his motives.

Most days Claire and Chase took off their employee name tags and sat in the public area with me to have their meals. I'd started bringing my lunch to cut down on expenses.

In related news, if I had to eat another PB&J, I might vomit. I was going on almost a week straight of eating them twice a day. I changed up the jelly flavor, but that didn't help much. I was on PB&J overload.

Oddly, Chase and Claire didn't talk about our upcoming trip. With Claire that didn't surprise me as I'd figured out avoidance was her coping mechanism when something was unpleasant, but Chase wasn't like that. He seemed to be somewhat of a planner, so that made it even more surprising.

By Thursday, though, I felt like the topic needed to be

addressed. I'd wanted to stick around for a while in case Xavier showed up, but that had turned out to be a bust. If he was going to show, I felt like he would have done it by now. The other reason for sticking around was so Claire could get used to the idea. I wanted to see how things were going on that front.

"So," I said as I choked down my PB&J, "What's the plan for leaving?"

The pleasant expression immediately fell off Claire's face and she crossed her arms, looking away.

Chase spared her a glance. "I was thinking we could leave early Monday morning. I have a lead on an apartment we can sublet for the fall semester. It's a two bedroom, so it will be tight, but it's affordable."

"What's affordable?" I asked. "I don't have a whole lot of money."

"Claire and I have enough to last a while," Chase said. "We got a small insurance payout when Mom died. I also have money saved from working the last year. It won't last forever, but it should be enough to get us by until we can find jobs."

"Do you have any leads or connections on those?" I thought back to how hard my job search was when I ended up working for Shenice. Job hunting wasn't an endeavor I looked forward to taking on again, but it was a necessary evil. Since college wasn't in my future, I needed to figure out what field I wanted to get into. Unfortunately, with no discernible skills or certifications, the pickings would be slim. I also didn't think Penn State would be my final settling point. I had no idea where I wanted to end up, but even still, I viewed that as temporary.

"No." He frowned, rubbing his chin. "And jobs can be hard to come by in a college town."

"Damn," I said, realizing he was right. There would be thousands of teens and young twenty-somethings all vying for the same jobs. "Are you sure that's the best place for us to go? Maybe we should go farther north to a bigger city."

Claire's eyes widened for a moment and Chase squeezed her hand. "Bigger cities mean more expensive apartments," he said. "Let's stick with this for now."

I could tell there was more to it than what he said, but since Claire seemed distressed by the idea of going farther, I didn't push the issue.

I considered for a moment. It wasn't a permanent move anyway, so we could try it out for a while. Except if we signed a lease for an entire semester, we'd be stuck there until December. "If we don't find jobs, do you have enough money to get us by until the end of the lease?" I asked.

Chase squinted as he mentally calculated. "Yeah, it shouldn't be a problem. If we have to, we can go farther out to look for jobs."

"Good point," I said. There was no reason we couldn't drive thirty or forty-five minutes if we had to. The commute would suck and it would cost more in gas, but if the job paid enough it would still be worth it. The trouble would be finding a job that paid more than minimum wage for the reasons I already mentioned. *Sigh.*

Claire had been silent through the conversation, so now I turned to her. "Are you okay with this, Claire?"

Tears glistening in her eyes, she nodded. "Chase convinced me it's the right thing to do. I just don't like change."

"I'll be there," Chase reassured her. "That part won't change."

She plastered on a brave smile that didn't reach her eyes. "Are you guys done with your trash? I'm going to the ladies room, so I'll take it."

We nodded and she gathered up our food wrappers, then walked away.

Watching her, Chase sighed. "She's right. Change freaks her out. That's one of the things that's different about her. She used to love surprises and new experiences, but now they give her anxiety."

"Are you sure she'll be okay with this?" I asked.

"Yeah. She's been to Penn State lots of times for different volleyball things. That's why I picked it. That and because it's not a long drive."

"Why does the drive matter? Do you plan on coming back here often?"

"No, but Claire freaks out if she's in the car too long. For a while after the accident she wouldn't even get in a car. That's why I drive my mom's old van. Since it's bigger, it doesn't bother her as much."

Chase had been the one driving during the accident, so I was surprised he didn't have anxiety about getting behind the wheel again. My guess was that even if he had, he'd swallowed it down years ago so he could be there for Claire. And probably his mom. I didn't know how much she was able to do while she was sick, but a lot of responsibility must have fallen on Chase.

"Poor Claire. It sucks for her that she has so many issues."

"She hides them well and like I told you before, she doesn't want anyone to pity her or treat her differently. Most of her friends drifted away after the accident. They started out being supportive, but Claire was so different. The only thing she was able to keep up with was volleyball. Now that she's done with school, she doesn't even have that anymore."

"I don't have many friends," I said. "My mom and I moved around a lot, which made it hard, and once I learned I was a seeker, I pushed people away."

"Yeah, it's hard to maintain relationships." Chase's voice was harsh, giving me the feeling there was more to it, but I didn't ask. We were all entitled to secrets. I had Cole and he had whatever caused the closed-off look on his face.

All of the seekers I knew had totally messed up lives. Granted, my sample pool was small, but I would like to meet just one seeker who was living a normal happy productive life. I didn't think it was possible.

Maybe what we were doing would be easier if we knew for certain we were contributing to some greater good. Was there happiness in being an angel? The only true angel I'd met was Areli and he seemed miserable. Knowing everything I knew now, I'd especially like to see him again and talk to him. I wondered if I ever would. Since it was forbidden, I doubted it.

The three fallen angels I'd met—Xavier, Xena, and Linda—didn't seem particularly happy either. Xavier was filled with so much hatred he couldn't see past it to anything else. I hated him so much I'd never stopped to wonder why he was like that. I had no interest in understanding him—I just wanted to end him. Even if I knew his story, he would never get my sympathy. Nothing he'd been through could be a good enough excuse for what he'd done to my mom and Cole. And me. I usually didn't include myself in his list of victims, but I'd definitely suffered as a result of his actions.

Xena wasn't exactly unhappy but she definitely didn't seem content with her lot in life. She'd once told me that being a fallen angel wasn't necessarily a bad thing and that some angels asked for it. But she never told me if she was one of them.

I'd only spent about ten minutes with Linda, but that was enough for me to discern she was a bitter woman. I did not want to be in her cross hairs. Too late for that. She had to know I was gone by now. I wondered if looking for me took precedence over finding the seeker who had no limits. For Cole's sake I hoped so.

Chase looked at his watch and stood up, presumably to go back to work. I wasn't looking forward to idling away the rest of the day in the park by myself, but I had nothing better to do. I'd actually enjoyed doing my laundry yesterday because at least it was a change of pace. Maybe I would leave the park and try to find a thrift store to buy a cheap paperback or two. Granted, I didn't pack my bag when I left, but even if I had packed it myself, I wouldn't have thought to bring entertainment. I never imagined I'd have this much downtime. Though, I didn't know why. What had I expected to be doing?

As I stood, I saw Claire walking toward us with a man by her side. She appeared perfectly comfortable chatting with him except for the slight wringing of her hands. It seemed like she knew him. Maybe another park employee? He wasn't wearing a uniform but perhaps he had the day off.

He was a hipster, but not of the usual variety you'd see at coffee shops. No, he was the real deal. He looked like he belonged on a black and white television show. It was like he'd come from another time. I couldn't gauge his age. He had a baby face that couldn't be hidden, even with his thick beard. He could be twenty or thirty-five. Probably not older than forty, though.

"Oh, shit," Chase said.

"What?" I asked, immediately alarmed.

"Niles," he said under his breath as Claire and the man approached.

Niles. It took a moment for the name to register. This was their handler. That explained the outdated look. He probably *was* from another time, maybe the fifties or sixties.

"Hello," Niles said, only it came out like *haaaalllloooo*. He was definitely British.

Chase nodded curtly. He wasn't openly rude, but he definitely communicated he wasn't happy to see Niles. If Niles noticed or was put out by it, he didn't give any indication.

"This is A—"

"Amy." I cut Claire off before she could finish, holding out my hand, hoping to make Niles think I was simply too forward and perhaps a bit rude instead of hiding something.

Shaking my hand, he flashed a cursory smile that

clearly indicated he had no interest in me.

Whew.

I didn't know how the handler network worked. Could Linda have put out some kind of APB to all the other handlers to keep an eye out for me? Unlike their search for Cole, they could easily identify me.

Or perhaps I was overestimating my importance. I doubted it. Not if I was "the one," as Claire had referred to me. That was wishful thinking on my part.

Until now it hadn't occurred to me the significance of the fact that my family tree was a straight line. My dad wasn't in the picture and my mom had no family to speak of but that wasn't unusual. Lots of people had small families.

But lots of families weren't the descendants of an angel.

So when Claire had referred to me as "the one," maybe she was being literal. I was the only seeker left who had been born and not made. I felt like a semi-truck had suddenly been dropped on my shoulders. I was the last of my line.

"So, Niles," Chase said with his arms crossed, "what are you doing here?"

Niles looked at me briefly then jerked his head to indicate he wanted to talk to Chase and Claire alone, but Chase didn't take the hint, even after Niles widened his eyes and not-so-subtly jerked his head again.

It was kind of rude, actually. I obviously knew why he wanted to talk to them alone, but if this were a normal conversation and I was the sensitive type, my feelings would definitely be hurt.

But don't worry, Niles, old chap. I don't want to interact with a handler any more than you want to interact with me.

Chase merely leveled his gaze at Niles and Claire continued wringing her hands.

"Well," Niles said with an awkward laugh. "It's about

that time again."

"We'll have to talk about it later," Chase said. "Claire and I need to get back to work." He took hold of his sister's arm and led her away, leaving me alone with Niles.

I shot an angry look in Chase's direction, but of course he couldn't see it since he was leading Claire away with gusto. But dang it, why the heck would he leave me alone with Niles?

I turned back to Niles and he seemed really uncomfortable, clearing his throat and avoiding my gaze. If I didn't know better, I'd think he was shy. Or timid even. Maybe he was. I never thought in a million years a handler would be shy. It made me view him in a much different light.

Niles tucked his hands in his back pocket and rocked backward on his heels. "Right, then. I'll just be—"

"How do you know Chase and Claire?" I asked, curious to see what he'd say. Other than him looking like he belonged in another decade, Niles seemed really normal and I suddenly wanted to know if that was possible—for a handler to be "normal."

"Oh, we go way back, you know." He cleared his throat. "Friend of the family."

"Where are you from?"

"Oh, um, er—" He coughed, and I got ridiculous joy knowing I was making him squirm. It was such a reversal from the norm.

He blushed, the pink spreading from his cheeks to his ears. It was adorable in a totally nerdy way. I could see why Claire didn't want him to get in trouble. Because she was fond of him, I'd cut him some slack.

"Nice meeting you." I hid my grin until I turned and walked away.

CHAPTER 19

I STOPPED BY THE MERRY-GO-ROUND to let Claire know I was leaving. Then I went in search of a thrift store. I didn't find one, but I did find a library. I lucked out and they had one of those "friends of the library" sales where they sold used books. The pickings were slim, but I was able to find two that looked decent and were worth parting with two dollars.

I tucked those under my arm for later and made myself comfortable in one of the armchairs in the magazine section with a stack of back-issue *People* magazines. I skipped over all the doom and gloom articles and focused on the ones about people doing good deeds, like the kindergarten class that raised money to buy a therapy dog for one of their classmates with epilepsy.

That was exactly the kind of good we needed in this world. I bet a lot of the children's auras were pure or close to it. Generally speaking, children tended to have purer auras than most because they hadn't been corrupted by society yet, but I had to believe that some of those kids would continue to be good Samaritans.

When pure souls became angels, the goodness in their souls became a fixed entity. But wouldn't actions based on love and compassion be more powerful than a fixed entity?

There was so much I didn't understand, and I truthfully hadn't cared to ask the right questions because I was too focused on how everything affected *me*. Now that I was away from home and on my own, my eyes were opened to the fact that it was a great big world with a lot of seekers and a lot of handlers and a lot of people. The collective actions of handlers and seekers affected more than just us and those connected to the names we turned in.

What kind of person chose the life of a seeker? Obviously, one who was faced with a difficult choice—die or choose to submit names for reaping for the rest of your life. It came down to the value of life, meaning whose had more? Yours or those with pure souls? Obviously since there were seekers, a lot of people choose themselves. I thought of Reggie. He was a bitter and angry man. Had he always been that way or had years of seeking made him like that? I had no way of knowing how long he'd been a seeker. But in my limited interaction with him, I'd peg him for the type of person who'd value his own life above others.

I replaced the magazines and went to the grocery store to pick up a pre-packaged salad. I could not stomach another PB&J, and since I was already out, it wasn't a waste of gas to drive to the store. There was a little park up the street, so I took my food there and relaxed with one of my books. I got lost in it—a story with vampires and witches and star-crossed lovers. I was peering at the pages and squinting before I realized how late it had gotten. Of course I was having trouble seeing. It was nearly dark.

I hesitated for a moment before dog-earing the page, cringing as I made the fold. It was a used book that had already seen better days, but even so, I hated doing it.

I was glad my hotel was only a few minutes away so I'd be able to get back to my book. But when I pulled into the parking lot, my spidey senses went on full alert. I didn't know what made me look to the far side of the lot because I hadn't paid it any attention before, but a shiny red sports car was parked there. Inside was a lone figure, but in the darkness, I couldn't tell who it was. Even though it wasn't super close to my room, the person in the car would have a perfect view. *If* that was what they were looking at.

Coincidence? Maybe. The person wasn't trying to hide or anything, but I wasn't taking any chances. The hair on the back of my neck was usually—and strangely—intuitive. And it was at full attention.

I parked on the other side of the hotel and crept around the side, keeping close to the building and circling around to get a good look at the car. I pressed my body up close against a dumpster, not even caring when some other guests gave me odd looks. Taking a deep breath—which was kind of a bad idea this close to the dumpster—I peered around the corner.

Linda.

Shit, shit, shit.

How had she found me? Holy crap, had I been right about there being a handler network? I mentally calculated how long ago I'd seen Niles. It was nearly nine now. I didn't know exactly what time it had been that I had lunch with Chase and Claire because I never did buy a watch, but it couldn't have been any later than two. So that was seven hours—more than enough time for Linda to drive up here if she'd still been in Tidewater.

But that still didn't explain how she'd found my hotel. It couldn't be by chance. But I'd worry about it later. I had more important things to worry about at the moment, like now what should I do?

If I went anywhere near my room, she'd see me. No doubt she was expecting me to waltz up to my door where she could pounce on me. She didn't give me much credit.

I'd have to wait her out. *Dang it.* One thing was certain—I couldn't stand by this dumpster much longer. The stench of rotting food and I didn't even know what else was seeping into my pores and taking up permanent residence in my nostrils.

As I circled back around the building, I wondered if she'd noticed my car when she came to Bill's the other day. Geez, was that really less than a week ago? It seemed like so much longer.

Obviously, she'd seen the car, but did she remember it enough to pick it out? Since I was in Pennsylvania, the Virginia plates might stand out, but other than that, it was an ordinary sedan with no distinguishing characteristics. Even still, staying in the parking lot just thirty yards from where she was parked would be stupid. I didn't make it this far to be dragged home by Linda.

I returned to my car and got out of there as quickly as I could, pulling into a busy restaurant parking lot about a mile up the road. I'd give it an hour, then drive back and see if she was gone. At least her car was easy to pick out. I would never have guessed Linda to be the flashy sports car type.

Flipping on the overhead light, I pulled out my book. The words blurred together on the page and after looking at the same paragraph for a solid five minutes I gave up.

Stupid Linda. I was so freaked out by her arrival I couldn't even read. It made me hate her more.

This was all her fault. If she weren't such a scheming hag and stuck to her own damn assignment, I'd be home right now with Cole instead of sitting in a steakhouse parking lot, smelling the scents of delectable fried foods that should have made my mouth water but were instead making my stomach churn. Her appearance ruined everything. First with Cole and now when I'd actually made some friends and headway on a new life for myself.

I closed my eyes for a minute, letting the hatred flow through me. When I opened my eyes, I blew out a breath, wanting all the bad feelings to escape with it.

This totally sucked, but allowing my anger to eat me from the inside out wasn't going to make it any better.

Think glass half-full, Ava.

Since Linda was here, that meant she wasn't going after Cole, which was good. I'd much rather have her focused on me than him. After all, that was the whole reason I'd left.

I gave it an hour and five minutes for good measure, then drove back to the hotel.

The sight of her obnoxious car dashed my budding hope. She hadn't moved. *Damn it!*

My room was paid up until tomorrow, so I didn't want to spend money on another hotel, but that wasn't the only thing stopping me from going somewhere else. All of my cash was locked in the room. I thought it would be safer to keep it tucked away in the room safe, so I only had twenty bucks on me.

I cursed myself for spending money on dinner and the books. Not that the eight dollars would have made much difference. Any hotel room that was only twenty-eight dollars a night was probably one I didn't want to set foot in.

I decided to give it another hour, so I repeated the process of parking at the busy restaurant and watching the clock. An hour later, same deal. This time I parked my car and crept around behind the dumpster again. I wished I had a set of binoculars so I could get a better look. From what I could see, she showed no signs of leaving.

I watched her for a few minutes, hoping that status would change, but she merely sat with a content look on her face, like staking out a wayward teenage seeker was her idea of a good time.

Creeper.

She turned her head in my direction and I jumped back behind the dumpster, accidentally hitting my heel hard against the rusty metal. If the pain weren't bad enough, it made a loud noise, so I hobbled as quickly as I could to my car, my heart pounding. I half-expected Linda's red car to come racing around the corner, but thankfully, that didn't happen.

By now it was nearing midnight. I couldn't keep doing this. Either Linda would see me or someone at the hotel would call the cops about my weird behavior. I'd already gotten several dirty looks.

Shit, shit, shit.

What were my options? I could call Claire, except for my moronic insistence of not using my phone. I could look for a pay phone, except those were few and far between and I didn't have any change on me. I didn't even know how much a pay phone cost, anyway. I'd never actually used one. I could try to find an open business that would let me use their phone, but at this hour, most of the open businesses were bars. Since I wasn't twenty-one, would I even be allowed in? I had no idea.

No, I'd have to figure this out myself. I was on my own.

And I should figure it out on my own. For the past week, things had been smooth sailing. I'd gotten really lucky finding Chase and Claire like I did. Insanely lucky. This was the first real hiccup I'd encountered. If I couldn't get through this, then how the heck did I expect to survive on my own?

Think, think, think.

Walmart. That was the answer. The store was open twenty-four hours.

I drove there and as soon as I walked in, I realized the store would have a phone. But it was after midnight and my mother raised me better than to call someone this late. If it was an emergency, I wouldn't think twice, but this wasn't an emergency. Not really.

Or perhaps I should say, *not yet*. I wanted to keep it that way.

I went into the store and browsed. First books, then movies, then clothes and finally art supplies. Not that I was an artist, but they were neat to look at. I steered clear of the automotive department. Too many reminders.

Wandering around solo in the middle of the night at Walmart was enough to make anyone lonely and I was no exception. If I'd been at home, I could have called Cole no matter what the hour. He would come get me, no questions—

Well, that wasn't true. He'd ask a million questions, but only after I was safe.

Not that I was in danger right now. Maybe in danger of falling asleep, but that was about it.

I yawned, the bottles of nail polish I'd been looking at for the last twenty minutes blurring together. My head had that tired dull ache and it was getting worse by the second. I had to try to get some rest. Part of me wanted to drive back to the hotel to check on the status of Linda, but there would be even less people in the lot than before, which would make my skulking more conspicuous. Also, I didn't expect her to be gone, even though it was the middle of the night. She didn't need sleep—she ran on pure sourness alone.

I really hated her.

I'd parked under a light in the parking lot, as was my habit at night, so I felt relatively safe inside my car. I cracked the windows to allow some air flow and locked the doors, then I stretched out in the backseat, tossing and turning in the small space, trying to get comfortable and willing my brain to turn off.

CHAPTER 20

MY ARMS FLAILED AS I awoke with a start, nearly falling off the seat onto the floor boards. My shirt was damp and it clung to my skin and the air inside the car was stale. I reached for the window control before remembering they were automatic, so they wouldn't work unless the car was on.

I'd been dreaming I was stuck in a coffin, and the satin walls were suffocating me. I took deep, cleansing breaths, focusing on the roof on the inside of my car.

What I saw made me forget to breathe. The roof was closing in on me, coming down on top of me. For a moment, I stared at it, paralyzed. Then I inhaled sharply and sat up, reaching for the door latch. But it wouldn't give. It was stuck.

I was trapped.

As the ceiling slowly lowered, the doors also began invading my space until I was stuck sitting upright in the middle of the backseat, boxed in. Panic started in my chest, spreading to the rest of me until I was having a full on panic attack.

I choked, trying to suck in enough air to scream.

My eyes sprang open and I panted heavily, my hand on my chest.

It was a dream. A dream within a dream.

Even though my brain told me this, tears still streamed down my cheeks and I had trouble breathing. I reached up and yanked on the door latch. At first it didn't give and I went into a frenzy, pulling the handle so hard I was lucky I didn't break it.

Then common sense kicked in and I realized it was locked. I unlocked it and tumbled out onto the pavement, gulping in air.

Resting my elbows on my knees, I hung my head, giving my heart time to stop racing. Tears burned my eyes as I tried to hold back sobs.

I thought I'd gotten over my claustrophobia since I hadn't had an incident in quite a while. Apparently I was wrong.

"Miss, are you okay?" An elderly man had stopped beside me and was peering down, a concerned look on his face.

I forced a smile. "Fine. Thanks for checking." I climbed to my feet and brushed the stray gravel off my butt.

The man looked skeptical, but he shuffled along.

His stopping had actually helped—it made me pull myself together and remember I was sitting in the middle of a Walmart parking lot. Granted, it was nearly empty, but still. I liked to keep my shit together in public.

I must look a wreck. I ran my fingers through my hair, trying to make it look somewhat normal. As I did, I tilted my head to the side, causing a sharp pain to shoot through my neck. I winced. I must have slept on it wrong.

Figures. I'd only gotten a few hours sleep, and I'd managed to both have a nightmare and injure myself. Heck, I'd probably projected my aura, too.

Sigh.

I headed toward the Walmart bathroom but thought better of it and changed course for the health and beauty aids section. I selected the cheapest toothbrush and toothpaste I could find and went through the self checkout. No need to subject anyone to my morning breath. Then I went into the bathroom.

My eyes were bloodshot and the skin underneath was puffy and a light purple hue. I had drool crusted on the side of my mouth and my hair was sticking up at all angles despite my attempt to smooth it out. I looked exactly like I'd spent the night in my car. It was not a becoming look for me.

I did the best I could to make myself presentable before going in search of breakfast. I hadn't bothered to check the time, but after my second time checking out, I saw it on my receipt. Yikes. Just past six. I had some time to kill before I could go to Hershey Park.

As I ate my breakfast of a banana and yogurt—which was quite a feat considering I didn't have a spoon—I calculated the odds of Linda still being at the hotel. Would she have stayed there all night? I didn't know her well, but I wouldn't put it past her. She'd have to sleep at some point, though.

I drove to the hotel with fingers crossed, hoping the shiny red sports car would be nowhere in sight. How the heck did she afford a car like that anyway? I wasn't aware handlers made a salary. So where did they get their money from? They didn't work traditional jobs, so was their some sort of angel fund that paid for stuff? And if so, where did *that* money come from?

As I got into the turn lane for the hotel, I groaned and switched on my signal to get back into the straight lane. The car was still sitting there. I couldn't spare more than a glance at it because I was driving, but I thought I saw someone in it. Maybe she had someone with her. Maybe they were taking turns staking out my room.

Either way, it didn't matter. As long as that car was parked there, that meant Linda wasn't far away. She might have even gotten herself a room at the hotel, maybe the one right next door.

Back to Walmart I went. I'd wait until eight and then

ask to use their phone to call Claire. Hopefully she'd give me her address and let me come over. I did *not* want to sit in the Walmart parking lot anymore.

It took a little convincing and more begging than I was comfortable with for the customer service rep to let me use the phone. While I dialed, she gave me the eye, so I turned my back and prayed Claire would answer because I wasn't going to be able to call again. At least not from here.

"Hello?" She sounded like she was still half asleep.

"Claire," I said. "I need to come over."

"What? Why?" Her speech was slurred and I felt bad for waking her up.

"I'll tell you when I get there."

"Are you okay?" She was alert now and I could picture her sitting up in bed, wrinkles forming on her forehead.

"Fine," I said. "What's your address?"

I jotted down the address and vague directions she told me, assuring her I'd be able to find it. I quickly thanked the Walmart employee again and trotted out to my car.

Her house wasn't hard to find—only one missed turn. It was in a nice neighborhood, the kind where kids left their bikes out in their front yards without worrying someone would steal them.

I'd never had a bike. Apartment living made having a bike difficult because I'd have to carry it down and up the stairs every time I used it. Plus, our apartments were usually tiny and we didn't always have a good place we could have kept it.

I parked in front of her house and peered into the rearview mirror one last time to make sure I was still somewhat presentable.

I knocked on the door lightly, not wanting to wake anyone in the house who was still sleeping. And let's be honest—I also didn't want Chase to come to the door. While I wasn't interested in him in *that* way, I would still like to maintain my dignity.

There was a scuffle behind the door, followed by a loud crash. A few seconds later the door was flung open. Before me stood a middle-aged man who had probably been handsome once—he had the same piercing blue eyes as Chase. His hair was thin, his eyes were bloodshot, and his face was puffy, reminding me of the Pillsbury Dough Boy. He wore a brown suit and his white dress shirt was only partially buttoned, except it wasn't the top buttons that were undone. Three random buttons were done, but they were matched with the wrong holes. Only half of the shirt was tucked in and there were several stains on the shirt and jacket.

"Who the hell are you?"

I nearly gagged at the stink of alcohol on his breath. If he breathed on me again, I might end up drunk myself. Holy crap.

Though he was obviously intoxicated, his blue eyes were able to focus on me with such an intensity I took a step back. I could see where Chase got that from.

"Dad." Claire came up behind him and wrapped her arm around his waist. "Let's get you to bed."

She shot me an apologetic look and guided him away from the door. He crashed into a table, knocking over a glass that shattered on the floor. I winced at the sound.

Claire lost her grip on him, nearly falling herself. He clumsily leaned down to pick up the pieces, only he gathered them up in his fist, squeezing it tightly.

"Dad, no." She pried his hand open, but the damage had already been done. Shards of glass were stuck in his skin. *Ouch.*

At the sight of the blood, I squeezed my eyes closed.

Cleaning that out was going to hurt like nobody's business. Of course, he might be past the point of pain. Perhaps it was good he was drunk.

But if he wasn't drunk, he wouldn't have ended up with the injury in the first place.

"Do you need help, Claire?" I asked hesitantly, selfishly hoping she'd say no. I didn't want to come any closer to his bloody hand.

"No, I've got it."

I didn't think she did. Her father probably weighed twice what she did, and he seemed to have lost full function of his legs. She was the only thing keeping him upright.

I stepped into the house and closed the door, not sure what to do. A second later, the door opened behind me, causing my heart to jump into my throat.

It was Chase, dressed in shorts and a loose, sweaty t-shirt. He looked like he'd been out running, probably giving the ladies in the neighborhood an eyeful. He really was good looking and I hated that I noticed.

Putting his hands on his hips, he surveyed the scene. "Guess he finally made it home." There was bitterness in his voice.

"Claire's taking him to bed," I said. "I think she might need help."

Chase stepped forward, and I put my hand on his arm to stop him. "Careful. There's glass there."

"I see it."

I yanked my hand back, feeling stupid. Of course he saw it. You couldn't miss it. "Is there a broom somewhere? I can clean it up."

"In the pantry," he called over his shoulder.

I carefully sidestepped the mess and found the broom. It didn't take long to clean up the glass, and I was glad I could be useful. I was just dumping the contents of the dustpan into the kitchen trash when Claire reappeared.

"Sorry you had to see that," she said, leaning against the counter.

"It's no big deal," I replied as I put the broom away. "Besides, it's not your fault."

"He didn't come home last night," Claire said in a way

that told me this wasn't an unusual occurrence. "He got back right before you came. I have no idea where he was."

"I'm sorry."

I could tell his behavior bothered her, but I could also tell she was somewhat desensitized to it. I wondered how long he'd been this bad. Chase had said Claire covered for him with his job, but I didn't see how that could possibly go on. If he was like this a lot, he was bound to lose his job, no matter what Claire did.

I could understand why Chase wanted to get away. Unless their father initiated a change himself, it wasn't going to happen. It must be horrible to have to sit and watch him ruin his life. But from Claire's perspective, I could see why she'd want to keep an eye on him. There was no right answer in this situation.

She pushed her hair out of her face. "I'm used to it."

"It still sucks."

She looked down at her nails as she picked at them. "Yeah, I guess so. So, what's up with you?"

"It's a long story."

Chase walked into the kitchen. "Then start talking." His tone was gruff and a little short, but I didn't hold it against him. Not after he'd had to deal with his father. That was enough to put anyone in a sour mood.

"Have you had breakfast?" Claire asked.

I nodded.

As I watched them prepare their food—Claire, a bagel with cream cheese and Chase, some kind of protein shake—I contemplated where to begin. In the end, I gave them the short, sweet version of everything, sans Cole.

I couldn't talk about him.

But his part in the story wasn't essential. Oh, his part was definitely essential in *my* story, but I wanted to keep that for myself. My feelings where he was concerned were all over the place. I didn't think I'd be able to put them into words right now, anyway.

And yes, I was glad Linda was here because that

meant she wasn't hunting Cole, but Chase and Claire didn't need to know that. All that mattered was that Linda was after me. The reason was superfluous.

"So all my stuff is essentially being held hostage in the hotel room," I finished.

Claire swallowed her last bite. "Where did you stay last night?"

"Uh...in my car," I muttered. I obviously hadn't been too proud to do it, but I didn't like admitting it.

"Ava! You should have called!"

I shrugged. "It was late. I didn't want to bother you."

"Seriously? The next time you're thinking about sleeping in your car, *bother me*." Claire shook her head.

"Okay," I said easily. I had no plans to wind up in the same situation again, anyway. For one thing, I planned to keep my money on me. In hindsight, I realized it was stupid to keep it all in one place. And in cash, no less. I was so used to being a minor that I forgot I was able to do things as an adult, like open a new bank account. So as soon as we got to Penn State, I would open an account that would give me a debit card. I'd need a permanent address for that, but I could use the address of the apartment we rented. I just had to be there long enough for them to mail the card to me. That would make life so much easier.

"I think we should leave now," Chase said.

"We still have a few days," Claire protested. "I need time to stock the pantry and clean the house before we leave."

Chase crossed his arms, his gaze speaking volumes.

"What?" Claire said defiantly. "If we're going to leave him to fend for himself, I can at least stack the deck in his favor."

I wouldn't say it because I didn't want to hurt her, but until her father wanted to be brought out of his self-harming spiral, nothing Claire did would make a bit of difference.

"He's an adult," Chase said. "He's supposed to be able

to take care of himself."

"There's nothing wrong with helping him out," Claire retorted. "Besides, I'm an adult now, too."

"*Exactly*. That's why we need to leave and take control of our lives. The decision to become seekers was made for us, and it's time we started making our own decisions."

This conversation had many parallels to my situation with Cole, except in his case, I was the one who made the terrible decision. But my options—Cole becoming a seeker or dying—didn't leave me much choice. Chase and Claire's mom had to have felt the same way.

Of course, I hadn't decided to become a seeker, either. It was my birthright.

It was easy to say what you would do in a given situation when you weren't actually in that situation. I wondered what it would be like to have to make that decision for myself. For instance, if I had terminal cancer with only six months left to live, would I choose to become a seeker to save my life?

I'd like to think I wouldn't put more importance on my life than others, but hadn't I basically done that when my mom was sick and needed Xavier's blood? I'd put more value on her life than those I would have turned over to Xavier. Comparing this scenario to being between a rock and hard place didn't begin to do it justice. It was more like being stuck between a diamond and Captain America's shield. Those were the two hardest things I could think of and even that didn't fully describe it.

Choosing between death and death wasn't a choice— it was a misfortune no one should have to bear.

Claire sighed. "You're right."

I was glad to see she was coming around to Chase's way of thinking because I sided with him. Unfortunately for me, I was stuck.

"I might have to catch up with you guys, later," I said. "I have to wait out Linda." It was on the tip of my tongue to ask to borrow some money. I hated to do it because I didn't like being in people's debt, and aside from that, I'd known them less than a week. But I had few options. I didn't want to stay in my car again, but I wasn't above doing it. However, I needed to eat and I'd prefer not to dumpster dive. I had to draw the line somewhere.

"No," Claire said firmly. "We all go together or we don't go at all."

All for one and one for all. That was us—the three musketeers. Three teenage seekers who were going to stick it to the man by *gasp! Not* leading innocent people to their deaths. We were such rebels by wanting to be decent human beings.

"I don't know how long Linda will stick around," I said. "And all of my stuff is in that room. I need to retrieve it first and it could take awhile."

And shit, I'd need to pay for the room so my stuff would stay there. I was paying by the night and I imagined if I missed a payment, they'd clean out the room to get it ready for the next person, which meant my stuff would end up in the trash and my cash would line the maid's pockets.

"Describe the hotel to me in detail," Chase said. "And tell me exactly where Linda is parked in relation to your room."

I told him as much as I could recall, but he started asking specifics, like how many parking spaces were in the row and how many feet the lane was in front of the parking. I thought I'd been paying better attention to my surroundings, but geez, I didn't know all that. I had been feeling pretty good about seeing Linda before she saw me.

Now? Not so much.

Chase stared at me for a moment and I thought he was going to berate me, but instead his mouth stretched into a Cheshire cat smile.

"I know what to do."

CHAPTER 21

CHASE'S PLAN WAS MORE THAN a little crazy. But it was better than my plan, which was more of a non-plan.

It took Chase less than an hour to put all the pieces in place, then we set off in their van.

I had to hand it to Chase—he somehow rocked that mini-van and made driving a soccer mom mobile look cool. I think it was probably because he honestly didn't give a shit what anyone thought. Confidence had a way of canceling out things that might otherwise be uncool.

I doubted I could make even a fancy car like Linda's look cool.

I crouched in the second row as we pulled into the parking lot, a small part of me holding out hope the red sports car would be gone. But nope. It was in the same place as before. Why hadn't the hotel employees called the cops on her? Wasn't it suspicious that she was simply sitting in her car staring at the building?

Perhaps she'd paid them off. That would explain how she knew exactly what room I was in because I hadn't shared that information with anyone.

I pointed to her car as Chase drove around the side of the building. "There she is." Since I wasn't driving, I was able to study her as she sipped a cup of coffee like she was waiting on a friend instead of staking out a teenager like the creeper she was. She seemed perfectly relaxed, like this was a normal day in her life.

Claire squinted, turning in her seat as Chase drove to the far side of the parking lot where I'd parked yesterday. "She looks so...*matronly*."

"Yeah, but she's no Mary Poppins."

"It'd be a lot cooler if she was," Claire said.

"Agreed," I commented.

Chase looked at us like we were weirdos. I didn't care. The medicine I'd been given lately was vile, and I'd love to have a spoonful of sugar to help it go down. And I'd take any manner of make-believe magic nannies, fairy godmothers, or genies if they could help me fix things.

"When will Zach be here?" Claire asked.

Chase checked his phone. "About ten minutes."

Zach was a guy Chase went to high school with who owed Chase too many favors to count. He'd agreed to help us and Chase would consider them even. What we were asking him to do was pretty crazy—not life threatening or anything, but strange. Part of the deal was Zach simply had to do as instructed, no questions asked.

It kind of made me wonder what kind of favors Chase had done for Zack in the past. When I asked, Chase told me I didn't want to know. Which of course made me want to know even more.

We sat twiddling our thumbs for about five minutes before getting out of the van to get in position. Well, Chase and I did, anyway. He and I agreed Claire should stay in the van. Neither of us wanted to risk Linda seeing her.

I wished Claire was comfortable driving so she could act as our getaway driver, but she didn't even have her license. We told her to keep the car running and act as a lookout. She stuck out her lower lip in a pout but didn't argue. There was no time for that.

Chase and I waited behind the dumpster. At least it had been emptied some time since last night, so the stench wasn't quite as awful. It was still pretty darn putrid.

A large soda delivery truck pulled into the parking lot, and I sucked in a breath. That was our cue.

We crouched down low and ran up the stairs to my door. Chase had done some kind of geometric calculation and he figured the truck wouldn't completely block the view. Everything would be visible from about doorknob height up.

As I reached into my back pocket for the key card, I was tempted to tell Chase I forgot it, just to mess with him. He had to have asked me at least half a dozen times if I had it on the drive over. But wanna-be smartass that I was, I knew better than to waste time with that. Or irritate Chase since he was the one who'd planned this and was taking a risk on my behalf.

The sound of the lock clicking was a relief. I'd half-expected the door to jam or my key card to no longer work because that was usually how things went for me. Once we were inside the room, Chase took position at the front window, peeking through the curtain.

"Be quick," he snapped.

My nostrils flared and I clamped my mouth closed so a snarky comment wouldn't come flying out. Because seriously? What did he think I was going to do? Take a shower and do my make-up? I could stand to do both, but come on. He should give me some credit.

But I kept my mouth shut because Chase was going out on a limb to help me, despite only knowing me less than a week. He easily could have said screw it and left me to fend for myself. Although, our relationship was symbiotic—I made it easier for him to convince Claire to leave. If that weren't the case, would he still help me?

Maybe...if Claire talked him into it.

I flung open my suitcase and threw my clothes in, wishing I'd kept them packed. I hadn't expected to have to flee like this, though.

"Can you see anything?" I asked.

"Zach got out of the truck. He's talking to her."

"Was that part of the plan?"

"Not exactly."

"I bet she's pissed."

Chase shrugged. "Her face looks like she's choking on some lemons."

"That's just her normal face."

"Maybe she's like the Hulk and she's angry all the time."

I snorted and cracked a smile. Did Chase just make a joke? And at a time like this? High-five to him.

In the bathroom, I shoved all my stuff in my toiletries bag. I came back out to the bedroom and placed that on top of my clothes. Then I keyed in the code for the safe and pulled out my baggie of money. That was right—I was keeping my entire life savings in a Ziploc. What could I say? I was classy like that.

Taking one last look around, I zipped up my suitcase. "That's it. I got it all."

Frowning, Chase looked down at his trusty watch. I leveled my gaze at him. He'd better not complain I took too long. It had literally taken me two minutes to gather all my worldly possessions.

I brushed past him, pulling my suitcase. Just as I put my hand on the doorknob, I gasped. *Shit.*

"What?" Chase's voice was alarmed.

"I almost forgot my phone." I marched over to the dresser drawer to retrieve it.

"I thought you didn't have a phone." Now he sounded annoyed. I could understand that. Things would have been easier if I'd used it the last few days, more for me than him. For instance, I might not have had to spend the night in my car.

"It's complicated," I muttered, feeling like an idiot. I was doing the best I could in a crappy situation. He could judge me all he wanted, but later, after we'd gotten away from Linda.

Chase looked outside one last time. "Let's go."

He opened the door slowly and as I tried to fit my suitcase through the small opening he'd made, the wheel got caught on the edge of the door and it fell over, making a thump sound. I winced, even though it wasn't that loud.

Chase shot me a look that could kill, as if I'd purposefully sounded a gong instead of accidentally knocking over my suitcase. I rolled my eyes. *Whatever.* If he had opened the door wide enough, it wouldn't have gotten caught.

He yanked the suitcase away from me, picking it up and carrying it under his arm like a football. And this was no small bag, either. He crouched down, going back the way we came. I gently closed the door behind me and followed.

At the bottom of the stairs, the knots in my stomach uncoiled and I let out the breath I'd been holding. I grinned. All we had to do was circle around the building to the van and we were home free.

In your face, Linda!

Suddenly, the truck's engine rumbled, going from the idling sound to something else. It started to pull away.

Shit! That wasn't part of the plan. Zach was supposed to keep his truck there until Chase texted him with the all clear.

As the truck ambled past us, Zach glanced over our way from the driver's seat and shrugged.

Asshole. The murderous look on Chase's face told me he shared the sentiment. Perhaps Zach was still going to owe Chase some favors after all. But if we managed to get out of town like we wanted, Chase would never be able to collect anyway.

Chase and I looked at each other and as our eyes met, we both took off. The truck picked up speed and it was nearly past us.

We weren't going to make it around the corner in time. I looked over my shoulder just as the truck cleared us.

And there next to Linda was Xavier.

I SKIDDED TO A HALT.

Xavier.

I'd been on the lookout for him all week and he showed *now*?

His face was just as messed up as the mother from the park said it was—he did indeed look like Freddy Krueger. The skin on his cheeks was taut, like a burn victim's and there were angry red ridges and valleys. His ears were misshapen, almost like someone had ripped them off and put them back together incorrectly. If I hadn't gotten grim satisfaction from knowing my mother did that to him, it would have been frightening to look at.

Linda and Xavier appeared to be having some kind of an argument, but I couldn't tell what it was about because of the deafening pounding of the blood in my ears. If my head was clear, I would've been able to hear since I was close enough.

"Ava!" Chase hissed. He'd made it around the corner and he beckoned me to join him, probably wondering what the hell I was doing.

I was wondering that myself.

But I couldn't let this opportunity pass me by. I hadn't seen Xavier in months, not counting the minor run-in at Hershey Park. Who knew when he'd show again?

Maybe if I were a better person, I could let bygones be bygones and move on with my life.

But I wasn't. I couldn't.

I stepped toward him and Linda looked in my direction.

"*You.*" Her face scrunched up in anger as she stared me down. She looked like an angry schoolmarm in her long skirt and buttoned-up blouse, like she wanted to rap my knuckles with a wooden ruler.

I ignored her.

"Xavier," I called. "We have unfinished business."

We certainly did, but as I got to within a dozen feet of him, my head cleared and I realized how foolish I was being. I had no plan. There were two handlers who both hated me, one of which had freaky, deadly powers. And who knew? Maybe Linda had them, too. They'd definitely suit her personality.

Xavier's eyes bore into me in a way that would have made me squirm a year ago, but not now. I'd already lost everything. There was nothing he could do to me that would be worse than what I'd already been through.

My hand slipped into my pocket and squeezed my pocket knife with sweaty fingers. I wouldn't be able to kill him, but I could make him bleed. That wouldn't be enough, but for now it would be immensely satisfying.

Xavier and I stood staring at one another—a showdown.

I was so focused on him I barely noticed Linda advance. It didn't escape Xavier's notice though, and like a super villain with super reflexes, he whipped his arm out, soccer mom style, slamming it into her chest. She flew back several feet, hitting her car and landing on her butt. Xavier pivoted so he was facing her and he bent his knees and spread his arms out, like he was preparing for battle.

What...the...?

My mouth hung open as I watched it unfold, until a hand clasped on my shoulder. I spun around, drawing my pocket knife. The only problem was the blade was still sheathed.

"Come on," Chase said urgently.

"But—"

"What are you—crazy? Let's go."

I didn't argue that time because what could I say? *No, I want to stay and watch these villains who are supposed to be good guys duke it out.* Because *that* was perfectly sane.

Even still, he had to drag me away while I tried to watch over my shoulder. It wasn't until I almost ate pavement that I focused on the task at hand—getting away.

We ran around the building and as soon as the van came into sight, I felt like I'd been punched in the stomach. *Claire.* I'd totally forgotten about her waiting for us in the van. What if Linda and Xavier had seen her? What if she'd come over to investigate because we were taking too long? Chase could fend for himself, but Claire was another story.

Claire opened the passenger door, then climbed into the backseat so I could jump right in. Chase quickly deposited my suitcase in the back, then jumped into the driver's seat. He peeled out of the parking lot, going away from Linda and Xavier, so I didn't get to see what happened.

I hoped they killed each other.

CHAPTER 22

WE GOT A FEW MILES down the street before anyone spoke.

"What happened?" Claire asked. "You guys took so long I was about to go look for you."

Chase gave me the side eye, and I knew he was thinking the same thing I was. If anything had happened to Claire, he never would have forgiven me. But he would have to get in line because I would never forgive myself, either.

"Why the hell did Zach drive away?" I asked.

"*No...he...didn't*," Claire said, her eyes wide.

"Are you surprised?" Chase said. "He's always been a piece of shit."

"I don't know why you hung around him." Claire shook her head. Those were strong words coming from her, a person who always saw the best in people.

But I could probably guess why. If your friends were assholes, there was no danger of them ever having a pure aura.

"It would have been fine except Xavier showed up," I said. Or maybe Xavier showing up was the reason Linda hadn't noticed us at first. So maybe if I hadn't stopped, he would have provided the diversion we needed to get away.

I hated coming face-to-face with him to leave things as I always did—unfinished.

"Oh my God," Claire said, "did he sneak up on you or something?"

"No." Chase looked straight ahead, and I could all but hear his teeth grinding. "We were about to get away when Ava turned back to taunt him."

"I wasn't..."

Okay, I guessed I had taunted him, just a little. But Chase didn't understand. He didn't know my history with Xavier. They hadn't had to deal with a psychopath like I had. Their handler was a nice, normal kind of guy.

I gasped sharply.

"What?" Chase asked, looking over at me, then in the rearview, probably checking for a tail.

"Niles," I whispered, realizing I hadn't told them my suspicions about how Linda had found me. The only other possibility was that Xavier had told her, but somehow I didn't think that was the case.

Chase picked up on what I was thinking right away. "Damn it," he said.

"What?" Claire's brow was furrowed, then she shook her head. "No way. Niles wouldn't rat her out."

"Why wouldn't he?" I asked. "He's not loyal to you."

Claire reeled back like I'd slapped her. "He's our—"

"*Handler*," Chase said firmly. "He's not our friend, Claire. He's not on our side."

"Did you see him after I left the park yesterday?"

"No," Claire said.

"Me neither," Chase agreed. "And it's kind of odd because once he shows up, he normally likes to get down to business. I'm surprised he wasn't waiting for us when we got off work."

"Wait..." Claire sighed. "After work last night when I took my purse out of my locker, my wallet was in the wrong section. I always put it in the middle zippered section, but it was in the unzipped part. I thought it was weird, but I'm so forgetful these days I didn't dwell on it."

"Let me guess," I said. "My hotel information is in

your wallet."

Claire nodded. "I'm sorry."

"It's not your fault," I said.

"We need to leave," Chase said. "We can't wait any longer. As soon as we get back, let's pack up and go."

"Wait," I said. "What's to stop Niles from leading Xavier and Linda to your house?"

Chase switched lanes. "Nothing. But I'm going to call him and set up a meeting. We need to know if that's how she found you."

"He won't tell the truth," I said.

"You'd be surprised," Chase said. "He's kind of a pansy ass. Not much of a spine. He'll tell us. And if he doesn't, I'll beat his ass."

"You can do that?" I asked.

Chase looked at me like I was a moron. I rolled my eyes. Yes, I knew he was a big, buff guy who could probably kick most other guys' asses, but this was a handler we were talking about, not a normal person.

"What I mean is, if you can do that, then why haven't you done it already and been done with all this seeker stuff? What hold does he have over you?"

"Seeking is the condition for us living," Claire explained in a somber tone. "If we don't, then we forfeit our lives."

"So, what? Niles will kill you?" I couldn't imagine Niles being violent. A snitch, yes. But a killer? No. And for goodness' sake, he was a fallen angel, emphasis on *angel*. Angels weren't supposed to kill. They were supposed to be the embodiment of good, and correct me if I was wrong, but killing was pretty much the worst thing anyone could do.

"He wouldn't hurt us," Claire said, sounding one-hundred percent sure about that statement. "I'm not entirely sure how it would work because we've obviously never defected and no one we know has, either."

"Our mom was sick," Chase said. "We couldn't leave

while she was still here."

Now *that* I understood perfectly.

Chase turned into a parking lot and pulled out his phone. "Where are you?" he barked into it. "Niles, I swear to God, you'd better tell me."

Yikes. If I was on the other end, I wouldn't want to tell Chase my location, either.

"Stay there." Chase put the van into gear and pulled back into traffic. "He's only five minutes from here."

Chase drove us to a coffee shop. Niles was leaning against his car, a silver Mercedes. What was up with handlers lately and their fancy cars? Geez.

Chase flung open the door and stalked over to Niles. To his credit, Niles remained perfectly composed, and I wouldn't have thought Chase's death stare affected him except for the way his coffee shook in his hand.

"Hello everyone," Niles said a bit too cheerily. Oh, yeah. He was definitely guilty.

Chase knocked the cup out of Niles' hand and grabbed the front of his shirt, hauling him to a standing position.

"What...did...you...do?"

Niles let out a noise that sounded like *eep*, and Claire rushed over, putting her hands flat against her brother's chest and pushing him back.

"Relax, Chase."

Chase backed up a few feet. I hung back, letting them handle things. Though this directly involved me, it wasn't my territory. And Chase seemed to have it under control.

"You spilled my coffee," Niles said indignantly, fixing his shirt.

"I don't give a shit about your coffee," Chase growled.

Claire shot her brother a look, then turned back to Niles. "Tell me you didn't rat out our friend. Tell me you didn't sic Linda on her." When Niles remained silent, Claire groaned. "How could you?"

"There are rules," Niles protested. "A hierarchy. You don't understand. Everything isn't so great on this side of things, either."

"Explain it, then." Claire crossed her arms. "Help us to understand."

"Look, not all of us agree with what we're doing. Some of us are forced into it. You two are the youngest seekers they ever made and it caused the ranks to split. Half thought it was brilliant, while the other half—myself included—thought you were much too young, especially since you didn't consent to it yourself."

"Get to the point," Chase said.

"I don't give you two the number of assignments I'm supposed to. I've been flying under the radar, so to speak. I have a few friends who are higher up who've turned a blind eye. Linda found out and so far I've been able to put her off, but I wouldn't be able to keep it up much longer. When I met Ava, I figured she was the seeker Linda was looking for. So I made a deal with her. It was to keep you safe."

When he said that last line, he raised his hand, like he wanted to touch Claire. Abruptly, he dropped his arm at his side, having thought better of it. But I didn't miss the tender gaze in his eyes as he looked at her. My eyes widened as I realized what the real deal was.

Chase must have realized it at the same time because he glared at Niles, then shook his head and closed his eyes, putting his fingers up to the bridge of his nose.

"You scumbag," Chase said when he opened his eyes. "You're in love with my sister."

Niles blushed about eighteen shades of pink but didn't deny it. It wouldn't have made much difference, but good for him. At least he owned up to it. But still, it was so inappropriate.

Claire stayed silent, her gaze fixed on the pavement.

"And you knew!" Chase said to his sister. "Please tell me you didn't—"

"No," Claire said, anger in her eyes. "Of course not. But there's nothing wrong with having some compassion."

Chase turned back to Niles. "How old are you?"

"Twenty-four."

Chase laughed bitterly. "No, that's how old you were when you became an angel. But you've been an angel for much longer than that, you sicko. Claire is barely eighteen! She was only fourteen when you met her!"

I wondered if Claire realized Niles had been bending the rules for them. If she was strategically taking advantage of the situation. Perhaps Chase hadn't been giving his sister enough credit.

"I haven't done anything improper," Niles protested.

"If I thought you had, you'd already be dead right now," Chase retorted and Niles paled.

I didn't think now would be such a good time to let Chase know handlers couldn't be killed easily.

"Does Linda know where they live?" I asked, wanting to get the conversation back on track.

"Not that I know of," Niles said. "At least, I didn't tell her."

"This is what's going to happen," Chase said. "You're coming with us. I don't trust you not to call her the minute we're gone. Get in the back of the van."

Niles looked like he wanted to protest, but like Chase predicted, his invertebrate nature took over and he did as he was told.

"We're going back to our house," Chase told me and Claire quietly. "We'll pack while Ava keeps an eye on Niles to make sure he doesn't make any phone calls. Then we'll get the hell out of here."

I nodded and we headed toward the van. Just as Claire was about to climb into the back, Chase said, "No. Claire sits in the front with me."

I quickly switched places with her as she rolled her eyes. I stifled a grin. Chase had given the big speech about how Niles was a pansy ass, but now Chase considered him some great threat to his sister. It was laughable. Claire might have difficultly with math, but she could certainly handle Niles and his little crush on her.

When we got to Chase and Claire's house, their father's car was still in the driveway. I pulled Chase aside to ask if that was going to be a problem. He gave me one of his "you're a moron" looks.

"He'll be passed out all day," Chase said. "You could drive a bus through the house and he wouldn't notice."

Well, okay then.

Chase and Claire went to their respective bedrooms to pack, which left me in the living room with Niles. Awkward silence ensued.

I didn't blame him for what he did. Wanting to protect the people he cared about was definitely something I could identify with. Of course, I wished he hadn't screwed me over in the process. I didn't have much to say to him.

I'd never guarded anyone before. When he shoved his hands in his pockets, I almost yelled at him to keep them where I could see them. I was a little jumpy.

"So you're the one, yeah?" Niles asked.

"Shouldn't you know that since you ratted me out to Linda?"

He blew out a breath. "It was nothing personal. She's going to catch up to you sooner or later, so I figured I might as well help out Claire."

I noticed he didn't include Chase. It seemed there was no love on both sides.

"There's more ways to do that than being a snitch," I said. "If you don't agree with seeking, then why are you part of the system? Why don't you try to change it?"

He laughed. "No one listens to me. Not even Chase most of the time. And you expect me to convince a bunch of angels to change the system they've been using for years? Not bloody likely."

"Change has to start somewhere."

"Angels are stubborn. Good luck to anyone who tries to change their minds."

I peeked out the window, looking for signs of Linda.

But also, I didn't want to look at Niles anymore. He disgusted me. Because he wasn't part of the solution that he knew needed to happen, he was part of the problem. He might be a nice enough guy, but Chase was right. He had no spine. And I couldn't respect that. I'd made a lot of stupid choices in the past year, but at least I'd acted based on what I thought was right.

It only took Chase and Claire another ten minutes to finish packing. He piled their stuff by the front door, then went into the kitchen to pack up a cooler full of snacks, which was great thinking on his part. Claire probably wouldn't like it since she'd wanted to stock the pantry, not raid it, but I was definitely pro-snack.

Claire disappeared upstairs once more, and I heard a door open and close. She was probably saying good-bye to her father, even though Chase had been right and he hadn't stirred. And Chase hadn't exactly been quiet as he pulled their suitcases down the stairs.

Claire came back downstairs and we waited inside while Chase loaded everything in the van.

"Claire, I was only trying to help you," Niles said, sounding pathetic.

She shook her head sadly. "That's the thing, Niles. I appreciate what you were trying to do, but you went about it all wrong. You don't know me at all if you'd think I would want you to help me by hurting one of my friends. That's unforgivable."

Niles recoiled like he'd been slapped.

Less than fifteen minutes after arriving at their house, we were back out front, ready to go. Niles approached the sliding door of the van, but Chase put a hand on his arm, stopping him from getting in the vehicle.

"This is the end of the line for you."

"But...how am I supposed to get back to my car?" Niles sputtered.

Chase got into the driver's seat, sparing Niles one last look. "I don't know and I don't care. Maybe you can ask your new handler friends."

"Good-bye, Niles," Claire said. "For what it's worth, thanks for everything."

His eyes widened as he realized what was happening. I didn't know how he hadn't figured out what was going on when he saw the suitcases. My guess was Niles wasn't the brightest crayon in the box.

"But what am I supposed to do?" he asked.

"Whatever you think is best," Claire said. "We're doing what we have to do. You do the same."

She shut the door and fastened her seatbelt as I got into my own car. I didn't bother to say good-bye.

CHAPTER 23

LUCKILY FOR ME, CHASE WASN'T a crazy driver, so I had no problem following him. I didn't know exactly where we were going—just Penn State—so if I lost them, I'd be screwed without a way to contact them. Even if I wasn't being all weird about using my phone, it was in my suitcase. Which was still in the back of the van. Not my smartest move.

After about an hour, Chase pulled into a gas station and I pulled behind him at the pump. Claire hopped out of the van and walked back and forth, shaking out her arms and doing neck circles. Chase hadn't been lying when he'd said she had a phobia of long car rides.

"I'm going to take a walk," she said, setting off.

"I'll come with you," I chased after her. I didn't want her to be alone.

"No, I'll be fine." She quickened her pace.

"She's okay," Chase said quietly. "She just needs a minute."

Still unsure, I watched her walk away. But if Chase said it would be okay, then it would be. He wouldn't do anything that put Claire at risk.

I stood with Chase as he pumped gas. I had about three quarters of a tank, so I wasn't going to bother filling up right now. It was always a pain to pay for gas with cash, so I'd wait until I was nearly out.

Chase replaced the gas nozzle, and I noticed he'd only pumped about eight bucks worth.

"We didn't actually need gas." He must have noticed me looking. "But Claire can't handle being in the car for more than an hour at a time."

"How long are we stopping?" Even though I had no idea what awaited us, I was eager to get there.

"As soon as she gets back, we'll go." He snapped the gas tank closed. "We need to talk about Xavier. What was he doing with Linda?"

"I have no clue." That was something I wondered about myself, though I hadn't had much time to actively think about it. "They were arguing about something, but I have no idea what. Xavier went rogue a while ago, and at least one soul he was responsible for is unaccounted for. Linda is so straight-laced I would think she'd have a real problem with him because of that. So it could be that simple."

"But you don't think so."

I sighed. "In my experience, nothing is ever that simple. But I've also learned that there's no point searching for Xavier. He'll turn up again when we least expect him. It's what he does best."

"What do you think he did with the soul?"

"Again, I have no idea. Nothing good."

Chase crossed his arms and leaned against the side of the van. "All the more reason to get the hell out of dodge. Turning in names is bad enough under normal circumstances."

A green SUV pulled up to the other side of the pump and a man got out.

Chase's face broke into smile. "Holy, shit."

The man looked over at Chase and his face mirrored Chase's. He wasn't much taller than me, and his head was shaved in a military style cut. I'd put him in his mid to late twenties. He crossed over the barrier to our side.

"Chase, what the hell?" They did the guy hug thing, clapping each other on the back.

"I thought you were down in Florida," Chase said.

"Pops died, so I decided to move back here."

"Sorry to hear that, man."

"Thanks. It's a total bummer, but it was expected. Tell me what's up with you."

This whole time, my gaze had ping-ponged between them, but Chase made no move to introduce me. At first, I was annoyed. Because what the heck? It was kind of rude.

Then I remembered the trouble that came from being introduced to Niles. Maybe it was better if I just sat this one out.

I headed into the convenience store part of the gas station to hit up the ladies' room while we were stopped. While I washed my hands, Claire came in. I waited for her while she did her business.

"Chase is out by the van," I told her. "He's talking to some guy."

She squirted soap onto her hands. "Yeah, I saw. That's Lance. He's a seeker Niles introduced us to at the beginning. He taught us how to differentiate between the souls."

Damn it! I'd been standing just a few feet away from another seeker and I'd had no idea. The special seeker *energy* or whatever the hell it was wasn't registering with me. Lance hadn't seemed any different than a normal person.

"You don't think he'll tell anyone about us, do you?" Niles had caused a lot of trouble for me. Granted, he was playing for the other side, but you never knew where people's loyalties lay.

Claire snorted. "Not a chance. Heck, if he knew we were going into hiding, he'd probably want to come with us. He hates being a seeker."

"Then why did he decide to become one?"

"He needed a kidney transplant, but his name wasn't coming up on the list and it wasn't looking good for him. His parents are both gone and he's the caretaker for his grandfather. He's the only one his grandfather has."

I remembered his comment about Pops. That must be the grandfather Claire referred to.

Another thought occurred to me.

"Hey, can you show me how you determine he's a seeker?" I asked.

Claire shook the water off her hands and reached for a paper towel. "Sure. It's not hard. I honestly can't believe you don't know how to do it."

We went back out into the convenience store, but just before Claire went outside, I held her back, shaking my head. "Let's do it here where he can't see us."

Claire peered through the smudged glass window, then glanced over at the clerk who was giving us the eye. The only thing Claire and I might be guilty of was loitering. We weren't stealing or vandalizing anything. He needed to cool it.

"Okay," Claire said in a low voice, even though there was no one close enough to hear her. "You see how he has like a translucent shimmer around him?"

I slowly lowered my guards. It felt strange doing it since I hadn't looked at auras in a long time.

When I looked at Lance's aura, all I saw were dark colors. It wasn't quite black, but the colors were so dark they were barely differentiable. For all intents and purposes, he might as well have a black soul.

That surprised me. Normally I could guess at what color a person's aura would be and nine times out of ten, I'd be right. Even though I only heard Lance and Chase talk for about a minute, I wouldn't have pegged him to have a black aura. I hadn't been around him long enough to predict an exact color, but definitely not black.

But that was all I saw, which meant I also wasn't seeing the shimmer Claire was talking about.

I lightly pounded my fist on the glass, earning a dirty look from the clerk. "Damn it. I don't see any kind of shimmer. Just his aura."

Claire cocked her head at me, like I'd said something crazy.

"What do you mean?" she asked.

"I don't see any kind of shimmer. His aura looks just like everyone else's." Well, except for the fact that it was nearly black. Most people's were more mixed.

"What do you mean, just like everyone else's?"

Now it was my turn to look at Claire like *she* was crazy.

"Just what I said. His aura looks normal. There's no shimmer or anything."

"But..." She seemed at a loss, her mouth hanging open as she stared at me. "I can't see his aura."

"What do you mean?" We'd totally reversed roles.

"There are no colors. Just a translucent shimmer, like an energy field or something where his aura *should* be. I can't see seekers' auras." She paused for a moment, and I slammed my guards firmly into place in anticipation of the question I knew was coming. "Can you look at Chase's aura? And mine?"

Her eyes were wide and her expression hopeful. But when I'd lowered my guards a moment ago, I'd purposefully *not* looked at her and Chase's auras. It felt wrong to look at other seekers' auras, and I didn't do it lightly. It felt like spying, especially now that I knew they couldn't see mine. Even though she was asking me, I still didn't want to.

I tore my gaze away from her face, trying to figure out how to let her down gently.

She put her hand on my arm. "Please," she whispered, anguish in her voice.

I knew her fear—that seeking would make her own soul black. I had the same fear. So how could I deprive her of the peace I could provide.

Sighing, I closed my eyes. When I opened them, I took a quick peek at both their auras, just enough to see they weren't dark.

"They're not black," I said. "That's all I'll tell you."

Her shoulders slumped a little as *something* left her— fear, despair...I didn't know what.

She squeezed my hand. "Thank you."

IT WAS A MIRACLE I didn't fall asleep behind the wheel. Spending the night in my car was finally catching up to me now that some of the adrenaline had left me. I also felt grimy and nasty, still in yesterday's clothes and in desperate need of a shower. I'd done the sniff test too many times to count, and I wasn't getting any fresher.

Chase pulled into a fast food restaurant, and I said a silent prayer of thanks. My eyelids were struggling to stay open.

"What's the plan?" I asked, getting out of the car. Claire was already out, pacing and shaking her arms. This time she didn't move to go for a walk, though.

"I made an appointment to look at the apartment this afternoon," Chase said. "So we have some time to kill."

I closed my eyes as I stretched, trying to ease my stiff muscles. Even though we'd only driven two hours, between that and last night, I was ready to *not* be in my car for a while.

When I opened my eyes, I was nearly blinded by the sea of colors—the few people in the parking lot, the people I could see in the restaurant through the glass windows, the people whizzing by in their cars. Their auras were overwhelming, and my head began pounding before I could get my guards in place again.

I put my hand up to my temple, letting out a low moan at the pain.

I was so darn tired. Between that and the stress of the

last twenty-four hours, I must have let my guards slip without realizing it.

"Are you okay?" Claire asked, still shaking her arms.

"Yes. I just let me guards down for a minute and the auras caught me by surprise. They're so freaking bright."

"What guards?" Chase asked.

I closed my eyes, knowing I was about to learn something else that would make me different. "The guards I put in place to block the auras." I opened my eyes to see blank looks on both their faces. "Don't you use something to block them out?" Perhaps this was just a misunderstanding due to them using different terminology.

"No," Claire said. "Auras are really dim. It's a struggle to see them most times."

"Are you kidding me?" I couldn't stop my annoyed response.

Chase maintained an even expression, leveling his gaze at me. I sighed.

"Sorry," I muttered. "It's just frustrating to finally find people like me, only to learn I'm still different."

"So the auras are bright?" Claire asked.

I nodded. "They're overwhelming. If I don't block them out most of the time, I wouldn't be able to function."

Claire gave me a sympathetic look, but walking into the restaurant, I ignored it. I couldn't handle her sympathy. I didn't need it or want it.

If I gave into it, I'd start feeling sorry for myself. I'd start feeling like maybe they were right, that maybe I was the "one." And that wasn't a good thing. It meant a lifetime of loneliness, never having anyone who truly understood my existence.

I'd never missed my mom so much.

I marched up to the counter and focused on reading the menu, the exact components of each value meal suddenly having major importance.

Anything to keep me from crying. Because crying

wasn't going to fix it and it wouldn't make me feel better, either. At least not for the long haul.

And I owed it to Chase and Claire to keep it together.

CHAPTER 24

"MY FIRST WAS A FIFTEEN-YEAR-OLD BOY," Claire said quietly, so quietly I had to lean forward to make sure I'd heard her correctly. It was the first words anyone had spoken since we'd gotten our food and sat at a corner table.

When most teenage girls made a statement like that, they referred to something else entirely, but I knew Claire was referring to the first name she'd turned in.

I wondered why she was saying this. What prompted this confession?

I did know it was a big deal, so I stayed quiet, letting her get out the words she needed to say.

"He was from the next town over." Her voice was mechanical, but the tears streaming down her face gave away her true emotions. "It turned out he was the cousin of a girl we went to school with. He died in a car accident. Dead on impact. The similarities of his accident to ours are crazy. It always made me wonder if he died that way because we lived."

I didn't say what I was thinking—he *had* died because they lived. The cause of death was irrelevant.

"After all these years, I've never said his name beyond giving it to Niles. Not his or any of the other souls I turned in. I've been part of this horrendous thing and too scared to even admit what I'm doing."

Whatever veil she'd been holding in front of her eyes, it had been stripped away. She was raw as the truth crashed down on her, and she finally began to accept it.

I'd only known her a short time, and I didn't want to seem condescending, but I was proud of her.

"You can't change the past, Claire," Chase said gruffly. "There's no point looking back."

"I disagree," Claire said. "We have to look back so we can learn from our mistakes."

"We're doing the right thing now," he said.

"What was his name?" I asked. She'd mentioned she'd never said his name, but she still hadn't said it. It would do her good to get it out.

Claire drew in a shaky breath. "Trevor. Gina. Marcus. Those were my three."

I reached across the table and squeezed her hand, knowing how hard it was for her to say those names out loud.

We could play the blame game all day long, but the truth was we'd all made bad choices. Their mother never should have made that decision for them. I didn't want to be too judgmental, but I had to wonder about a woman who would knowingly put that burden on her children.

Of course, my mother had done the same thing. Yet, she'd attempted suicide when she was pregnant, trying to kill us both. It hadn't worked—the Reapers had saved her. I once again had to wonder why. If seekers could be made, then why were we so important? Did being part of Areli's line make us special? Indispensable? *Why?*

I wished to God I knew.

THE APARTMENT CHASE FOUND FOR us was a basement level two bedroom unit. Fortunately, it was furnished, but no dishwasher and no washing machine. Ugh. Going without a dishwasher was no big deal, but having to pay per load to do my laundry would get expensive fast. Most of the apartments my mom and I had lived in had a washer and dryer. It was one of our few requirements. But for the few units that didn't, my mom would do our laundry while I was at school, so I never paid much attention to how much it cost. I was shocked by the prices when I'd used the laundromat a few days ago.

While Chase finalized the details with the apartment manager, I dozed on the couch. When the front door slammed, I jolted awake, my hand going to my pocket where I'd stowed my knife.

"Home, sweet home," Chase said.

Claire came out of one of the bedrooms with a frown on her face. "It's furnished, but there's no bedding. Or towels." She walked into the kitchen and opened a cabinet. "No kitchen stuff, either."

"Shit," Chase said.

He could say that again. The three of us looked at one another in despair. Apparently none of us had considered we'd need stuff like that.

"I wish I had brought some from home," Claire said with a sigh. "We have so many of those things."

"Well, we can't go back now," Chase said. "I guess we're going shopping. But first I want to unload the van."

"I'll help," I said.

Claire grabbed the apartment complex branded notepad and pen the landlord had given us. "I'll make a list of what we need."

Out at the van, I used the opportunity to ask Chase about something that had been bugging me since Claire told the story of her first. I hadn't wanted to ask her about it since she was distraught.

"Claire only mentioned three names," I said.

"Yeah, so?"

"Is that it? She started when she was fourteen, right?"

"She was fifteen when we got our first assignment."

"Still only three?"

"Niles gave us assignments about once a year. So every six months, one of us got one."

"Wow," I said slowly. "He really was covering for you two." Despite everything, I was glad for it. It was that many less people who had to die. So perhaps Niles had been good for something.

"How many assignments did you have?" Chase asked.

"One every few months."

"Damn."

I couldn't have said it better myself. I was glad Chase left it at that. Even though Claire had the need to get it off her chest, I was fine keeping my track record to myself.

After depositing our bags downstairs, there was something else I realized the apartment lacked—a TV. So that really kind of sucked. I wasn't a huge television watcher, but it would be nice to have one. But since it wasn't a necessity, I doubted we'd be picking one up.

We found everything we needed at Walmart, including groceries. Chase paid for everything, even though I offered to chip in. I had to admit I didn't protest too much because it seemed like he had a lot more money than I did. I'd have to make sure to pull my weight when it came to cleaning and stuff like that.

Once back at the apartment, it was nearly dinner time. Claire offered to cook, but Chase quickly said he'd do it. At first I thought that was gracious of him, but then I realized he just didn't want to get stuck going to the apartment complex laundry to wash the new towels and bedding.

Apparently I wasn't the only one who had an aversion to laundromats.

Claire and I gathered up everything, including the detergent she'd picked up at Walmart. Just before heading out, I slipped my still turned-off phone in my pocket.

The laundry was only one building away, so that was convenient, at least. I ripped into the brand-new pack of sheets and she tore the tags off the towels before stuffing them into two washing machines. Then we both hopped up on the decrepit counter, hoping it would hold our weight.

All the while my cell phone felt like it was burning into my skin. Listening to the sound of the swishing washing machine, I kicked my legs, my heart heavy. Was I ready to take this step? I'd only been gone a week, but it felt like so much longer than that. What was going on at home? Was Bill okay? Did Cole miss me? Or was he just angry at me?

What I'd done was shitty. The reasoning behind it was solid, but I'd literally run out on him—straight from his bed. If our roles had been reversed, I didn't know that I would ever forgive him for sleeping with me and then disappearing. Was it any different because I was the virgin and he was the experienced one? Or because I was the girl and he was the guy?

No, it wasn't. We'd shared something—given one another a part of ourselves—and on the surface, it looked like I'd cast his offering aside.

Damn it, I'd never wanted to do that.

I was such a coward. I should have found a way to contact him, to let him know how much it meant for me for him to be my first, how much *he* meant to me.

And always would.

But hearing his voice would break me. Seeing his face would ruin me. Reliving his touch would undo me.

So I'd pushed it out of my mind—self-preservation at its best.

When I'd grabbed my phone, I'd known what I planned to do but that didn't make it any easier. Before I could talk myself out of it, I handed the phone to Claire, hoping there was enough battery power for it to turn on.

She looked at me with a question in her eyes.

"I need you to do something for me," I said. "I need you to delete all voice mails and text messages."

"Okay," she said slowly. I looked away, focusing on

some clothes going around and around in a dryer across the room. It soothed my nerves.

I listened as the startup music of my cell phone played, a sound I hadn't heard in quite a while. I jumped off the counter, too anxious to stay there.

Claire looked at me. "Who's Cole? There's—"

"Don't tell me." I closed my eyes and rested my forehead in my hands. "Please just delete them."

She cocked her head. "Not until you tell me who he is. I want to know what I'm doing."

I opened my mouth to protest, to try to talk her into doing my bidding, but I could tell by her stern expression that wasn't happening. Claire might be nice to a fault, but she could be tough when she wanted to.

"He's..."

How did I describe him? Define him? A simple explanation wouldn't do it. He was everything and then some.

So I went with the simplest truth I knew.

"He's the love of my life."

CHAPTER 25

CLAIRE GAPED AT ME, THEN glanced down at the phone. "Are you sure this is what you want?"

No, it wasn't what I wanted. What I wanted was to listen to every message he left. Read every text he sent.

Then answer them all in person.

I would wrap myself around him and never let him go. Which was precisely why I needed to do this.

"Do it."

She placed the phone facedown on the counter next to her. "No. Not until you tell me why."

"It's a long story."

She glanced over at the washing machines. "You have twenty-seven minutes and however long the dryer will take."

I told her everything. About how Cole died. About how I agreed to make him a seeker to bring him back. About him wanting to take care of Kyle.

I explained that no one knew who Cole was, but Linda was on the hunt for the "seeker with no limits." I explained that if she found him, he'd never live a normal life.

I explained that it was all my fault.

But most of all, I talked about us. How he drove me so crazy I didn't know if I wanted to punch him or kiss him. How he understood me like no one else. How we'd do anything for one another.

All the while, my fingers ran over the angel pendant I never took off.

Telling her all of this made my heart hurt, made it clench and squeeze so hard I thought for sure it was breaking, never to beat again.

But when I was done, I also somehow felt lighter.

She stayed silent for a few moments before letting out a whispered, "Wow."

The wash cycle ended and I was grateful for the distraction of moving our items to the dryer. I was exhausted in every way I could be—physically, emotionally, and spiritually. The physical could be fixed with some sleep, but I didn't know what it would take to fix me emotionally and spiritually. However, confiding in Claire was a good first step.

"I don't think I want to do it," Claire said.

"But Claire, you have to," I pleaded. "I can't go without my phone anymore and—"

"Why do I have to?"

"Because I obviously can't do it. That would defeat the purpose." I didn't mean for my words to come across as being annoyed, but didn't she realize if I could've done it myself I would have last week? It would have saved me a lot of trouble.

"No, I mean why does it have to be deleted? Maybe you should hear what he has to say."

I crossed my arms and turned away, feeling betrayed. Though it had been good for me, it wasn't easy to open up like I did. And now she was judging me. I hadn't expected that.

"And what about Bill and Xena?" she asked. "Are you going to ignore them forever?"

I whirled around. "You act like this isn't hard for me."

She shrugged. "I'm not saying it isn't, but it was your decision. They didn't ask for this. I can't imagine how hard it must be for them not knowing why you left. That's all

I'm saying."

I took a moment to push down my anger and think about her words. I wasn't worried about Xena. She knew exactly what was going on. But I hated hurting Bill. I wished I'd handled things better. I supposed it wasn't too late to send him a letter to explain, and it was selfish of me not to. I made up my mind to do that as soon as I figured out what to say.

I should probably do the same for Cole, but I'd never be able to figure out what to say. Honestly, it might be better for him if he didn't hear from me. If he knew the truth, knew the sacrifice I was making for him, he'd feel honor bound to make the sacrifice himself instead because that was the sort of person he was. But the thing was everything we'd gone through was all my fault. He shouldn't have to make any sacrifices on my behalf. It wasn't fair to him or Kyle. His brother needed him and who was I to stand in the way of family?

"I'm doing what I think is best for everyone," I said. "So will you help me or not?"

Claire sighed, then looked down at the phone she still had clutched in her hand. "I just hope I'm not helping you make a big mistake."

It seemed lately almost everything I did was a mistake, so if this was another one it would be in good company. Still, my mind was made up.

"I won't hold it against you. I made the decision."

Claire tapped on the phone a few times then looked up at me. "Last chance."

For a fleeting second, I had a change of heart and I ached to hear Cole's voice. This was it. I was metaphorically erasing him from my life. Or at least Claire was on my behalf.

But it was the only way I knew how to protect him. So even though it sucked and it totally hurt, I had to go through with it.

I leveled my gaze at Claire. "Do it."

BY THE TIME WE MADE it back to the apartment, Chase had dinner ready. As soon as I saw it, I wished Claire and I had insisted on cooking and sent Chase to the laundry. He'd made bland baked chicken, quinoa, and broccoli. I'd only had quinoa once in my life and that was enough. Healthy eating was overrated.

Claire shot a look in my direction and I knew she was thinking the same thing—the two of us would definitely have to pull our weight in the kitchen if we wanted to eat things that didn't resemble cardboard.

"This looks good," I said to Chase. Totally two-faced, but he did cook, so I wasn't going to complain. A little white lie never hurt anyone.

We filled our plates directly from the stove and sat down. The food actually wasn't nearly as tasteless as I'd expected, but I could practically hear my stomach scratching its head in confusion. *Health food? What's going on out there?* Other than the occasional salad, which was generally loaded down with fried chicken and cheese, my tastes ran to the more indulgent.

"I'm going to start job hunting tomorrow," Chase said.

"Do you have any leads?" Claire asked.

Chase shook his head. "But as soon as the students come back to town, it's going to get that much harder to find something close by."

"True," I said, remembering how hard it was to get my job with Shenice, and I'd only actually gotten that job because Xena bribed her. So who knew if I was actually employable? It wasn't like I could even list her as a reference.

"There's bound to be something," Claire, our resident optimist, said. "I'm not above scrubbing toilets if that's all that's available."

I nodded in agreement. I also needed to find a bank

and open an account. Shenice was old school and issued me paper checks, but most places probably did direct deposit. I knew most of my mom's jobs did. So I'd need that info in order to fill out the paperwork.

I gasped and pounded my fist on my forehead.

"What is it?" Chase asked.

"I don't have my birth certificate or social security card," I said.

Chase looked at me with his *you're-an-idiot* expression, one I'd gotten way too familiar with in the short time I'd known him.

Damn it, I hadn't packed my own bag. But even if I had, would I have thought to take those important documents? Nope.

This adulting stuff was turning out to be more difficult than I'd thought.

"You might be able to get some babysitting jobs or something like that that pays under the table." Claire was trying to be helpful, but her comment just made me feel worse. Besides, in a college town, there were unlikely to be a lot of families in need of child care.

I looked over at my phone sitting on a table in the living room. When Claire had given it back to me, I hadn't looked at it. I was still only planning to use it when I had to.

And now it looked like I did.

I'd have to call Xena and get her to retrieve the documents for me. I had no doubt she'd be able to get into Bill's house undetected and find them.

Guilt hit me. I'd been such a bitch to Xena and here I was—asking for another favor. But what choice did I have?

Mistake after mistake after mistake. Would I ever get it right?

I DIDN'T CALL XENA THAT night. After dinner, I showered—

finally—and by then it was nearly nine. Too late to call. Or so I told myself.

But in all actuality, I was exhausted. I would give myself some much needed rest before dealing with that issue.

Since it was a two bedroom apartment, Chase took one bedroom and Claire and I decided we'd share the other one, which had a queen sized bed. It was a little odd. As a kid, I'd never had sleepovers because of my random aura projecting. So the only person I'd ever slept in a bed with was my mom.

And Cole.

But I wasn't going there.

In any event, I was so tired I didn't even notice she was there. A T-Rex could have climbed in bed with me and I wouldn't have noticed. I slept hard, but more importantly, I didn't dream.

While Claire and Chase bustled around the next morning getting ready to go job hunting, I sat at the kitchen table with my bowl of Cheerios. There was no point in me going if I didn't have the needed documents because it would be just my luck that I'd find a place that wanted to interview and hire me right away. I hoped the two of them would be successful though. Since it was Saturday, their plan was to hit up stores and restaurants. Ideally, we wanted to get office jobs or something that paid more than minimum wage, but none of us had any experience so it was a long shot. Still, we had to start somewhere. Now that I was officially back to using my phone, I could research temp agencies to see if there were any in the area hiring. That seemed like the best bet.

Once they left, I washed my dishes and left them to dry in the strainer. Then I sat on the couch with my phone. It was turned off. As I pressed the power button, butterflies powered to life in my stomach, knocking into each other and my insides. I didn't know why I was nervous. It was just Xena—she already knew everything. I had no confessions to make, no apologies.

I looked at the screen through slit eyes, only opening them fully when I saw there were no messages and no voice mails. *Thanks, Claire.*

I dialed Xena, half-hoping she wouldn't answer. I needed my birth certificate and the sooner the better, but I'd been surviving by blocking out what I'd left behind. Calling Xena just made me think about everything.

And everyone.

Xena picked up on the fifth ring, which made me wonder what she was up to. When my name came up on her screen, did she have to walk away to a private place before taking my call?

"What's wrong?" she hissed.

Damn. Perhaps I was right. Who was she with? Cole? My heart clenched at the thought of him being on the other side of the line.

"Everything's fine." I paused, thinking of Linda and Xavier. Always freaking Xavier. "Sort of."

"Then why are you calling?"

"I need my birth certificate and social security card. I can't get a job without those."

Xena let out a huff and for a moment I was totally annoyed. She was the one who'd packed my stuff and shoved me out the door. Granted, I'd already come to the conclusion I probably would've forgotten them if I had packed, but still. She'd inserted herself into the situation. I hadn't asked her to get involved.

"I should have thought of that," she muttered. I relaxed, realizing she was irritated with herself and not me.

"Bill has them," I said.

"Okay. Text me an address and I'll send them."

Then she hung up. I looked at my phone in disbelief. Thinking about calling her, I'd nearly broken out into hives. The whole conversation had taken less than a minute. She hadn't even wanted to know how I was or where I was, other than the address for the purposes of mailing the stuff. I was miffed.

And a total hypocrite. I'd cast her aside, so I was lucky she was willing to help me at all. It was just that even when I was rude to her, she'd never changed. She'd still treated me the same way and I'd taken that for granted.

In addition to her not asking how I was, she hadn't shared anything either. I'd worried about what to do if she started telling me about Cole because my soul was hungry for information, but as hard as it was to wonder what he was doing—and if Danielle had gotten her perfect little claws into him—it would be harder knowing.

What if he desperately missed me?

What if he didn't?

And here was the million dollar question—when would I stop wondering about these things? I'd only been gone a little over a week, so perhaps I should cut myself some slack, but I didn't see myself moving on anytime soon.

I SPED THROUGH THE TWO books I'd picked up at the library sale over the weekend, so when Claire and Chase left Monday morning for more job hunting, I was left with no TV and nothing else to do. I was bored out of my mind.

College wasn't in my future, but we were less than a mile away from a major college campus, so why not explore? I quickly showered and set off in the direction of the campus, after turning my phone on. I did that whenever I was separated from Chase and Claire, just in case. Every time I pressed the power button, I cringed, expecting there to be new messages. I at least expected to hear from Xena about the status of my documents, but other than her quick reply of "got it" when I sent the apartment address, there was nothing but radio silence on her end.

And nothing from Cole and Bill. I didn't know how to feel about that. So I just wouldn't think about it.

Penn State's campus was beautiful. And huge. Perhaps essentially going on a hike in the middle of summer wasn't my brightest idea. But if I drove through campus I wouldn't be able to look around because I'd have to focus on the road. Besides, there were parts of campus that couldn't be seen from a car. And anyway, I didn't want to waste gas on sightseeing, especially when I had no job prospects.

Dang it, what was taking Xena so long? I hadn't asked how she was going to send the documents, but this was my birth certificate we were talking about. I hoped she wouldn't put it in an envelope, slap a stamp on it, and drop it in a blue box. If it got lost in the mail, I didn't know what I'd do.

If it hadn't arrived or I didn't hear from her by Wednesday, I decided I'd call her again to find out what was going on.

The campus was relatively empty, which was to be expected since it was summer. My favorite building was Old Main, a really old stone structure with eight super tall columns in front and a clock on top. Standing where I could only see it and nothing else, I felt like I'd stepped back in time.

The entire campus was awesome, though, and I never regretted not being able to go to college more than at that moment. I wandered around for nearly two hours, working up a sweat. I followed some students into a building, hoping to find some air conditioning. I found myself in a huge lecture hall that had to seat several hundred students. No one paid me any attention, so I slid into a seat in the back, ready to make a quick getaway if someone realized I didn't belong there.

But that didn't happen. The professor didn't say the name of the class and it wasn't posted anywhere, but I figured out it was an introductory sociology course. It wasn't at all what I expected. When I thought of sociology, I thought of social workers, kind of like the ones who were dealing with Kyle. Or should I say *failing* him.

That was an entirely different issue.

Anyway, it was super interesting.

So the next day, I did the same thing. Well, not exactly. I went to a different class. This one was on early American history. It was good—not quite as good as the sociology one but definitely worthwhile. I stuck to the large lecture style classes so I could blend in. Even still, I sat in the back. The third class I went to was geology. I had to admit I dozed off in that one. I felt bad. The professor seemed like a nice man and was so enthusiastic, but there was nothing he could do to make rocks exciting.

The classroom had been dim, so when I walked outside, I squinted, putting my hand up over my eyes to block the sun. I wished I hadn't forgotten my sunglasses.

Trying to get my bearings, I spun around. After three days of walking all over campus, I mostly knew my way around, but I was having trouble today and had already gotten mixed up once.

I started in the direction I thought led toward home.

"You're going the wrong way," someone behind me said.

I'd know that voice anywhere.

I whirled around, coming face to face with Xavier.

CHAPTER 26

"WHAT ARE YOU DOING HERE?" I asked stupidly, when I should have asked how he knew I was going in the wrong direction.

He'd lost a little of the Freddy Krueger look. Now he resembled Deadpool, which wasn't much of an improvement. He wore black pants and a black long-sleeved shirt. The color was not surprising, but it was a little unnerving to see him out of his normal attire of suit and red tie—always the red tie. Not counting the red scars on his face, he wasn't wearing the color.

It was an odd thing to focus on.

He also wore a baseball hat, which he had pulled so low it almost touched his dark tinted sunglasses. The hat didn't cover his ears, though, which were as gruesome as they were the first time I saw them at the hotel.

"You know why I'm here." He walked toward me in the same gait he'd always had—one that exuded arrogance. Even his ruined visage didn't strip him of that.

My hand felt for the knife in my pocket, coming up empty. *Damn it.* I hadn't been bringing it to campus because I didn't feel right having a weapon with me. Plus, I didn't know if it was allowed and since I was already sneaking into classes, I didn't want to do anything else against the rules.

"I *don't* know why you're here," I said. I never knew what the hell Xavier wanted. How could he even begin to think I knew what went on in his mind?

It was absurd.

Something else that was absurd was the fact that Xavier was standing right in front of me, and I had no way of ending him.

It was like we were involved in a complex dance for which I didn't know the steps. Despite that, I was ready for the grand finale. Only one of us was going to make it to the final bow.

"Walk with me." He turned and started down the path, not bothering to make sure I would follow. But of course I did.

As I hurried to catch up, I noticed some students looking at him with disgust. Did he notice? Did it bother him?

If he did notice people's reaction to him, he gave no indication. He never did care what people thought of him, anyway.

"What do you want?" I asked, falling into step beside him.

"Believe it or not, Ava, we want the same thing."

"Bullshit," I spat, loathing myself for giving him the time of day. "Because I never wanted my mom to die."

"I didn't either."

"*Bullshit!*" Some passing students eyed me, their gaze shifting between me and Xavier as they scurried away.

Damn it. I never could keep my cool with Xavier, which caused me too many problems to count. But I couldn't listen to him tell lies involving my mom.

"I never wanted her to die," he said. "I wanted you to give me souls. That's what I wanted."

My nostrils flared as I realized he actually had a point, not that I would admit that to him.

"You knew I didn't want to turn in any more souls."

"Yes, but I also knew you would do anything for your

mother. I know you better than you realize. Probably better than you know yourself."

I'd grant him that he knew me well. After all, he'd known me my entire life. But he did not know me better than I knew myself.

Still though, I had to pause and think about it. Would I have gone through with turning in a soul every month in exchange for my mom's life? I'd never know. It was easy to say what I *would* do. It was another thing to actually be in the situation.

My mom sacrificed herself so I didn't have to make that decision.

"What did you do with the last soul my mom turned in?" I asked, changing the subject.

Xavier sat on a bench, but I didn't join him. I still didn't trust him, but aside from that, he was crazy if he thought I could just casually relax next to him, like he hadn't killed the two people I loved the most.

He stripped off his sunglasses and I was startled by what I saw. His eyes—normally so cold and calculating— were dead inside. Just void. I couldn't describe it.

"You know Areli's tale," he said. "Now let me tell you mine."

"Why do you think I care?" I said coldly. Sitting there on the bench, resting his elbows on his knees, he was pathetic, not at all the strong, dynamic force he once was. I was looking at a broken man. Or being. Or whatever the hell he was.

But no matter how pathetic and broken he appeared, I would not pity him. He didn't deserve it.

Somehow, he'd still managed to maintain an air of arrogance. Even broken, he held himself above others.

"Because you want to understand," he said.

He was really pissing me off. Every time he made a valid point, I hated him more. But damn it, he was right. I did want to understand. I wanted to know the reason for everything I'd been through.

Also, no one knew what he'd done with that last soul and here he was, offering an explanation. I'd be a fool not to listen.

"Fine." I crossed my arms, remaining on my feet in front of him. He was significantly taller than me, but in our current positions, he was the perfect level for me to punch him in the face. Or the throat.

I couldn't guarantee I wouldn't do just that.

A light breeze skated by, and I caught a faint whiff of cinnamon. I couldn't believe I hadn't noticed it before—Xavier's smell had always been so overwhelming, but now it had faded to nearly nothing. What did it mean?

"Areli and I were friends. We had a lot in common then, but mostly it was our love of humans. We wanted to be around them, spend time with them, develop relationships with them."

As Xavier spoke, I couldn't help but think of Areli. Right now, Xavier sounded a lot like him—his tone, the way he spoke. It was so weird.

Everything about this interaction was weird.

"We decided to spend some time on Earth. Areli immediately fell in love."

I already knew this story. He fell in love with a woman, but when she died after giving birth to their child, he asked to go back to heaven. That was the beginning of seekers.

"While Areli fell in love with one woman, I fell in love with all of them." Xavier's mouth stretched into a smile, and he paused like he was reminiscing. A light chuckle escaped his lips. "By the time Areli went back to heaven, we'd already gone our separate ways. Eventually I'd had enough, and I wanted to go back as well. But I wasn't allowed. Areli was, but I wasn't. Do you have any idea how that felt?"

Did he have any idea how much I didn't care? Was he actually expecting sympathy from me?

But he was talking and though I hated to admit it, I

was intrigued. He'd wreaked so much havoc in my life, and now I was finally going to learn *why*.

Even still, I couldn't bring myself to utter any kind of words that might be construed as sympathy. Luckily, he didn't seem to actually want an answer.

"I was doomed to be fallen until I redeemed myself, but nothing I did was ever enough. And it never would be, but by the time I realized that, it was already too late. Angels are inherently good but the more time we spend with humans, the more we take on their characteristics. The longer I stayed, the lower and lower I fell until all the goodness was gone."

"Are you saying being around humans made you evil?"

He seemed to consider my question for a moment. "Yes."

I shook my head. "Then you were hanging around with the wrong people. Most people are good." Now I sounded like Claire. But I refused to accept his explanation that humans were responsible for his reprehensible behavior. *Talk about not taking responsibility for your actions.*

"Good and bad are two sides of the same coin," he explained, which essentially explained nothing. He didn't seem to care if I actually understood what he was saying. Although he sounded eerily like Areli, he was still Xavier, which meant he liked to hear himself talk.

And for once, I was content to let him.

"What did you do with the soul?" I asked, wanting to get back on track. I was tired of his stupid story.

"I absorbed it," he said.

My eyes bugged out and my jaw dropped. There was no hesitation on his part. Just *"I absorbed it."*

What the hell did that even mean?

"I decided that if I was doomed to stay with humans, then I might as well become one. I needed a soul for that. Unfortunately, it didn't work the first time."

"The first time?"

Oh my God, he'd done this more than once?

"It didn't make me human, but it did conflict with some of my gifts." He gestured to his face, allowing me to put it together. He'd absorbed the soul—or at least attempted to—shortly before my mom shot him. So his healing ability must have been damaged.

I wondered if his freaky pain-causing ability was also damaged. Could that be why he hadn't used it since the last time he'd hurt my mom?

"How many souls did you try to absorb?" I cringed as I waited for his answer. There was only one unaccounted soul that I was aware of, but I very rarely had all the facts.

"Only two. After the first one, I realized the soul was too old. I needed a much younger one. They're purer than old souls. That's why I needed you. But you know how that turned out."

I would always regret my mom's death, but now I was more grateful than ever I hadn't had to give Xavier any more names. I was also grateful my mom never found out what happened to the last name she'd turned in. It was bad enough turning in names for reaping when they had the potential to become angels. But turning them in for this monster to *absorb* them? It didn't get any worse.

"If younger souls are purer, then why—"

"I know," he said like he was commiserating with me on some wrong. "Younger souls are purer because they haven't had enough time to get corrupted. But it's not that simple. If the person hasn't faced adversity and hasn't had to make choices, then how can you determine if the soul is actually pure or if it simply hasn't gotten sullied yet? So sixteen was set as the minimum age souls could be reaped for our purposes."

That didn't make sense. I could have sworn Claire said she was fifteen when she started seeking and that the boy she submitted was also fifteen. She could be mistaken, but I doubted it. Those weren't the sort of details a person messed up.

The system was flawed beyond belief. Even the so-called rules weren't always adhered to. I'd bet anything Claire and Chase weren't supposed to be turned into seekers at their young age, either. Someone else probably broke the rules.

"Where did you get the other soul?" I asked even though I already knew the answer. Why else would he be hovering around Claire?

"Niles gave it to me."

Before I'd felt kind of sorry for Niles, but now I outright despised him.

"Did this one work?" I peered at him, trying to determine if Xavier was human. That would make it a lot easier to kill him once and for all, but though he was changed, I didn't think he was human. He still had an ethereal quality.

Though he reminded me of Areli now, he didn't exude the same vibe Areli did. Being in the angel's presence was like being enveloped in warmth and love.

Xavier's vibe was more...apathetic, maybe? He was definitely different, and I was having a hard time reconciling the Xavier I knew with this one. Gone was the sinister creep, and in its place was this broken creature.

"Not exactly. Instead of making me human, it restored some of my angelic qualities."

I couldn't help it—I snorted. Where were his angelic qualities when he knocked that little girl to the ground in Hershey Park?

He was a warped twisted version of himself—neither the being he'd started out as nor the sadistic monster he'd become.

"I need you to do something for me," he said. "And now that I've done some things for you—"

"What?" I exclaimed, totally and utterly flabbergasted. He thought he'd done me a favor, and now he wanted one in return?

He was more than just a warped version of himself—he was also living in a warped reality.

"I took care of Linda for you," he said. "Had I not shown myself, you wouldn't have gotten away."

He was right. *Damn it.* But I couldn't accept he was trying to help me. He could have been there for any number of reasons, and any of them were more likely than him wanting to help me.

"I don't believe you."

"Fair enough."

I blinked. Was he actually being reasonable?

"I also led you to Chase and Claire," he said.

I hated hearing their names come out of his mouth. It scared me. I didn't want anyone else I cared about on his radar.

"No, you didn't. I found them on my own."

He cocked his head. "Do you like roller coasters, Ava?"

"What does that have to do with anything?"

"Didn't it seem odd that you had a sudden urge to go to Hershey Park when you don't even like rides?"

"I..." I trailed off. Then I shook my head. "No." I wasn't letting him get in my head. My logic had been sound. Amusement parks had lots of people, and lots of people meant a higher potential for seekers.

But so did other tourist destinations, like the beach. It would have made more sense to get farther away from Shenice. And being near the beach made me feel closer to my mom.

Why *had* I been so hell bent on going to Hershey? Had he somehow planted thoughts in my brain? He'd said he'd lost his abilities. Mind control had never been one of them, anyway.

"No," I said again.

"Believe me or not, it's true." He paused. "To be fair, Areli did help with that, but he never would have intervened if I hadn't alerted him."

I didn't like the idea of Areli getting into my head much better than Xavier getting in. Even more I didn't like the thought of Areli and Xavier working together. Areli was supposed to be on *my* side.

But wasn't meeting other seekers my ultimate goal? So if Areli really had gotten involved, then he'd helped me get what I wanted. I just didn't understand why he would work with Xavier, especially to manipulate me. And why would Xavier have gone out of his way to help me?

"Areli wouldn't do that," I whispered, wondering if my words were lies.

"You can believe it was pure luck you ended up at the park if it makes you feel better," he said. "But you have to admit I led you to Claire, one of the only other seekers your age."

I'd been chasing him when Claire found me. I never would have found her on my own. The merry-go-round attendant station wasn't visible from the walkway, so it was unlikely I would have seen her unless I'd gone on the ride, which I wouldn't have done. The commotion Xavier caused by knocking the girl down was what had put me in Claire's path.

Though Xavier had undergone some sort of transformation, there was still enough of the old Xavier left in him that I didn't trust him. Even if God Himself came down and declared Xavier trustworthy, I still wouldn't trust him. Short of him undoing everything he'd done to my mom and Cole, there was nothing he could do to earn my trust.

Xavier never did anything that didn't benefit him, so even though it appeared on the surface like he was helping me, his motivation was self-serving. It had to be.

"Why?" I asked.

"Because I want the same thing you want."

"Bullshit." How did we get here again? We'd already done this. "Just tell me what you really want."

Something flashed in Xavier's eyes—those eyes that

until now had been dead inside. They flared to life momentarily, and I saw a shadow of who he used to be. Then just as quickly it was gone and the apathy was back.

"I want to die."

CHAPTER 27

"WHAT?" I WHISPERED. WAS THIS some kind of cruel joke?

I began to feel light-headed, so I fought to keep my breathing even, to keep the panic attack at bay.

Although why my body would respond that way to the news that Xavier had a death wish was beyond me. Because if he really did want that, then he had been right—we wanted the same thing. Every thought I'd had about him in the past six months involved ending him.

"I have nothing to live for," he said simply.

I gaped at him as he sat with his hands primly folded in his lap. Even his mannerisms were different than what I'd come to know as classic Xavier. It was one of the freakiest things I'd ever encountered—he was both Xavier and *not* Xavier.

Though it went against every fiber of my being, I tried to see things from his perspective. He had a miserable existence. If he hadn't used his power to inflict pain on my loved ones, I might have been able to feel sorry for him, but I didn't have it in me.

Now that *he'd absorbed two souls*, he'd apparently had a come-to-Jesus moment and was now himself, for lack of a better term, a tortured soul.

Good. I was glad. He deserved every bit of misery he'd brought on himself. And I didn't feel one bit guilty or petty for thinking that.

"You seem surprised and I understand that," he said, taking on his angelic persona. "Absorbing that soul didn't make me human like I'd wanted, but it did make me see what I'd become. It makes me sad to see how far I've fallen."

His expression was forlorn, like he thought *he* was the victim in all of this. Everything that had happened to him was a result of his own actions. He was not in the same class as me and Cole and Claire, not to mention the countless people who were affected by seekers.

He was no victim.

I might have been one, once upon a time, but I refused to play the victim again. I made my choices, knowing full well the consequences.

"What do you want from me?" I asked.

"Every day I continue to exist is torment. I want to die. And I want you to kill me."

EPILOGUE

I LET MYSELF INTO THE apartment, my hands still shaking as they had the entire walk home.

"Are you okay?" Claire asked, rushing over to me. I must have looked as shaken as I felt.

"Fine," I said. "Just maybe too much sun."

I couldn't tell her. She'd only just been able to say the names of the souls she'd turned in. How could I tell her what had happened to the last one? That Xavier had absorbed it?

I didn't fully understand what that meant, but it was bad. That much I knew.

"I'll get you some water," she said.

I sat on the couch next to Chase, who said nothing. He was perceptive enough to know something was up, but we didn't have the sort of relationship where he could ask.

Could I actually do what Xavier asked of me? It wouldn't be as simple as putting a bullet in his brain. That would be too easy. It would be a long, gruesome, painful process that was sure to mar my soul.

My gut had been burning with a thirst for vengeance, and now it was being handed to me on a silver platter. But was it really vengeance? He *wanted* to die. If I killed him, I'd be giving him exactly what he wanted. If I didn't, he'd continue to exist and who knew how he'd end up. Sure, he had some perspective now on right and wrong, but would that last? It was a warped perspective at best.

If I killed him, I wouldn't even be killing Xavier. Not really. He was just a shell of who he used to be. A stranger wearing his skin.

I couldn't win. Xavier had boxed me in. I was damned if I did and damned if I didn't. I would get no satisfaction or resolution from this situation.

Claire handed me a glass of water and I took a big gulp, focusing on the cold liquid as it slid down my throat. I felt dead inside.

I'd thought Xavier had already stolen everything from me.

I was wrong.

I hadn't realized how strong my need for vengeance was. And now he'd even stolen that.

"Are you sure you're okay?" Claire asked.

Before I could answer with another lie, there was a knock at the door. Claire gave me one final concerned look before walking over to open it.

She peeked through the peephole, then swung the door open wide.

The sight of our visitor made me lose my grip on the glass of water. It fell to the ground, splashing icy water on me and Chase.

But I didn't even feel it. How could I when my heart felt like it was going to explode?

Because there in the doorway was Cole, his cool gaze taking in Chase and me sitting together on the couch.

Finally his eyes locked onto mine and he held out a white envelope. "I have your birth certificate."

Thank you for reading *Sacrifice*! I hope you enjoyed it. If you did, please help other readers find this book by telling your friends and leaving a review on Amazon, Goodreads, or your favorite book retailer. Word of mouth and reviews help authors more than you know!

ABOUT THE AUTHOR

 Jessica lives in Virginia with her college-sweetheart husband, two rambunctious sons, and two rowdy but lovable rescue dogs. Since her house is overflowing with testosterone, it's a good thing she has a healthy appreciation for Marvel movies, Nerf guns, and football.

To learn more about Jessica, visit her website jessicaruddick.com. Connect with her on Twitter at @JessicaMRuddick or on Facebook at facebook.com/AuthorJessicaRuddick.

Other Books by Jessica Ruddick

Birthright: The Legacy Series, Book One
Retribution: The Legacy Series, Book Two
Letting Go (Love on Campus #1)
Wanting More (Love on Campus #2)

CPSIA information can be obtained
at www.ICGtesting.com
Printed in the USA
LVOW07s1404300717
543157LV00001B/52/P